A
BONE STREET
RUMBA NOVEL

BATTLE HILL
BOLERO

DANIEL JOSÉ OLDER

NEW YORK TIMES BESTSELLING AUTHOR OF *MIDNIGHT TAXI TANGO*

$7.99 USA
$10.99 CAN

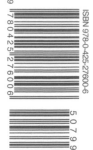

santa clara
county
library district

Renewals: (800) 471-0991

www.sccl.org

PRAISE FOR
THE BONE STREET RUMBA NOVELS

"[Older's characters'] cadences are musical and real, their thoughts unflinching and sometimes unabashedly graceless. . . . Wonderful."　　　　　　　—NPR.org

"Richly detailed and diverse."　　　　　　　　　—io9

"A damn good read . . . Daniel José Older takes aim at a whole bunch of familiar targets and hits them hard in new and interesting ways."
　　　　—Simon R. Green, *New York Times* bestselling author of
　　　　　　　　　the Secret Histories Novels

"As real as fresh blood and as hard as its New York streets. A Lou Reed song sung with a knife to your throat."
　　　　—Richard Kadrey, *New York Times* bestselling author of
　　　　　　　　　the Sandman Slim Novels

"Simply put, Daniel José Older has one of the most refreshing voices in genre fiction today."
　　　　—Saladin Ahmed, author of *The Thousand and One*

"Smart and gripping, funny and insightful. It kicks in the door waving the literary .44. Be warned: This man is not playing."
　　　　—Victor LaValle, author of *The Ballad of Black Tom*

"Vividly imagined and rendered."
　　　　—Jesmyn Ward, National Book Award–winning author of
　　　　　　　　　Men We Reaped

continued . . .

Titles by Daniel José Older from Roc Books

HALF-RESURRECTION BLUES
MIDNIGHT TAXI TANGO
BATTLE HILL BOLERO

BATTLE HILL BOLERO

A Bone Street Rumba Novel

DANIEL JOSÉ OLDER

ROC
New York

ROC
Published by Berkley
An imprint of Penguin Random House LLC
375 Hudson Street, New York, New York 10014

Map by Cortney Skinner
Illustration by Mildred Louis

ISBN: 9780425276006

First Edition: January 2017

Printed in the United States of America
1   3   5   7   9   10   8   6   4   2

Cover art by Gene Mollica
Cover design by Adam Auerbach

For Jud, Tina, and Aya

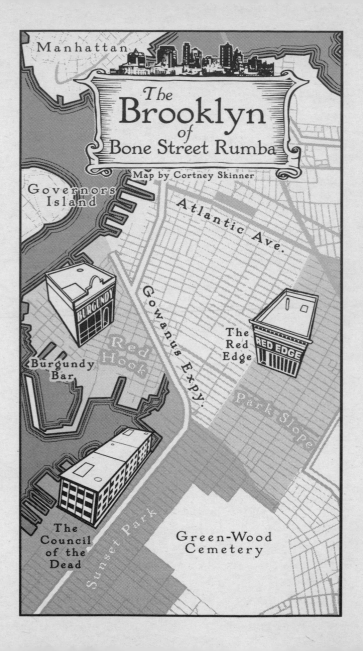

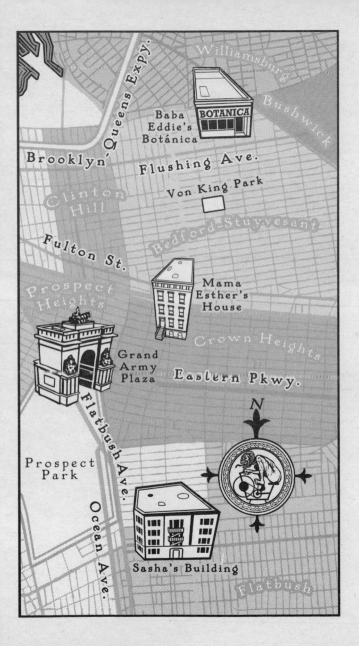

DRAMATIS PERSONÆ

DRAMATIS PERSONAE

Carlos Delacruz—an inbetweener, a Soulcatcher Prime for the Council of the Dead, and undercover member of the resistance.

Sasha Brass—an inbetweener, founding member of the Survivors.

Trevor Brass—an inbetweener, Sasha's brother, killed by Carlos on orders from the Council.

Krys—a Council soulcatcher, undercover member of the resistance.

Victor Torres—a friend of Carlos and FDNY paramedic.

Jimmy Torres—Victor's teenage cousin.

Kia Summers (the Iyawo)—runs the counter and online shop at Baba Eddie's Botánica.

Baba Eddie Machado—consummate santero extraordinaire.

Russell Ward—his husband.

Ernesto "Gordo" Quintero—big ol' Cuban cat who can see spirits.

Cicatriz "CiCi" Cortazar—member of an ancient order of story collectors. Badass.

Charo Velazquez—runs the Medianoche Car Service and its underground gangster affiliate.

Rohan Baksh—member of Reza's crew, also rolls with the Revolutionary Dead.

Mama Esther—grounded house ghost, keeper of the largest supernatural library in New York City.

Rathmus AKA Blardly—One of the ancient spirits of Garvey Park and an ancestor of Carlos.

Ookus—a river giant.

Reza Villalobos—lead enforcer with Charo's crew, driver for the Medianoche Car Service.

Dr. Charlotte Tennessee—archival librarian at the Harlem Public Library. Reza's boo.

Janey Vega—Gordo's future daughter-in-law, Sasha and Reza's friend. CiCi's acolyte.

Miguel Mirabela—driver for Medianoche Car Service.

Quiñones—barkeep at the Burgundy Bar

THE REVOLUTIONARY DEAD

Cyrus Langley—old-time conjureman, busted out of the African Burial Ground with a crew of spirits from old New York.

Riley Washington—former Soulcatcher Prime gone rogue, Carlos's ex-partner and best friend.

Damian Ray—a child ghost, distant relative of Cyrus Langley.

Big Cane—Soulcatcher Prime, secretly working with the revolutionary forces.

Moco—leader of Remote District 17.

La Venganza—RD 17 ghost.

Rosali Ayala—RD 17 ghost.

Angelina Martinez—RD 17 ghost.

Vincent Jackson—killed by the NYPD, leader of the Black Hoodies.

Darius Blay—a Black Hoodie.

Tolula Brown—a Black Hoodie.

Alice—a Black Hoodie.

Father Desmond—leader of RD 5.

Saeen Moughari—leader of RD 4.

Kaya Doxtator—coleader of RD 7.

Breyla Phan—coleader of RD 7.

Forsyth Charles—a Burial Ground ghost.

Redd—a Burial Ground ghost.

Dag Thrummond—a Burial Ground ghost, Cyrus Langley's bodyguard.

Sharon Bentley—coleader of the Ghost Riders.

Brit Terry—coleader of the Ghost Riders.

THE NEW YORK COUNCIL OF THE DEAD

Botus—Chairman of the NYCOD, one of the Seven.

Bart Arsten—A Council subminister, middle management.

Juan Flores—a Soulcatcher Prime.

Caitlin Fern—formerly of the Blattodeons, current necromancy consultant to the Council.

Dr. Calloway—one of the Council's leading scientists.

Harrison Range—a soulcatcher.

CYCLE ONE

◦∞∞◦

FRAANG PA KONSEELI

En una tarde de inquietud
Quisqueya vióse de pronto de pavor sumida.

On a tumultuous afternoon
Dread suddenly inundated Quisqueya.

"El Trío y el Ciclón"
Trío Matamoros

CHAPTER ONE

Sasha

I open the door, blade ready, and the first thing I think is, *Oh, Carlos, what have they done to you?*

The thought comes with a startling pinch in my chest, and I step back from the shimmering, hunched-over figure, suddenly sadder than I thought I'd be.

Thought I'd be if ever—

Because surely one day—

Shit.

I shake off the threads of worry and sorrow, and blink once at the ghost in my doorway.

His flowing cloak and notched helmet mark him as one of the Council of the Dead's Soulcatchers Prime. He's tall—Carlos tall—but his shoulders slump forward, one lower than the other. His head slumps down like a hanged man, face hidden behind the caged face guard. He clutches a cane, just like Carlos. And he's trembling. But the energy is all wrong; something vastly more desperate and mournful radiates from this wraith. And for Carlos, half-dead like me, to be a ghost, they would've had to catch and kill

him the rest of the way, and somehow, deep inside myself,
I'm sure I would've known if that had happened.

"The Council pardoned me," I say. It comes out hoarse,
like I've been crying. "Almost a year ago." Nine months
and seven days. The last time I saw Carlos. "Maybe you
didn't get the memo."

"My lady." The ghost bows. His voice is a thin, unrav-
eling whisper.

Definitely not Carlos.

Tiny muscles I didn't know I had unclench themselves.
But if not Carlos, who?

"What do you want, soulcatcher? I don't politic with
the Council."

He shakes his head. "A word, is all. I'm not here on
Council business. Not exactly."

Down the hall behind me, the twins sit perched on
their big, old babysitter's lap. I shut and locked the nurs-
ery door as soon as I'd heard the knocking. Baba Eddie
has ghostproofed, sanctified, cleansed, and spiritually
booby-trapped their room hundreds of times.

And still, it's never enough. Still my slow, slow heart
cantors into overdrive at the gentlest hint of something off.

I narrow my eyes. "I have no words for Council goons."

"You don't have to have any," the soulcatcher assures
me. "The words are all mine."

"Not interested."

Just before I slam the door the ghost says, "I knew you."

He says it very quietly. It's not desperate, not a plea.
Just a fact. I glare at him through the crack of the doorway. "Excuse me?" A fury rises up and I push it away.

"I knew you," he says again. "In life."

A moment passes, then another. My stare doesn't waver.

It could be a lie. A trap. I could somehow force it not to matter, but I'd be pretending. No matter how many ways I try to ignore it, the truth about my life matters.

Still, I already dislike this phantom. First of all, he's with the Council. I'm inbetween—full flesh and blood but neither fully dead nor alive—and the Council has no tolerance for folks like us, unless we're doing their dirty work.

Like Carlos.

Who I murdered once—a lifetime ago, before we fell in love.

Who this ghost strangely resembles.

"Wait here," I say, and shut the door.

I unlock the twins' bedroom and poke my head in.

Their babysitter sits like a giant Cuban Santa Claus, a toddler on each leg. He squints at the handwritten letter through his bifocals. I don't know if it's old age or all that coffee he drinks, but his hand trembles slightly. "It was maybe the fourth time Mrs. Overbrook has called me," Gordo reads. "I think she just likes having someone to talk to." He makes it sound like a fairy tale, Carlos's never-ending cycle of ridiculous adventures. Xiomara and Jackson are enraptured. There's no way they can grasp what's going on, but their wide eyes are glued to Gordo's face as he reads.

"I'm going out," I say.

The twins train their *how dare you interrupt story time, Mami* faces on me, and I almost come curl up with the three of them, the Council's limping ghosts be damned.

But no. My life—even if it's a cruel joke, it's one I need to get to the bottom of.

"We know this," Gordo says. "You already said goodbye."

I puzzle at him for a half second and then remember: it's Saturday and my friend Reza gives me what she calls "offensive driving" lessons on Saturdays. That's why Gordo's here in the first place. I'd been on my way out when the knock at the door sounded.

"Right." I smile, but it's forced and Gordo knows it. I'm already off my game.

"Everything alright?"

I shake my head but say, "Yeah. Change of plans, though."

Xiomara cocks an eyebrow at me, because she was apparently born knowing everything. I come back in the room, a flurry of jingling keys and all my weird stress, kiss both their foreheads—little Jackson squirming already at his mommy's love—and Gordo's cheek. He's so warm; they're all so warm and wholesome, and I'm so aware of my chilly skin against theirs.

Gordo smiles at me, takes my small, cool hand in his big, hot one. Of all the fully alive folks I've met, Gordo is the only one who never missed a beat realizing how neither/nor I really am. Without a word spoken, he just gets it, and I will always love him for that.

"Ten cuidado, nena," Gordo says.

I nod. "Always."

I start to leave but he doesn't let go. "Yes, Sasha, always. But much more so now."

He lets go and turns back to the letter, suddenly Santa again. "And then we had to help a group of suicides out of the riverway. What a mess that was!"

Xiomara giggles; I shake my head and walk out of the room.

Carlos

"Should I cut him?" Harrison Range's voice shivers. "I mean, I mean . . . I feel that I should probably cut him, right? I'm not sure though, to be honest."

I hate new guys.

Harrison is clinging to a support beam of the Manhattan Bridge. He's a ghost, and ghosts don't really fall unless you push 'em, so there's really no need to be clinging. But that's not what's put the tremor in his voice, at least not the only thing. A river giant stands astride the Manhattan-bound lane of traffic, sobbing.

The answer to Harrison's question is an unequivocal and enthusiastic yes, according to Council protocols. But it's Saturday, and I haven't had any coffee yet, and I'm not in the mood for even the pretense of following these inane bylaws. Anyway, I think I know this river giant. Got into a tiff with a group of 'em not too long ago on the west side—they were trying to resurrect an ancient serial-killer god. We murked the whole squad except one, who disappeared back into the dirty waters of the Hudson. I *think* this is that one, even though my friend Krys warned him not to come back with the business end of a ghost bazooka.

Then again, all river giants look alike to me, so what do I know?

"Do what you want, Harrison."

Harrison whimpers. The giant sniffles and sobs.

Traffic is snarled, mostly because our lumbering, distraught friend caused a fender bender. No one can see him, at least not most folks, but his very presence sends discord rippling through the congested air above the East

River. It's the third mash-up this week, and the Council finally caught wind, and, well, here we are.

"I'm not sure I should cut him," Harrison reports.

Surely one of these passing cars has a spare cup of coffee in it.

"The thing is, according to Council Bylaw 89.2, the river giant is a Causal Disturbance Entity, and I should thereby cut him and send him to the Deeper Death, thereby ending his existence entirely and for good."

I peer through the crisscrossing tension wires, into the window of a black SUV. That guy has two coffee cups in his drink holder and no one in the passenger seat. Dickhole.

"However, there are two complications: the river giant has not technically made himself visible to the general public, and he hasn't caused any mass loss of life or property damage in excess of forty thousand dollars—not by my guess, anyway. Wouldn't you say, Carlos?"

"Not unless that Winnebago that got trashed at the exit ramp was full of cocaine." My arm doesn't quite reach, so I slide my cane through the steel crossbeams.

"Ha, no, we probably would've heard about it if it was."

"What's the other thing?"

"What other thing?"

Success! The tip of my cane clacks against the side of the SUV. The window slides down with a whirr. "What the fuck!" the driver yells. He's burly and wearing those Terminator sunglasses that grandmas realized weren't cool in 1994. I'll take the L.

"You said there were two things, Harrison." I walk a few steps out of range while the driver continues his curse-out. "What's the second one?"

"Oh! River giants are almost extinct."

"How can a dead thing be—"

"Therefore, as per subguideline 91a, they are technically protected entities."

Didn't seem like that a few months ago when we were trying not to get stomped by them on the banks of the Hudson. "Well, damn. Didn't realize that. So what you gonna do, man? I'm cold, and I gotta be somewhere at two."

Above us, the river giant lets out a warbling cry—something like a thousand dying goats simulcast through a screechy megaphone. I scowl. I'd forgotten about that shit. Harrison squints, steeling himself.

"I'm gonna cut him!" he announces.

As it turns out, I have my own little set of protocols, and one of them is don't announce you're going to cut a gigantic river demon before you do it. It's too late for all that though; the warbling peaks in intensity and then cuts suddenly short. The giant looks at Harrison.

Harrison says, "Oh sh—" and then the giant backhands him off the bridge.

Fuck.

Then the river giant looks at me.

Double fuck.

"You!"

There aren't enough fucks in the world. I turn around and run.

Sasha

For a dead guy, Juan Flores is remarkably ungraceful. Most ghosts flit around with that edgeless, flowing aban-

don you'd expect from a being that's all soul. Even the
ones that stride, like Carlos's friend Riley, strut like walking water in a seamless swirl. It's a glory to behold, when
you stop to take it in, and soulcatchers more than anyone
else are supposed to be unflappable, ferocious, and yes,
graceful.

Not Juan Flores, though. He limps along beside me
like a busted San Lázaro / Darth Vader mash-up, phantom
cane clacking on the pavement as his bum leg drags along
behind.

"Anyway," Flores says, "the Council is in the midst of
a lot of change. Several Remote Districts are in open
rebellion. No one knows when they'll replace the slain
minister . . ."

"I hate the Council, Mr. Flores."

"Juan, please."

"I want nothing to do with them. Ever. I told them as
much when they brought me in to say they wouldn't be
trying to kill me anymore. You said you weren't here on
Council business."

The ghost sighs. Snow from a blizzard three days ago
still covers the park in pristine blankets. Some kids run
around a playground, squealing, and I think of Xiomara
and Jackson, wonder briefly if they'll ever know a life so
perfectly simple.

"You're right," Flores finally says.

"You said you know me, Flores. Out with it."

He stops walking, turns to face me. "April nineteenth,
Grand Army Plaza."

My back straightens without me telling it to. Tiny beads
of sweat form along my spine.

"A rainy night."

Even hunched over, Juan Flores's face reaches a little higher than mine.

I nod.

He lifts the visor of his soulcatcher helm. Inside, it's just a hazy fog.

"We were seven," Flores says. "All died. Five survived."

It's the only information Carlos could track down about the night we died—the resident house ghost at the plaza told him before being annihilated by a powerful sorcerer named Sarco, who orchestrated the whole thing. Then Carlos and I killed Sarco.

"You were there?" I try to make my voice sound unimpressed. It doesn't work.

Flores nods.

"But you . . . you remember?"

"My passing was less violent than yours. Or the other four."

The other four. Carlos and my brother Trevor, who Carlos later killed on orders from the Council. Marie and Gregorio, who formed the Survivors with Trevor and me, and died in the infighting last year.

My blade is out; it's pointed at that swirling emptiness where Juan Flores's face should be.

"Who was I?"

"Sasha . . ."

"Before I died. You said you knew me."

Juan Flores nods. "Aisha," the ghost says in that trembly, soft voice. "Aisha Flores."

I lower my blade, raise it again. "I was . . ."

"My wife," Juan Flores said. "My dearly beloved wife."

Carlos

I shove through a gaggle of tourists—German, I think. I grunt an apology without stopping. None of them mind too much—apparently assholes are just part of the local flavor. One even snaps a picture, but then the river giant is on them, which must feel like some huge, invisible tornado just dropped out the sky. They collapse, screaming.

The river giant doesn't apologize; he just roars toward me with those humongous strides, crashing along the walkway like a deranged oak tree. I turn back to look where I'm going just in time to see the cyclist I'm crashing into.

For a few seconds, everything is a tangle of gears and sudden aches and the biker's cursing. Then I'm right side up again and still running—my odd, lopsided gait even more slanted.

"You can't goddamn just do that, man!" the guy yells. "I mean! I mean!" And then he too is swept aside with a yelp. The whole fence shivers, the cyclist grunts and collapses, and me? I run.

I'm only halfway across the bridge when I start running out of breath. Blame the Malagueñas. But I still hear the thing clambering along behind me, even if a little less enthusiastically now. I steal a glimpse and then stop entirely, leaning my hand against one of the huge concrete support pillars to catch my breath.

The giant's wild flush forward has slowed to a pathetic, uneven clamor. He keeps stopping to wipe his eyes like he has something in them and then hock giant ghost loogies into the river below.

The bumps-and-bruises carnage we caused is far enough back not to trouble us, and besides the gridlocked traffic and passing seagulls, we're alone on the bridge. The giant stops a few feet away from me and just breaks down sobbing. One hand clutches the tension wires above him, the other massages the center of his wide face, right between those two beady eyes.

"Ay," I say. My cane unsheathes to reveal a blade, and it's a blade that deals the Deeper Death to spirits like this with a quickness. Plus my breath is back, mostly. I take a step toward the river giant. "You alright?"

He snorffles and sniffles, wipes the two slits where his nose should be, and looks up at me. For a second, I think I'm gonna have to make a break for it again. Then he says, "Ookus," and goes back to sobbing.

Man, I've had days like that. More than a few, in fact, especially since I murdered the brother of the woman I love before I'd even met her, and then fathered her children. And then found out she murdered me. I just usually stay in my apartment instead of terrorizing a major throughway, though.

I don't know what "ookus" means, but I know what I do when I'm sad. "Ookus," I say, retrieving two Malagueñas from my inside pocket. "Ookus."

He looks up again, wipes his eyes. Then the river giant reaches those long fingers out and daintily accepts the gift. I'm wondering if I'll have to explain what to do with it, but he just puts it right into that big ol' mouth and leans forward, putting his face all up in mine, for a light.

"And then she showed me her memory," I say, two hours and six Malagueñas later. "The one memory she had of her life before she died. And it was me, Ookus. It was me. My final moment. She . . . she killed me, man."

Small, gated-in enclosures line the upper level of the
Manhattan Bridge. Empty forties, crumpled paper bags,
and cigarette butts cover the ground, and graffiti commem-
orates the many exploits each alcove has witnessed. But
the view is unparalleled: the shimmering towers of Manhattan's Financial District stare down Brooklyn's newly
converted warehouse apartments as the East River swirls
between toward the scattered islands of the open bay.

Ookus looks down at me, aghast. We've cleared the
trash out the way and sit facing each other, backs to the
colorfully cursed-upon stone walls of the enclosure. At
some point during the conversation, God or the orishas
or Nuyorican Jesus sent one of those foodcart guys past
on his way to catch the late lunch crowd and I snagged
two coffees for us.

"Ookus barabat kimbana shok," Ookus says, glumly.

"Right?" I don't know what that means, but it seems
genuine. He's probably been in a similar situation and
feels my pain. "Thanks, man." I shake my head, sip the
now-cold foodcart coffee. "I was pretty mad. I am. I
mean, I walked away, never looked back. Sorta. Sorta
never looked back? Is that a thing? Look." I pull a scrap
of folded, lined paper from my pocket and pass it to
Ookus. Then I relight my cigar while he reads.

"Baseena pos prana koolesi," Ookus says.

"Exactly. I just feel like, they should know something
about their father's life. Half-life. Whatever. So I pass
'em along with the old Cubano guy that babysits 'em. But
I know that what we did before we died—us halfies,
I mean—we can't be held responsible for it, not really. I
have no idea what I did or who I was before that night. I
coulda been a hellish human being. What matters is what

we do now. And in the now? I'm the one that was in the wrong more than Sasha. And I mean . . . when it comes to those letters, they're nice, I guess, but really and truly? I ain't shit for it. I know, I know I gotta suck it up and face them . . . her . . . soon."

Ookus peers over the lined paper at me. Nods. "Ookus."

"I know, man, I know. I'm gonna."

He passes the paper back.

"But I keep seeing that night, the night I killed her brother. And I really think she forgives me, to be honest. I just don't think I do. And you know what's really fucked up about it?"

"Ookus?"

"Behind everything that went wrong in my life, starting with that single night, lurks the motherfucking Council of the Dead."

Ookus's brow furrows.

"The Council sent me to kill Trevor." I relight the Malagueña and pass Ookus the lighter. "And when I did, the Council sent me to kill Sasha. Which I didn't, of course. The Council backed Caitlin Fern, whose fucked-up cockroach cult almost turned my babies into demon insect hives. My *babies,* Ookus. And when my best friend Riley had finally had enough, the Council wanted me to kill him too. And his ass already dead."

Ookus shakes his head.

"Hell, the Council sent me to kill you. You know what, Ookus? Fuck the Council. Fuck 'em in the face."

Ookus nods. "Fraang pa Konseeli."

"Exactly."

"Lareeni."

"Anyway, that's my story. What's got you so upset?"

CHAPTER TWO

Krys

There's a new girl working at the botánica when Jimmy and I stop by on the way to the meeting. She's all dressed in white, head to toe, and got a million beaded necklaces round her slender, dark brown neck, and it takes me like point eight seconds to fall in love. I mean: look at her! Eyes sleepy, mouth an unimpressed pout. Her hair's all hidden away beneath a white head tie, and a white Kangol sits on top, perfectly crooked. Besides all that, some kind of ethereal glow pours off her like she's just emerging from some divine seashell and the holy light of God is awakening all around her.

Also, she sees me.

To her, I exist. She says "Hey" to Jimmy first, barely taking note of his tall-as-hell but truly flesh-and-blood alive ass. Then her gaze rests on me, floating translucent and fat: the dead black girl beside him. Still mohawked, still fabulous and unfuckwithable. But very dead.

And invisible to most.

Jimmy waves at her, and his voice cracks when he says

"Hi," poor dear. She nods, ever so slightly, at me, and then she's back in the glow of her laptop, and I want to be that glow, to bathe her face, receive her undivided gaze.

"You coming to the secret meet up, Baba Eddie?" Jimmy yells. So much for the secret part.

"Baba Eddie's giving a reading," the girl says without looking up.

"Oh," Jimmy says. "Are you new? I haven't seen you here before."

She turns to him, and those big eyes narrow to vicious slits. "I built this place."

"Oh, I didn't . . ."

She assesses him and then seems to decide to be merciful, returns to her laptop. "I've been away."

"Well, welcome back. I'm Jimmy."

"You're not gonna introduce your friend there?" She nods at me. My face catches fire. I manage a smile through the flames.

"Oh, you—" Jimmy starts.

"I'm Krys," I say.

The girl lets loose a wide, adorable smile. She's got a gap: two front teeth just fully doing their own thing, side by side but not touching. "You can call me Iyawo."

"Ayo?" Jimmy says.

"Yee," she pronounces.

"Yee," we echo.

"Ah."

"Ah."

"Whoa. Iyawo."

Jimmy puzzles his face. "I've never heard that na—"

"It's not a name; it's a title."

"Oh!" He's doing the thing he does: the thing where

he's just oblivious to all that shade. It's either charming as hell or frustrating as fuck, depending on who he's dealing with and how much coffee they've had. The Iyawo seems to be softening to him, though. I'm just hovering in a corner amidst herb packets and dangling necklaces, trying to catch my breath.

"Well, nice to meet you, Iyawo." He pronounces the fuck outta it, and she seems to appreciate that, right up until he reaches out a hand.

She frowns at it. "I can't shake your hand."

"Oh, my bad."

"It's alright. It's a iyawo thing."

"Iyawo!" Baba Eddie calls from the back.

The Iyawo cocks her head and raises her eyebrows. "Awo?"

"Bring me some efun, por favor."

She grabs two little cups of chalky white stuff—the million bracelets on her wrist jangling a song directly into my heart—and then she heads to the back.

"Fuck," Baba Eddie says. "Make it a lot."

She whirls around, rolls her eyes.

"Know what? Just bring the whole bucket of 'em. This shit gonna need a real . . . yeah."

The Iyawo retrieves a plastic container and heads back through the aisles of sculpted saints and elaborate pots.

"The Iyawo is fine as fuck," I say.

Jimmy nods. "She aight."

"I heard that," the Iyawo calls from the back.

I cringe, then cringe deeper, then just give up because she didn't seem to mind, and anyway: it's true.

"I dunno if she's my speed," Jimmy says.

"Do you even have a speed?" Mina Satorius was the

only girl I've known Jimmy to have dated. She was a wee little white chick, and her satanic, doll-collecting grandma went MIA after Carlos busted her trying to steal Jimmy's soul. They messed around a few times after that, but really, that's a tough hurdle to overcome for a dweeby high school relationship. Jimmy and I check out ass on the street together, but his tastes have no rhyme or reason.

Jimmy shrugs. "I'm equal opportunity when it comes to the booty."

"You would be if you ever got any."

He's about to zing back when the front door opens just as the Iyawo reappears from the back. A tall bald-headed dude with a ridiculous goatee stalks in, smile first.

"What it do, my Iyaweezy!" he yells, crossing the store in a single stride and offering a fist bump to the Iyawo. "Dap? Ha! I'm kidding—don't touch me." He whisks his hand away, chuckling, then crosses his arms over his chest and bows slightly.

The Iyawo, who's been standing perfectly still with one eyebrow cocked and one hand on her hip, does the same, shaking her head. "Whaddup, Rohan?"

"Picking up Baba Eddie for the thing. You coming?"

She slides back behind the counter and pouts. "He says I can't cuz I'm a iyawo."

"Aw, man. Ah!" Rohan whirls around like Jimmy crept up on him. "What's up, my man. You mad tall! You almost as tall as I am, my dude. I'm Rohan."

"Jimmy," Jimmy says. They shake and Jimmy flinches.

"Ay, ghost." Rohan waves at me, smiling brightly.

"What it do?" I give him a salute. "I'm Krys." Guess I shouldn't be surprised that folks in a botánica can see spirits, but it still catches me off guard. Invisibility formed a habit with me.

Baba Eddie strolls in from the back. "Well, I see everyone's met." Jimmy and I call Baba Eddie the Puerto Rican Super Mario. He's short and shaped like a fire hydrant with a mustache. I've never seen him mad, but I have a feeling it's a terrifying sight—he's one of the nicest people I've ever met, and the ferocity hides deep in his eyes, but trust me, it's there. "Rohan, Krys and Jimmy are gonna roll with us to the thing."

"Fantastic," Rohan says.

"Iyawo." Baba Eddie pulls his jacket on and takes a cigarette out. "Baba Gene is gonna need a minute. He'll be along shortly. Just make sure you charge him for the efun and make a note we gotta restock."

"Already done," the Iyawo says. "Have fun at the secret meeting." She flashes a wicked smile at me, and even though it's a snowy winter day, for a second, everything is sunlight.

I'm still tingling with it when Baba Eddie leans over the front seat of Rohan's Crown Vic and says, "Listen, you two: do *not* under any circumstances fall in love with the Iyawo."

I frown at him. "Why would we?"

"Ha!" He turns back around. The cigarette still sits unlit in his mouth—Baba Eddie's big on savoring every little moment of his singular vice. "Why indeed." He raises the lighter, flicks it once, twice, a third time, and finally touches the flame to the tip, inhales.

"What's a iyawo anywa—" Jimmy doesn't finish cuz

I bap him on the shoulder. My translucent hand slides through his warm flesh, bone, and blood and he shudders.

"Not on the first drag, man, you know that."

Jimmy shuts up.

We hear the whisper of the kerosene, the embers crinkling, turning black like Baba Eddie's lungs must be, the slosh of cars driving through muddy snow, wet flakes from the sky slapping against the windows.

Baba Eddie lets out a sigh, his eyes closed.

"We going by Mama Esther's first, right?" Rohan says when it seems like the moment has passed.

The santero nods, eyes still closed. "Supersecret premeeting to prepare for the less-secret meeting."

Rohan grunts. "This is it, huh? We doin' it."

Baba Eddie chuckles wearily. "We doin' it. After this, there's no turning back. You got that, youngens?"

We nod.

"No turning back," he says again. Then he reaches his arm across the front seat and turns to face us. "A iyawo is a brand-new baby santero. Or in this case, santera. She just got made a few weeks ago, right after she got back from Brazil, in fact."

"Got made," I say. "Like in the mafia?"

"Heh, kinda," Baba Eddie chuckles. "But nicer. Usually. Anyway, her name is Kia, but for the next year, her name is Iyawo."

"*Year?*" Jimmy and I say together.

"And she will only wear white. She won't be going out at night, going to parties, drinking . . . none of that."

"Damn," Jimmy says. "Shut the whole thing down, huh?"

Baba Eddie shrugs. "She's brand-new and wide-open, spiritually speaking. Reborn."

"That's why she can't touch people?" I ask, trying to pretend like my whole entire shit isn't crumbling before my eyes. I wonder if I could wait a year. I wonder if Ki—the Iyawo could love a dead girl. Or any girl.

"Right," Baba Eddie says. "And that's why you won't be falling in love with her." He shoots a sharp look at Jimmy, who raises both hands and tries to look innocent. "Or making her fall in love with you." He glares at me.

I just shrug and look out the window.

"She's married to orisha," Baba Eddie says, turning back around. "'Iyawo' means wife. And orisha always wins."

Rohan just chuckles.

You can't feel lonely in Mama Esther's house. Trust me, I've tried. That ill emptiness starts to rise up, and then all that warm Mama Esther essence just lifts it and disperses it across the atmosphere like so many swirling dust motes. It's not that she lives in a brownstone on Franklin Avenue—Mama Esther *is* a brownstone on Franklin Avenue. She's a house ghost, which means she's like the cumulative spiritual energies of however many generations of women who lived there plus the actual building itself. She's gigantic and usually keeps to the top floor, where stacks and stacks of ancient and not-so-ancient books form some kind of epic spiritual library. I asked her once if she could ever leave, like just take off and go somewhere else, and she shook her head. "Not unless I take the house with me." That's what being a grounded ghost means, she told me: you a part of the place on a whole other level.

Mama Esther's smile always has a hint of sadness— that's how you know it's real.

The pre-meeting meeting is on the third floor, in an old wood-paneled room that's empty except for a huge claw-footed table surrounded by a bunch of foldout chairs and all the people, alive and dead, that I love the most in this world, except Carlos.

"Where's Carlos?" Riley asks when we walk in. He's a burly, bald-headed, brown-skinned former soulcatcher; he went AWOL when he cut down an ancient plantation-master ghost who the Council had designated a protected entity. He and C are best friends.

"Thought he was with you," Baba Eddie says.

I pull up a chair next to Riley. Jimmy sits beside me. "Probably got held up on some Council shit," I tell them. "They sent him and a new guy to handle some situation on a bridge this morning."

Big Cane sits on the other side of Riley—he's pretty much one of my favorite people, dead or alive. He's huge and white, which I guess explains why they call him that, and always knows when to shut the fuck up, which is why we're cool. We exchange a nod and smile. Across the table are Cyrus Langley, an old-time conjurer from the way-back-when days of New York, and his great-great-great-great-great-great-grandson Damian.

"And where's Gordo?" Riley demands. "Shit is too real right now for folks to just be playin' hooky."

"He had to babysit," Damian says. Damian's tiny, a child ghost, and it still bothers me a little, thinking of him dying so young and stuck in this little translucent, glowing form. He never told me how he went, and I never asked.

Everyone gets quiet after that, because the whole thing with Carlos having kids that he doesn't even see hasn't sat well with anyone since we found out a few months ago.

"You were waiting for me?" a great big voice says. "How sweet!" Mama Esther's gigantic head appears above the table, smiling that smile of hers. "Now let's get right down to it."

"That's what I'm talkin' 'bout," Riley says.

Cyrus Langley floats up out of his seat and leans forward on the table. His old, weathered face usually has a grandfatherly smile ready to shine out on the world, but today the conjureman is somber. "My people, we find ourselves at a crossroads."

"Amen," Mama Esther says.

"We been agitatin' and causing some mild mayhem for the Council for a few months now. They're down one chairman and there've been minor skirmishes in six of the remaining ten Remote Districts. The Council has begun to take notice, and they're vexed, my friends."

"A beautiful thing," Riley says.

The Remote Districts are small autonomous communities around the city that outright reject Council rule. "Crossroads moments are about crisis," Cyrus continues. "But the way I see it, we been in crisis for a minute now, just a very slow, painful one."

General mutters of assent from around the table.

"Now, we have three reliable folks inside the Council"—that'd be Carlos, Big Cane, and myself—"and the fools upstairs been beating us all down with their regulations, brutality, and corruption for long as anyone can remember. We've lost more souls than we can count. We've petitioned for change and demanded change and in reply they spat in our faces, ransacked our communities, murdered our living relatives. Should be no surprise that more than half the Remote Districts stand ready to bring havoc.

We have played by their rules long enough." The room
gets very quiet. I'm pretty sure we all knew this was coming, but still, it's the moment we've all been waiting for
for a while now. "It's time, I think, that we brought the
crisis to the Council."

There's a pause.

"Fuck yeah," I say. Then everybody laughs and cheers.

Cyrus clears his throat. "Which brings us to the meeting we're about to attend."

"Yeah, about that," Riley says.

Cyrus nods at him to take over, and Riley stands. "The
six Remote Districts that have been causing trouble—
that'd be RDs 4, 5, 7, 12, 15, and 17—have called for a
coordination meeting. They want to organize a unified
protest, basically send a message to the Council that
they're not going anywhere and not here for no COD bullshit etcetera, etcetera."

"But?" Baba Eddie says.

Riley scowls. "We're pretty sure the Council's gotten
to at least one of 'em."

"Wouldn't they tell Big Cane or Krys if they were
trying to sabotage the RDs?" Jimmy asks.

I shake my head. "Nah, man. They know we cool with
Carlos, and Carlos been getting the Council stink-eye
since Riley defected. We're all suspect, far as they're
concerned."

"They still giving you the big guns though, right?"
Riley asks.

I flash a winning smile. "They haven't given me any
new toys in a few, but they ain't asked for the old ones
back either." In Soulcatcher Academy, I pretty much
killed it—no pun—the whole way through; no one could

handle phantom ballistics like ya girl Krys. So they tried a pilot program on me, handing over all the good weaponry so I can test it out. "Anyway, they don't have much of a choice at this point, since no one else knows how to use the shit like I do."

"Excellent," Cyrus says, finally showing us that shiny smile that's somehow loving and menacing at the same time.

"More than being concerned about a mole, though," Damian says. "We're worried about a massacre."

"Ah," Baba Eddie says, and the room gets quiet.

Finally, Big Cane pipes up. He talks slow; it must take a while for the words to make their way through all the hugeness that encompasses him. "Thing is," he drawls, "I know the Council's foul much as any of us, but a massacre? Would they go that far before they even have a true rebellion on their hands? Seems unlikely. Risky, I mean, on their part. Let's say they slaughter a bunch of Remote District ghosts and then spurn a whole other uprising on the strength of that event, ya know?"

Some grumbles, and then Riley: "I wouldn't put it past 'em. They're tone deaf and bloodthirsty. Dangerous combination. And like Cyrus said, they're vexed. 'Specially now that they lost one of the Seven."

"Either way," Cyrus says. "We're proceeding with caution here. No warmbodies out in the field. I want Baba Eddie, Jimmy, and Rohan to hang back."

"Aw, man," Jimmy huffs. Baba Eddie looks relieved.

Cyrus continues. "Riley, Damian, and I will be in the meet. Council already knows who we are anyway. No one is to speak of any larger plan beyond the coordinated protest. We just there to listen and let everyone else play

their cards so we can see what we can see. And none of
our Council insiders are to make a showing, especially
not Carlos—if he ever shows up."

Riley snorts.

"So Big Cane, you and Krys and Rohan will post up
in the woods around the field where we meet. Any sign
of trouble, you all are the backup. Extract our folks and
get the hell out, yes?"

Big Cane and I nod.

"Good." Cyrus pounds the table one time. "We meet
at the park in one hour."

"What about me?" Mama Esther says. "You want me
to come, Cy?"

Cyrus flashes her his biggest smile yet. "I need you to
stick around, Miss Esther, so I know I'll have that pretty
face here to greet me when we come out of this mess
alive."

I think the whole room gapes at the same time. Did
Cyrus Langley just . . . flirt? We're all packing up to leave
and snickering with each other when Mama Esther calls
me over.

"Meet me upstairs," she says, her whisper warm and
mischievous.

I devoured books when I was alive. Ate my way through
whatever chapter books my parents bought me as a kid,
then their bookshelves, top to bottom. My dad was a history professor, and Mom had a thing for sci-fi, so between
the two of 'em I was set for a little while. Then I hit my
early teens and started building my own little library, a
kind of hybrid monster of them both, plus some brand-

new titles that were all me: bell hooks and Alice Walker; all the Song of Ice and Fire books and everything by Baldwin; Stephen King and Amiri Baraka, side by side.

That was one shelf. There were eight others, equally outrageous and fantastical, and I was dreaming of so many more when I got sick. My grandma usedta read to me from her grandma's Bible while I lay there, dying. It was boring as hell—she favored the ain't-shit-going on books like Numbers and boring-ass Deuteronomy—but the sound of her deep, old voice, rich and full and black and true, brought me peace. Anyway, the chemo made my vision blurry, and then I just didn't have it in me to lift my head, and then I was gone.

So up here—in Mama Esther's sacred temple of the written word—I am home.

There's a comfort in knowing I could never, ever read all these books. They're huge, first of all—most of 'em great unwieldy leather-bound tomes; some even have old, rusty locks sealing them shut. And beyond that, the stacks seem to go on forever.

Or, they used to. Today, Mama Esther's library looks a little thinned out.

"What's up?" I ask, plopping my translucent ass in one of her plush easy chairs.

"You tell me," Mama Esther says.

"Mama E, you asked me up here."

"And then I asked you what's up. So what's up?"

"Actually, I as—"

"Don't you *actually* me, girl." She's kidding—I know she's kidding. But it comes out sharp. My face must've registered some surprise, because she immediately softens. "Sorry, Krys. It's been . . . it's a rough time, this one."

I purse my lips and nod my head a few times. "Rougher than what Cyrus was talking about just now?"

Mama Esther points her gaze toward the darkening sky out the window. "I think so, child. Yes."

"What's up with you two, anyway?"

She lets out a soft chuckle. "As little Damian would say: Noneya."

"Fine."

"What about you, Krys? Who is he?"

"The hell you talking about, woman?"

She directs a long stare at me and I crumple. "She."

"Oh! My apologies. I've clung to some archaic habits in my old age."

I shrug it off. "S'fine. I just . . . to be honest, there are at least three great reasons why it couldn't happen, but I'm here focused on the one dumb one."

"Which is?"

"I feel . . . fat."

Mama Esther busts out laughing.

"I know, I know, shut up."

"No . . . It's just . . ." She tries to collect herself, fails. Throws her head back again. The whole building shakes with her silent chuckle.

"No, I get it. I'm a ghost. I don't even have *weight*. I literally weigh nothing. And like . . . so what if I am fat, right? I get that too. I mean, shit, I was fine as fuck, excuse me, fine as shit. Dammit, I was fine when I was alive. I'm still fine."

Mama Esther's eyes are still squeezed shut, and great ghostly tears slide down her face, around her wide smile. I don't even think she's listening.

"But this girl, she's just so lithe and slender. She's like

a fuckin' antelope. Grace just *lives* in her body. She could trip over her own feet and it'd be a ballet, Mama Esther. I feel huge beside her. Huge."

Mama Esther wipes her eyes with giant, glowing hands. "You think you big," she says. "Bitch, I'm a house." She cackles. "Literally!"

Old ghosts are so weird.

"I'm sorry, I'm sorry." She collects herself, wipes her eyes again. "I've always wanted to say that. I'm good. Listen, Krys, babychild. You beautiful. You more than fine—you reinvent grace. Trust me. It's on another level. And yes, there's so much of you to love. God just kept giving and giving, bless him. Embrace it. Please. It's all yours."

I sigh. I've told myself as much before, believed it too, but it's different coming from Mama Esther. "Thanks," I say, real quiet.

"Whenever you worried about being bigger than this li'l thing you interested in, just think about how much bigger I am than ol' Cyrus Langley."

"Whoa."

"And believe me when I tell you that doesn't stop him from loving the hell outta me, and loving me *right*."

"Jesus, Mama E, what happened to noneya?"

She rolls her eyes. "Just remember."

"Is that what you brought me up here to talk about?"

She coughs out the last little bit of laughter and straightens her face. "No, actually, that was just because you looked like you had someone on your mind. I wanted to give you these." She nods toward a small stack of books on the reading table.

"Give? Me? Wha—why?"

"Don't act like I'm miserly with the book now, Krys. Carlos probably has half my library tucked away in that little apartment of his. *Borrowed*." She makes little bunny ears with her fingers.

"Not half, though."

"Not by a long shot, no." She winks. "Anyway, take 'em. Call it an expansion."

"How so?"

"This way there'll be little satellite branches of the Mama Esther library all over the city."

"Okay," I say, putting the books in my bag. They're old and musty. I can't wait to dig in.

A morose silence settles over us, broken only by the shuttle train rumbling past. "You're worried, aren't you?" I say.

She nods, turning away. "Run along now, little dancer. They'll be waiting for you."

CHAPTER THREE

Sasha

The first face I saw when I came back to life was Trevor's. A thick ache swarmed my muscles and bones, and sharp flicks of pain danced up and down my sides like each nerve was exploding horribly back to life.

We were both crying; neither of us knew why. We didn't know anything, in fact. Memory wiped clean; all that was left was pain. So we sobbed, two newborn babies in full-grown bodies, lost and terrified. All we knew was that something was missing.

We were too weak to stand at first, so we lay there, sliding in and out of sleep and waking with bursts of terror, then sorrow. Trying to comfort each other. The walls were bare, no windows, so his breath and slow heartbeat became the only song I knew, my clock and compass.

And I knew he was my brother before I knew where we were or what had happened. It was never a question: this man beside me had grown up there. Later, when we saw ourselves in a mirror together for the first time, the unmistakable likeness wasn't even a surprise. We already knew.

A man who called himself Terra brought food and told us what had happened: we'd died, been murdered, and then brought back to life. Mostly. He looked away when he said "mostly," and no amount of pestering or threats could get more out of him. He put down our plates and slinked away. Later, two more showed up—a burly, bearded man and a middle-aged woman—and slowly we found trust, language, a kind of fragile connection.

When we were finally ready to venture into the world, it turned out that history had not been erased with memory. I knew this place called Brooklyn, her buildings and bridges, the streets and what they meant. I knew the wider world: messy, ongoing geopolitical melodramas and cultures thrashing up against each other. I knew the Middle Passage and arrogant gaze of expansionism, I knew the slow tide of peoples moving across this planet, by choice and by bullwhip.

But I had no idea where I was in all of it. I was a void amidst the thunderstorm, an empty woman-shaped shell in all that churning humanity. I was nobody. History was alive, but I had no part of it.

A few weeks after we were resurrected, Terra vanished. We scoured the city for him, but we had nothing to go on: no name, no information at all. All we know was what he looked like, and it's not like we could go to the police. The Survivors are all but wiped out now. Carlos and I killed Sarco, who set up the whole murder/resurrection tango. And I still don't really know where I fit, except to be a mother to two little babies.

"They're fine," Gordo insists into the phone. "Esleeping on top of me, in fact."

"Both of them?" Night has fallen around us, and the city sparkles to life on either side of the Manhattan Bridge. I slide the Crown Vic in and out of traffic; Reza keeps an eye on my maneuvering from the passenger seat, humming some salsa song under her breath. In the backseat, Janey chuckles to herself, her face lit with the spooky blue glow of her cellphone.

"Jes." Gordo chuckles. "I tried to put them in the crib but they wouldn't let go, even while they were asleep."

"You sure you don't mind staying later, Gordo? I feel bad."

"Ha! You should feel good, Sasha. I had a meeting to attend. Two in fact. I hate meetings. Meetings are Satan's way of balancing out all the beautiful things in the world, like music."

"Okay, man." Leave it to Gordo to make poetry out of a mundane ol' moment like that.

The Manhattan Bridge spits us out onto Canal Street and a clusterfuck of traffic.

"It's alright," Reza tells us. "The ferry leaves every hour, even on weekends." I don't bother asking how she knows that. It's Reza. She's probably dumped plenty of bodies in the New York Harbor.

We leave the car in a lot and make our way to the docks.

"He said Spine Island?" Janey asks when the ferry pulls off. "How is that even a thing though?"

The sky is black around us, the water blacker still. Manhattan's scattered lights twinkle in the ripples, and then they're mostly gone too and we're deep in the harbor and it feels like a million miles away.

"Apparently it's the Spine Islands," I say. "And we're to go to the sacrum."

"Yeah, they're mostly forgotten," Reza says. The frosty night wind cuts through us, and only Reza doesn't seem to mind. Janey and I, bundled up as we are, are still shivering our asses off.

"Aye," a voice says behind us. "Forgotten indeed." The ferry captain stands beside a big rusted anchor chain, smoking something hand-rolled and slobbered-on. "And what are you pretty ladies looking to find on such a forgotten archipelago?"

"Some peace and quiet," Reza says, her voice ice. The ferry captain fucks off accordingly.

"What *are* we looking to find though?" Janey asks when we turn back to the empty, dark harbor ahead.

"Flores said we'd know it when we got there," I tell them. "Guessing it's some high priority Council target they don't want anyone knowing about. He said something about it being a demonstration of his fealty to me." I affect some of the limping phantom's lilting drawl: "A gift for my lady."

"Not creepy at all," Janey smirks.

"And we trust this ghost why?" Reza asks.

"We don't," I say. "That's why I brought you along."

Janey's great-aunt CiCi been passing on some old-time magic to her and some white boy who lives next door. Janey doesn't talk much about it, trade secrets I guess, but I know she got some ferocious death-dealing power in those hands of hers.

And Reza's just Reza. She can't be stopped.

Besides being the best friends I have in the world, they're about as perfect a kill team as a woman could want. We must cut a mean tableau, strutting down the gangplank onto the deserted Spine Islands docking port. The snow flits through the night sky, a lackadaisical cascade coating the dilapidated shacks and skeletal trees.

"Looks cheerful," Janey says as the ferry hauls off into the darkness.

Reza puts a Conejo in her mouth, offers us the pack even though we always refuse. "Just wait," she says, her smile wry.

We stand on Cervical 1, the top island and the only one with an actual dock. The other six splay out in a loose arch that more or less evokes their namesake. Most are about the size of a baseball field, if even that big, and the only way to get between them is a fleet of rusty rowboats scattered throughout.

"You like this place, don't you, Reza?" Janey says as we unlatch the metal skiff at the far end of the island and set out. "This is like, totally your shit, isn't it?"

Reza shrugs, flicks her cigarette into the empty, snow-splattered world around us. "It's discreet. No record of our presence, no witnesses that I can see."

"No escape should shit go sour," Janey adds. "'Cept these dinky rowboats."

Reza's smile gets wider. "I'm ready for trouble." She pats the area just under her armpit where her Glock hangs.

"I dunno if the kind of trouble we're gonna find will care much about bullets," I say.

Reza just watches the snow. She told me the other day she hadn't been in a good shoot-out for a while, so she's probably happy to have some potential action in the works.

An eerie claustrophobia sets in, knowing the only way out is either to wait for the ferry or row like hell. Still, the

"That much is clear. Who are you?"

"Dr. Calloway," the ghost whimpers. "I don't . . . I don't want trouble, yes?" He's not lying—it's clear his only allegiance is to his own terror. "What do you need?"

"What is this place?"

"COD CentCom," Dr. Calloway says, brightening now that he can be of use. "Affectionately known as the Brain by Council higher-ups."

I had figured as much. "So each of these strands . . ."

"Connects the Council to one of their soulcatchers."

"Meaning they know where all their people are at all times."

"Ha . . . in theory," the doctor titters. He brings his hands down and rubs them together. "Of course . . . things don't always pan out that way. At the Sunset Park headquarters, there is a corresponding room where the information itself is broadcast, but it's not, shall we say, reliable?"

"That's comforting."

"Often the data is out of date, or just gone. But most people don't know that." He's pleading with me, proving his worth in secrets.

Carlos.

I walk along the edge of the Brain, avoiding the threads and keeping Dr. Calloway in my peripheral. "Seems important."

"Oh, very!" He falls into a glidey step beside me.

"Then why doesn't the Council care about it?"

"What's that?"

"Four soulcatchers to guard the central communication site of the entire operation? Seems low priority."

"Ah, no one can destroy what they don't know exists.

The Brain is one of the Council of the Dead's best-kept secrets." He's excited now, right back in his nerd-bro element. "Secrecy is the best form of defense, yes?"

"Apparently not," I say. I bring my blade down on the nearest glowing strand. It doesn't give right away, some tough ghost fiber, but with some added encouragement from my shoulders, the thread shivers and then collapses, the newly free strand floating off and disintegrating in the darkness.

"Oh no!" Dr. Calloway screams. He lurches toward the squiggly stump of thread left behind. "This is . . . treason! And the Council will . . . oh! I—" He stops short because my blade is in his face.

"Carlos Delacruz."

"W-what?"

"Show me the thread that's connected to Carlos Delacruz."

"But I—"

"Don't lie to me."

Dr. Calloway shakes his head, coughs, simpers, and then deflates a little and leads me to the other side of the Brain. At the far end of the room, a slightly open door lets a sliver of light into the dark warehouse. I nod at it. "Someone else here, Dr. Calloway?"

"No! I swear it! She's out."

"She?"

"I . . . It doesn't matter."

"Oh, but it does. Show me Carlos's thread; then we'll talk about this she."

He floats up amongst the glowing Brain strands, eyes squinted, mouth opening and closing around some inconceivable equations, and finally yells, "This one!"

"Bring it to me."

He frowns, looking back and forth between me and the thread, then eyeing the far door. "You won't make it," I say. "And if you do, my people outside will kill you. And if they don't, I'll find you later and kill you and everything you love."

Reza taught me that one. It only works if you really mean it when you say it. I do and it does: Dr. Calloway wraps his trembling ghost hand around the thread and pulls it down to where I stand. It looks like the rest except for a dim red hue.

"They'll know," he says, still holding on to it.

"I'm sure they will." I cut the thread—a strange gift, a strange kind of freedom for a strange man.

Dr. Calloway sighs, then looks at me with wide eyes as it dawns on him his usefulness has worn out.

"Who's this she?" I nod at the open doorway.

He shakes his head, backing away. "Please, don't . . . no. Just . . . do whatever you want, but I can't . . . don't make me . . ."

Chasing him down will be more trouble than it's worth at this point. "Go." I turn toward the door. "Believe that I can find you, wherever you end up. You have more to fear from me than the Council."

"Yes," Dr. Calloway whispers.

The door opens to a small office that's been converted into a crude kind of living space. There's an air mattress, an electric stove top, a Crock-Pot, and a space heater. On the rusty old metal desk in the corner: a laptop.

There isn't much time. At some point, the Council will realize their precious CentCom has been sabotaged. I'm

not sure how long it'll take them to get their shit together
and counterattack, but I'd rather not find out. I scoop up
the laptop, walk out the door, and freeze.

Dr. Calloway stands at the far end of the room. He
waves his hands over his head, then turns and runs toward
me, squealing in terror. Something huge emerges from
the shadows. It's carrying a long length of chain that glim-
mers in the glow of the Brain. Dr. Calloway turns back to
look, shrieks, and then trips over himself. The thing
lurches, and its chain lashes out, crashes down on Calloway in a tangled heap. A dozen screaming mouths open
across the monster's bulky, misshapen form. It's a throng
haint, a collected mash of spirits. And it's pissed. The
throng haint reels its chain back in, dragging Dr. Calloway
with it. When he lies writhing at its feet, the haint reaches
two long, bulgy shadow arms down and scoops him up,
extracting him from the chain. Calloway lets out one final
shriek as he's enveloped into the haint's flickering mass,
and then he's gone—another open mouth in the mire.

I drop the laptop and launch forward while the throng
haint is still taking Calloway in. It flicks a wrist and the
chain whips up to meet me. My blade cuts a long upward
arc, clanging against the chain. The chain doesn't shatter
like I thought it would—instead, the reverberations shoot
up my already-wounded arm, throw me wildly off-balance.
I hurl myself to the side just as the other end of the chain
crashes down where I'd just been.

The throng haint whirls, sending its whip in a low
circle across the room and shredding at least a dozen
ghost threads in its path. I hit the floor, barely in time,
and roll out of the way, panting. The haint lurches again,
throws a bulky, tumorous shoulder forward and the chain

comes flying over its head toward me. I roll again. I won't be able to keep this up much longer. I rise running, aim directly at the haint, and flush to the side at the last minute, dragging my blade across its midsection as I pass. An arm bursts out of its bulk, smashes clumsily against my shoulder. I spin at the ground but manage to slice it as I fall. Part of its shadowy hand disperses into the air.

The throng haint howls, a hideous Klaxon exploding inside my head. Then it hurls the entire coiled mass of chains at me. I clamber away, gasping. A dull, pulsing ache works its way up my leg.

I'm caught.

The haint is on me, faster than I thought possible, long, bulbous arms closing in on either side. I'm in no position to get leverage, but I swing anyway, clipping off a few fingers to clear those hands and then stabbing at its midsection. Mouths open, teeth gnashing, saliva dripping, and I shove my blade in one. The haint shudders, clobbers at my shoulder with one arm, but it's a sloppy attack. I swat its arm away, stab another open mouth, and then pull my blade upward, cleaving through ichorous haint flesh and slicing through a few mouths on the way.

The haint falls to its knees. The mouths keep opening and closing around me. If it collapses forward, we might go out together. I slash again, up and then across, opening generous new gashes in its bulk. The chain still has my ankle pinned though.

"Sasha!"

Janey. I can't turn to look, not with this monster still clawing. I get two more cuts in and then throw myself as far out of the way as I can when the haint falls forward in a muddled heap, barely missing my leg.

"The chain," I gasp as Janey runs up. She's on it, shoving the scrabbling creature aside with her glowing red hands. The thing's flesh dissipates at her touch. She grabs the chain, extracts my foot, pulls me up.

My sword comes down on what's left of the throng haint. Then again. And again.

"Sash."

"Shh."

It's scattered shreds of shimmering, empty flesh now. I splatter each one, watch them dissipate.

"Sash, we gotta go."

She's right. I close my eyes, bow slightly to the carnage. Shred as many strands of Brain matter as I can on the way to the door. "Thank you, Janey," I say quietly.

Outside, the snow cascades in relentless sheets. We're halfway down the hill when something prickles at the back of my neck. I look back, squinting through the snow and darkness.

"C'mon," Janey urges, but something's out there. Something watches us. "What is it?"

I shake my head. And then my eyes adjust and I see them. Eight more throng haints stand at the top of the hill, shimmering chains in hand. They don't move; they just watch us as we turn back toward the boat and run.

Carlos

There was this moment a few months ago, and I feel like it's been imprinted on my mind, lingering with me ever since. The Council had sent me to Remote District 17 to quell a potentially unstable situation. To the Council, anyone having a good time without permission constitutes a potentially unstable situation, but in this case, a bunch of ghosts had figured out how to immigrate into the district and they were flooding the streets—the living communed in the full public eye with their ancestors. And it was . . . it was beautiful. I'd brought Jimmy with me; he was still pretty new on the ghost scene, and for a moment I just stood there and took it in, this marvel of coexistence, this armistice in the war I carried within me. A dapper, middle-aged shroud accompanied a fully alive little old lady to the bakery. Three little ghostlings played hopscotch with some living kids, while teenagers both flesh and ethereal looked on.

Something in me almost broke right then and there. I pulled it together, though. There was a rebellion about to break out, and not the good kind—this one was a massacre waiting to happen. No time to get misty-eyed about what would never be.

I remember that happy street, as I do at least eight times a day, while I stand off to the side with Ookus, Riley, and Damian. One by one the Remote Districts send their reps to confer privately with Cyrus. The respect for the old conjurer is palpable; infighting and related bullshit falls away as each spirit takes a turn trudging through the falling snow to where Cyrus waits by the forest. First up is Saeen Moughari, the woman who butted heads with Moco. They confer quietly, and then she returns to the RD 4 contingent; they nod at the others and fade into the night.

Father Desmond reps RD 5. He's an older cat, doesn't seem to want any trouble, but his area sits along the southern reach of East New York and his folks have been fed up with the Council for ages now. He leans his old shaggy head forward to listen to Cyrus's whisper, then thinks quietly for a few moments, eyes closed. Cyrus waits, then smiles when Father Desmond mutters a final word and departs.

Kaya Doxtator and Breyla Phan are next. RD 7 sits nestled into a far corner of Harlem, and they've sent a large delegation. Kaya and Breyla always move as a pair— I think they're connected by some kind of unseen magic— so Cyrus doesn't bother trying to get one or the other to come. RD 7 has risen up a few times already, always with deadly consequences; I'm sure they've been waiting a long time for this day.

Vincent Jackson swaggers through the snow with that never-ending ease he always radiates. Like me, Vincent died so violently it tore every memory of his life away. But it was a high-profile case, and soon after he showed up as a spirit, all of Remote District 12 clamored to let him know what happened, who he was. They showed him his family, the corner he'd stood on when the cops blew him away, took him to the protests that had erupted in his name. Soon other spirits who'd been killed by cops gathered to him, and the Black Hoodies were born—one of the most badass ghost crews in open defiance of the Council. And the Council was predictably pissed—they'd lost control of the narrative from jump, but Vincent was too big a deal to snuff out. Cyrus embraces him like an old friend, and they chat amiably for a few minutes before getting down to business, Cyrus's reckless, cigar-stained cackle echoing through the park.

Moco staggers forward, always a little off kilter. I don't know if it's those wandering, bugged-out eyes or just a general awkwardness, but the dude can't seem to walk a straight line. He's with Cyrus the longest, nodding, then shaking his head, then nodding again. Finally, they part. Moco bows slightly, and then he fades away with the rest of RD 17 and we're alone.

"Nice of you to show up," Krys says, working her way out of the woods with Big Cane in her wake. Rohan follows close behind, his eyes scanning the snowy fields.

"I do what I can." She wraps me in a chilly hug. I would say I took Krys under my wing, but the truth is, I probably learn more from her than she does from me. She sought me out and slid seamlessly into our little ragtag posse. Plus she has a bazooka.

"What was that all about?" Riley asks.

Cyrus grins as we gather around him, his old eyes glassy. "That was called the New Amsterdam Rat Trap. That's what we usedta call it back when, anyway." Damian hovers beside him, looking smug.

"You had a chat with 'em each," Riley says, "and told 'em 'bout where the meet-up point is for the coordinated appearance."

"Ay."

"But how we gonna know which is the rat?" Krys asks.

"If any of 'em," Big Cane puts in.

"They all got different locations," Rohan says, looking wildly proud of himself. "If one spot gets flooded with soulcatchers, we got our rat."

Cyrus nods. "Indeed, young man, indeed."

"Reza and I usedta do that with rival gangs during the War Years. Play 'em off each other."

"So we got a stakeout to do tomorrow," I say.

"No." Cyrus's old face crinkles into a frown. "*We* got a stakeout to do tomorrow. You, Carlos, gotta go to Sunset Park and tell the Council you've been spying on us."

"With ya not showing up to the pre-meeting meeting ass," Riley mutters.

"Otherwise," Cyrus says, "as far as the Council knows, you just showed up at a meeting of subversives and are therefore in open rebellion against your own bosses."

"Story of my life," I say, but he's right. If there really is a mole, I'm blown. "Alright, I gotya."

"You want me to go with him?" Krys says. "In case, you know . . . they don't believe him."

"And then we lose two insiders instead of one?" Cyrus shakes his head. "Carlos is more than capable of fighting his way out of there." He winks at me. "And anyway, we need you on the stakeout, Krys. It might get ugly."

"Speaking of ugly shit," Riley says. "What if they had decided to come crush us while they had everyone here in one place at one time? I don't think Krys and them hiding in the woods woulda made that much of a dent against the full force of the Council. I mean . . . what are the numbers looking like?"

Damian steps up. "We estimate the Council at full force to be about a thousand soulcatchers strong. If the throng haint rumors are true . . ."

"They're true," I say. "We seen 'em."

"There probably aren't more than a dozen, from what I figure," Damian continues. "Of course, a dozen throng haints can do as much damage as a hundred squad of soulcatchers. And they get stronger as they kill, so that's not cute."

We grumble amongst ourselves.

"On the other hand: each Remote District has pledged seventy souls to the cause. Most of 'em won't be trained, but that still gets us to barely half the Council's force. Give or take. And there's no telling what kind of strength Ookus will be able to rustle up from the river giants."

Shrouds begin emerging from the woods around us: spirits. My hand is on my blade. A high-pitched wheeze stammers out into the night, and then I realize it's Cyrus. He's . . . he's laughing.

"What, man?" Riley asks.

"Wasn't gonna be no massacre tonight," Cyrus says when he catches his breath. "And we well over half the soulcatchers body for body."

We send him a collective gape. The figures sweep across the field toward us, a closing circle.

"Y'all ain't counting the new Remote District. The one nobody knows about."

I can make out their determined faces, their old clothes and jewelry. They carry pickaxes and shovels and swords.

"We rose up together as slaves," Cyrus says. "And y'all helped us escape the tombs beneath this city we were trapped in."

They are elders and little ones and everything in between. They arrive with a gentle, ongoing murmuring, something like laughter, something like tears, something like a river. It gets louder as they close around us, join our ranks.

"They've been making a life in this new city, this new world, the future, ever since. And this is their home, the eighteenth Remote District: Prospect Park."

The murmur grows to a reverberating thrum: a war song.

"And they're ready to fight."

CHAPTER FOUR

Caitlin

I t's been a difficult year, hasn't it?"

This simple, tawdry, milquetoast prick. Dr. Eldwin Shrug-Brannigan MD, licensed and board certified psychiatrist, according to the certificates on the wall. What kind of deranged hippies name their child Eldwin?

"It has," I say. I throw in a sniffle.

Behind his frameless glasses: sleepy blue eyes. Beyond that, comb-over, then the diplomas, and above that, a drab painting of a drab woman in a drab pink dress standing beside a flowerpot.

"Many tragic occurrences," Shrug-Brannigan continues, feeling, I'm sure, very clever about his little synopsis. "But also some triumphs, no? You have certainly taken the potatoes that life gave you, as they say, and made potato soup, if you will."

Is that what they say? I just blow my nose pathetically into a tissue and nod.

"Mr. Byron tells me you're the youngest senior VP the agency has ever had. That you've altered the entire course

of our trajectory as an organization even and, let me see"—
he adjusts his glasses and peers at the notepad in his
lap—"in so doing, perhaps helped usher the whole inter-
national adoption industry into the twenty-first century."

I shrug and sniffle and try to look humble. These egre-
gious pinch-faced savages were still using paper files and
floppy disks when I got here; ushering in 2001 really
didn't take much.

"And you spent the last six months in . . . let me see . . .
Dbradsk. Did I say that right?"

Butchered it. "Yes, Dr. Shrug."

"Shrug-Brannigan." He forces a smile to ward away
the awkwardness. It fails. "That's a city?"

"District," I say. "Eastern Siberia."

His mouth drops like he didn't already know that. "I
mean . . . Caitlin, that is just, that is amazing. I mean,
Siberia. Wow. Fantastic."

Forever snow, forever ice; a slow, never-ending death;
vodka that shreds your throat going down and burns coming back up; husky, bearded lovers with giant trembling
hands; stacks and stacks of files; resentful, traumatized
volunteers; and Monica Tannenbaum, an Australian aid
worker who got too curious. I had to do it myself; those
big burly men that climbed over themselves to prove their
worth to me turned out to be tepid simps when it came
to actually accomplishing things. Monica's eyes kept
pleading with me long after they'd dulled. The snow
landed on her face and she stopped fighting; her mouth
just hung open. Still I squeezed.

You have to finish things you start.

No one else will do it for you.

"It was quite a trip!" I flash a smile through the sniffles.

"And you brought the weather back with you." He gestures to the window, where snow spirals through the night against the sparkling Manhattan skyline. "Mr. Byron says you've had the agency tighten security protocols and block access to all employee and adoptee files."

Mr. Byron is a tragic waste of humanity shoved into a useless sack of skin.

"There were some . . . incidents," I manage. "In Siberia, I mean."

Monica Tannenbaum's bulging eyes went dull. Still I squeezed. For all the fuss and hubbub, taking a life really comes down to tenacity. It's like one of those Choose Your Own Adventure books Jeremy and I would read when we were kids. If you want to snuff out this meddlesome Aussie bitch: keep squeezing. If you want to let her live and then watch as everything you've worked so hard to build comes crashing around you in a blaze of self-righteous Australian fury: release.

Simple, really.

I take another tissue. Sully it. "You know how the Russian mafia is."

Dr. Shrug-Brannigan nods, brow furrowed, then shakes his head. "Terrible."

"The worst, Doctor. And of course, they have a long reach. Long fingers, they call the Russians. It's a metaphor of course, but you know . . . well, you never know. All that cabbage, I think."

He nods again, writes something down. Of course, the real reason for my security precautions is right here in this city. For a sudden, startling moment, I have the urge to just tell Dr. Shrug-B everything—the whole twisted truth with all its monsters and phantoms. I would spit it

all out in an unrelenting monologue and then just laugh
while Eldwin here gapes. And then they'd lock me away
forever, and that would never do.

Still, the notion has a certain devilish appeal.

"Let me ask you a question, Caitlin. How have you
been sleeping?"

"Oh, ha, you know . . . the truth is, not well." The truth
is, I've never slept so well. My little sideroom on the island
is surprisingly cozy, and the silence? Divine. On a night
like this, I could hear the snow fall. And the darkness back
there is complete. I shut out the light and the heater's single
red eye glares out of the black, but otherwise: nothing.

Bliss.

Of course, women who lost their whole family less
than a year ago aren't supposed to sleep well. We're supposed to be weepy, angst filled, skittish. So I sniffle again,
wipe my nose, and shrug. "I sleep some nights. Others . . ." I shake my head and tent one hand over my eyes.

The only nights I don't sleep well are when I'm with
Raj, but who ever finds peace beside another human?
We're such a foul and unpredictable breed, and in sleep
there's no chance to tuck all that away. In one night, Raj
will snore, fart, make little smacking noises—a fucking
symphony—and that's not even to speak of the smells.
But somehow, people do it—spend their lives doing it. I
figure the appeal must grow somehow; at some point, it'll
become familiar, just what is. That's how these things
work, isn't it? It's a small price to pay.

"It's a small price to pay," I say.

"Not sleeping?" the doctor asks, cocking an eyebrow.
"What is it exactly that you are paying for, Caitlin?"

What indeed? That normal life, I suppose. The one my

parents did such a stand-up job of pretending to have, with their lovely suburban Queens home and roachlord son. It's filthy, a shimmering, impossible dullness that radiates outward, metastasizing in mediocre waves across everyone and everything. But still, I crave it. In some deep part of me, I crave it. All this phantom intrigue gets old after a while, especially now that Jeremy's gone and Monica Tannenbaum's eyes keep going dull in front of me while I squeeze. And squeeze. Her bowels emptied out as she died, like one final fuck-you to me for killing her.

"Nothing," I whisper in a choked sob. "Just you know . . . surviving. I guess."

Shrug-B tut-tuts, his brow furrowed. One wisp of his comb-over has come free and flails back and forth like one of those giant floppy phalluses they use to advertise car washes.

"I'm writing you a prescription, Caitlin. You can pick it up at the pharma-desk across the hall. Sylflax is relatively new on the market, but the results have been excellent. It's a combined antianxiety and ACE inhibitor, which of course simply means it will make you feel better and hopefully help you sleep without actually making you drowsy." He opens a wide, grandfatherly smile at me like I'm ten.

This is unexpected and potentially fun. "Thank you, Doctor."

"Just make sure you don't drink any alcohol while you're taking it, and don't take more than one every four to six hours, with a meal. Okay, dear?" He tears the script off and hands it to me. "And hopefully I'll see you next week."

"Yes," I say airily. "Hopefully."

The Mexican girl at the pharma-counter looks about fourteen. I smile at her when I hand over the script.

She doesn't smile back.

"We've done a lot of work in Mexico at the adoption agency," I say, smiling even harder. "What part are you from?"

"South Central," she says.

"Oh, Oaxaca? We actually brought a grou—"

"Los Angeles." Her glare sharpens, then she heads to the back for my drugs.

I make a mental note to be sure we don't get any of her family members adopted if they should ever try. When she returns, I glance at her name tag: "Dr. Simone Hernandez, PhD." Guess they're handing out degrees to any teenager that comes sniffing at the gates these days.

She smiles when she hands me the bag. "Don't drink alcohol when—"

"And one every four hours—I got it." I snatch the meds.

In the elevator, I pop open the little orange canister and shove a handful of pills into my mouth. By the time I reach Luther's to meet the gals, I'm feeling right. Like, real right. I see I'm going to have to make it to my appointment next week after all, if nothing else to cry up a storm and get some more interesting little pills prescribed. Around me the city moves in slow, luxurious swaths of color, each hazy traffic light and blinking street sign a dancing tidal wave in the ebb and flow of Midtown's never-ending electrosymphonic bluster. Snow twirls and dances through the lights, speeds along in a clutch of wind through the great steel Manhattan corridors, and then swooshes upward like a billion particles of some formless superhero. And I'm one with it, entirely given over. For once, Monica Tannenbaum's bulging eyes, Jeremy's torn body sinking beneath the dark water, Carlos Delacruz's snarl—they all fade, swept away in a snowy deluge and then scattered amidst the polyrhythmic flashes of this living, trembling city on this singular night.

"You are late, bitch!" Samantha yells when I walk in. The other two cackle wildly and then rush to kiss my cheeks.

"A bourbon and a shot of vodka," I tell the waiter. Luther's swirls around me: dim, burnt-umber wood stain and old Guinness ads and drunken assholes and a football game on the screens. At the back, a pool table. Men who will say anything to sleep with you, men who are terrified of sleeping with you, men who will drug you to sleep with you. And my girls, Samantha, Gillian, Brittany. All from the adoption agency, all hilarious bitches once you get them out of the office and into the bar. Otherwise, drab and useless as three-day-old oatmeal with too much milk.

"I told Barry that he has three days to get his shit together," one of them says. Brittany, I think. I'm long past being able to tell them apart. "And do you know what he said?"

"Suck my uncircumcised dick!" another yells in a voice I can only imagine must approximate Barry's.

"No!" Brittany slaps her shoulder. "Oliver is the uncircumcised one! You're such a cunt."

We all burst out laughing, and momentarily my face becomes a disparate mass of spittle and brain matter exploding outward into the bar around me, coating the walls and these women and the lonely souls and rapists and busboys with cerebellum and skull. Then I blink as solidity returns, and no one's staring at me, so I guess my head didn't explode after all, but I am drooling, I realize, touching my own mouth and quickly wiping away the dribble. I finish the bourbon and hold up the vodka.

"To Oliver and Barry!" I yell. That gets 'em excited. It's easy really. The names were just mentioned, so they're right there on everyone's mind. It's not funny, but it is, because we all get it and laugh, and most of us probably had no idea someone named Barry or Oliver actually existed in Brittany's—let's be honest—pretty tepid and shallow life up till just now. If she had told us before, we forgot as soon as possible, because really, what use is that information to me—why allow it to share quarters in this mind with so many actually important thoughts?

"To Olly and Baliver," Samantha suggests. That was a good one, Samantha, and I kind of wish I'd said it but am content to have been part of the run-up, and anyway we're all cackling now and our glasses clink with a satisfying splash when half our drinks ends up on the sticky tabletop, and then Gillian, I think it's Gillian, puts her hand on my shoulder and says, "Does Raj have a big dick? I've always wondered that about Indian men."

I have to fight not to splortch my drink across the table, and then all the elements of that moment—Gillian's question and the unexpected upswing of hilarity it ignites inside of me—combine, and once I manage to swallow I realize with a gasp that I'm happy. Truly happy. Authentically present and alive and with my . . . my friends.

"Well, I guess that's a yes!" Sam cackles, mistaking my gasp for an answer. Then I cackle too and Brittany actually *does* splortch her drink, right on a passing waiter's crotch.

"Oh my God!" Brittany yells. "I can't believe I just did that! You guys!"

No one answers her, because we're too busy cracking up.

"I'm so, so sorry," Brittany pleads with the empty space where the waiter was just standing.

Sam, always ready with a clever joke, points out, "That was like a reverse facial, if you think about it."

"Oh my God, ew!" Brittany yells. "But yes! Oh-em-gee, yes!"

"Because like, you spewed on his dick," says Gillian, always ready with the overexplanation of Sam's jokes.

See? I know their little quirks and ticks, the oddities that make them who they are. They're more than just a cover story now. Brittany is shaking her head, saying, "I wonder if I have to confess to Brolliver that I reverse facialed a waiter," when Raj materializes in the crowd, and I wonder for a second if I didn't accidentally conjure him up when I wasn't paying attention.

No, Caitlin Fern, you had told him to come meet you at the bar tonight, because you wanted to spend some time with your friends and then go home and hop on that beautiful brown penis for a while before lying awake listening to Raj snore, fart, and sigh his way through the night.

No magic: I texted him earlier and then forgot.

"Hey Ra-aj," Samantha croons.

"Rajmataj!" Gillian says in a robot voice.

"Raj Mahal!" Brittany snickers.

Raj smiles in that lopsided, charming way of his and waves. "Hey, ladies."

"You can't just roll up in here all charming and hit us with the 'Hey, ladies,'" Gillian says. Her Raj impression isn't half-bad. "You gotta teach us some sexy yoga moves or something!"

Raj forces a smile. "You say that every time I see you, Gillian."

"I do?" She looks legitimately stunned, which is weird because she does mention yoga every time Raj comes around and he's told her he doesn't know the first thing about yoga at least twelve thousand times. "Oh my God, is that racist? Shit!"

The table is suddenly somber.

"I don't know," Samantha says. "It doesn't seem like you *meant* it in a racist way, and it wasn't like mean? So I don't think so."

Gillian and Brittany nod pensively. I down the vodka. "You want a drink, Raj?"

"Actually, I was wondering if we could talk." When everyone just stares at him, he adds, "Like, outside."

I stand, feeling strangely naked and furious at the same time. A furious naked woman, standing up in a crowded bar. My hands are so heavy, I have to concentrate on lifting them off the table and placing them into my pockets, then taking them out again because that's just weird.

"Outside?" Brittany says, not getting it. "But it's snowing!"

Sam, who always gets it, smacks her shoulder.

And then we go—a two-person procession of shame, shoving through the sweating, guffawing, alcohol-soaked men and women for whom everything works and makes sense and is normal and right.

A superhappy techno-pop ballad thunders out of the speakers, and I wonder why I hadn't noticed the music before; it's so loud, coats everything with its unceasing pulse and jabber. And then it's just a tinny bass-laden blur because we're outside and the snow is more like sleet, wet sheets of it, and Raj stands there in his long black overcoat and shiny shoes and moves his mouth around like he's not sure how to dislodge the words from inside it.

"I just . . . ," he finally manages. Then he stops, like he wants to swallow even that back up.

I shake my head, watch the city get wet.

"It's just not."

This is not what's supposed to happen. I didn't suffer through sleepless nights and snores, farts, and sighs for *this*. I'm Caitlin Fern, goddammit. I carry the last living fragments of the Blattodeon legacy in my blood. More importantly, I am Caitlin Elizabeth Fern—throng haints and ghostlings bend to my will. The mighty phantoms of Hell come crashing to their knees at *my* beck and call. *I* blanked all the pages and *I* wrote the book, and when the collective destinies of the Blattodeons shattered around me, *I* kept going anyway. *I* survived and fought off the demons of doubt and sorrow, and *I* took Monica Tannenbaum out into the snowdrifts when no one else would, and *I* kept squeezing when her eyes bulged and bowels emptied. *I* take life and I bring it at will. I rose from the tattered shitstain of my brother's failure and constructed a new life. This Caitlin Elizabeth Fern, who sat alone in her room, age twelve, contemplating life and death and Jeremy's destiny and my own and resolved to do what must be done, now, always, forever and ever, and then *I*, me, this Caitlin Elizabeth Fern, opened up to wild, impossible truth of spirits and the whole swirling phantom world, and I marked my resolve in blood, a single pinprick and then a shuddering globe at the tip of my finger—a smudge across the pink-lined paper of my diary and it was done.

"I just don't think."

I learned the ways and whims of spirits and how to slide along inside their cool, ethereal glow with my mind and bend them to my will. *I* did that.

"I did that." My voice a raspy growl. My throat already in shambles from the bourbon and vodka.

"What?"

"I did that. All of it. It's mine."

Raj cocks his head to the side, face scrunched. "What is?"

"All of this . . . These bitches. Mine." I shake my head, because he doesn't understand, could never understand, not even if I bothered being coherent. What's the point? "I should've known." I direct a withering scowl up and down his tall, adorable body, felt jacket now shimmering with precipitation.

"Should've known *what*?" Exasperated now; he'd already planned for an uncomfortable convo, but definitely not *this* uncomfortable convo.

If you go through the motions, the regular-people shit is supposed to work out. That's what Mom taught me. *Just pretend, Caitlin*, she'd say, sitting on my bed while I sobbed my little middle school heart out. *Watch what they do, and do it. You love to learn, deary.* Her hands running through my hair, picking out a bit of lint, rubbing my back. *Learn them. Know them, better than they know themselves. So you can be just like them. The rest will take care of itself. Be more them than they are, and then you can do what you need to with the family.*

"I did my part." A whisper. The snow is a whisper, the passing cars a rude *shushhhhh* in the soaking streets, the cruel, brown sludge, the flashing lights, the pounding bass beat of the cruel techno-pop ballad that is droll, as this man standing before me is droll, with his investments and takeovers and endless explanations about his droll, unfortunate days and his somewhat less droll beautiful brown penis.

"Bah!" I shove him aside, and then I'm marching through the street, the brown sludge, cars screeching and honking around me, rude, foul, incoherent, unappreciative, and in the way. "Get out of the way!" I hear myself yell at no one in particular and everyone ever.

"Caitlin!" Raj yells. "I didn't even . . ." But he doesn't come after me, doesn't even finish his sentence. He just shakes his head and walks away. Or watches me, perhaps. Pondering all he'll be missing out on with his unfinished sentences and investments and takeovers.

Halfway down the block I stop dead in my tracks because there's a ghost in front of me. A soulcatcher. He's tall and leans on a cane—unusual for a soulcatcher—as if Delacruz had been made fully dead and given the cloak and helmet.

"Whatdyou want?" I demand.

"Good evening, Ms. Fern," the soulcatcher says with a polite bow. "I'm Soulcatcher Flores. Juan Flores."

Soulcatcher Flores and Raj tag-teamed my now-shattered Sylflax high, but still, Central Park shimmers with an eerie, almost-living incandescence. Silvery icicles decorate the gloomy, snow-covered willows and oaks, and out past the unplowed jogging path: a shining field, bright white beneath the hazy, speckled sky.

We make our way up a hill, Flores strutting beside me with an erudite, phantasmic elegance. "I come on behalf of the Council," he says. "But also to pay you a visit personally. Your name is spoken with near-reverent tones at Sunset, and I wanted to meet you face-to-face."

I don't like his tone. Arrogance seeps through all the cracks of his false modesty. And I don't buy that limp either. "I'm off duty. The Council knows where to find me—hell, I *live* at the office when I'm not at my day job. You must've been watching me for a minute to find me, buddy, and I don't appreciate being stalked."

We come out from a grove of trees at the top of the hill, where a series of boulders sit turned inward toward each other as if frozen in some nefarious boulder conference. "Indeed, but tonight there seems to have been an event that requires your urgent attention, Ms. Fern."

I place a gloved hand on one of the rocks to steady myself. The buzz persists, however dampened by breakups and erudite, cripple ghosts. "Tell Botus I don't—"

"You can tell him yourself," Flores says. And then the chairman himself materializes over the boulders like some regal nature boy with too much chin.

"Caitlin Fern," Chairman Botus booms.

I'm unimpressed by his antics and I let him know with a curt "Chairman."

Bart Arsten, Botus's sniveling middle-management goon, appears on the stones beside him. He nods at me. I ignore him.

"How has your night been, Caitlin?" Botus says.

"Shitty."

"That's too bad. I'm about to make it shittier."

"That would be quite a feat."

"Just wait, Bart."

"The Spine Islands were attacked tonight."

Jesus. I hate when Botus is right. My home. The only home I've known since Delacruz burned down my parents' house with my parents inside. I keep my face impassive. "To what end?"

"Seems mischief," Arsten replies. "But our soulcatchers are still investigating."

"There's more."

"Dr. Calloway was . . ." He looks around, as if the word he's looking for might be hidden in the icy, drooping trees overhead. "Ingested."

Oh dear. "By one of my throng haints?"

"And the haint was then destroyed. It seems."

"*Destroyed?*" Fuck being impassive. "By who?"

"We don't know yet, I'm afraid. The problem is—"

"Who the fuck knows about the Spine Islands base?"

"That's exactly the question that *I've* been wondering about," Botus says. That's unusual: Botus almost always speaks in the plural when he says things like that. Something flickers at the corner of my eye—a soulcatcher. I turn and realize I'm surrounded. A full squad of eighteen 'catchers stand at attention around the summit of the hill.

I must be really cocked to let a pack of ghosts sneak up on me like this. I whirl back to Botus and find him smiling like the irritating prick that he is. "You can't think I . . . ?"

"I don't think anything," Botus says, his absurdly perfect teeth glaring in the glow of the park lamps. "Besides the surviving five other chairmen and the soulcatchers guarding it, there are only three people, living or dead, who knew about the location of the Council CentCom Brain."

The park sharpens into focus as adrenaline overrides whatever bit of joy was left from the Sylflax. I don't want to take my eyes off Botus—he thrives on weakness—but I don't like these helmet heads at my back either.

"Yourself, Subminister Arsten here, and Dr. Calloway." His grin widens as he gazes idly up at the trees. He'll wait on direct eye contact for some climactic finale, I'm sure, and my glare will be there to meet his. If the 'catchers make a move, it'll come from his cue anyway.

"And Dr. Calloway, of course, isn't here to give his side of the events in question." He shakes his head in a mockery of sadness.

I'm over these theatrics. It's late and cold, and Raj's unfinished rejection still burns a swath of wretchedness from my gut to my throat. I won't be humiliated *and* threatened in the space of an hour. I'm Caitlin Fucking Fern, and I've had it with this shit.

"The fact is," Botus begins, but then he stops. Why does he stop? Because I'm Caitlin Fucking Fern, that's why. His loyal soldiers have all slumped forward like sad puppets. Now they shiver, rattled by a spectral wind only they feel.

I am that wind.

The sharp tendrils of my mind slither through those dense, translucent cloaks. They worm into phantom skulls, burrow past glowing tissue and bone and then back through the cold and onto the next 'catcher. And the squad is mine.

I nod, not even looking at them, and all of the soul-catchers draw their blades and stand at ready.

Subminister Arsten turns an even whiter shade of pale,

and Botus lets out a contrived guffaw. Only Soulcatcher Flores stands completely still.

"Impressive!" Botus thunders. If he was intimidated at all, he's done a hell of a job concealing it. "But I'm afraid you misunderstand the purpose of this meeting, Ms. Fern."

"Explain yourself." A bead of sweat trickles down my forehead, despite the cold. Bending child ghosts to my will is one thing—I could swing two dozen around the training yards for a good half hour without tiring. The throng haints I've only dared to control one at a time. But this? Eighteen full-grown, thickly armored soulcatchers? I can probably hold them long enough to massacre Arsten, Botus, and Flores, but only if the killing's quick. With Botus in play, there's no promise of that.

And Flores, still unmoved, is an unknown quantity.

"Why would you, Caitlin Elizabeth Fern, reveal the location of your own secret hideaway?"

"Why indeed," I snarl.

He's stalling. I may have caught him off guard initially, but he knows even I can't hold so many 'catchers much longer. And now I've shown my hand.

"Especially if, as we suspect, the attackers were who we suspect they were."

"Sasha Brass?" The 'catchers lurch forward, spawned by my subconscious urge to kill that bitch. Arsten flinches and whimpers.

"It's possible," Botus muses. "But unconfirmed." My grip loosens, ever so slightly. If anything, I can set a few against the others and make a quick escape amidst the carnage. It wouldn't be the first time . . .

"Either way, it's unlikely you would give up such valuable information."

"I agree."

"Which means someone else must have."

He's right: this isn't going where I thought it would at all. And it's not a bluff; not even Botus is this good at lying. The 'catchers slump again, free from my grasp. They shake their helmeted heads and lean on each other for support, dizzy with their sudden freedom.

Botus frowns, shakes his head again. "I'm so very disappointed."

For a second, I think he means in me. Then he looks up sharply, nods at Flores.

It dawns on Arsten at the same time it dawns on me. "What?" the subminister squeals. "I didn't! How could—"

Flores draws a broadsword from the darkness of his cloak.

"I could never!" Arsten pleads. "I have been . . . for *decades* I have been a loyal servant of the Council and everything we stood for!" He stumbles backward over the boulders, rights himself, raises both hands. "I am the most senior subminister at Sunset! I won't stand for this!"

I was right about Flores's limp—he closes the distance to Arsten with a single, lopsided lunge. The injury may be real, but that humble old beggar routine he put on earlier crumbles as the warrior emerges.

"I don't even—" Arsten's words are cut short by his own high-pitched scream. Flores doesn't go for the core first, which would finish the job quickly. He takes one arm, then the other. Arsten's screams become almost unbearable, filling the chilly night air with gargled gibberish.

"Finish it," Botus says quietly. "We have things to discuss."

A true sadist, Flores pauses to take in his shattered victim. Then he plunges the broadsword through Arsten's open mouth and into his core. The last screams fade along with the subminister's tattered shroud, and then we all stand there in that icy silence for a few seconds.

Juan Flores wipes his sword in the snow and sheaths it. Returning to Botus's side without a word.

"Now," Botus says, releasing his smile back on me like the high beam of a Mack truck. "Let's talk business."

CYCLE TWO

❧ ❧ ❧

THE GHOST WITH NO FACE

Reinaba allí la lluvia, la centella,
Y la mar por doquiera embravecida.
Horas después quiso la aciaga suerte.

Rain and lightning took over,
And the whole world became water.
Hours later, the ill fated sought to survive.

"El Trío y el Ciclón"
Trío Matamoros

CHAPTER FIVE

❧

Carlos

She's back.

Dark brown skin and black curly hair. Full lips, one side curled up just slightly—a coy smile. That broad nose. She knows things, knows me, knows my secrets and lies, everything I've been and wished I was. She's spread out across me, hovering over me like a hummingbird; a languid, amber-washed universe stretches out behind her.

Carlos. My name a prayer on her lips, a glinting bead of sweat, gathering slow and then dropping to anoint me.

Carlos is my name now, not my name before. She knows me now, the man I have become, not the man I was. Or both perhaps.

Who are you? I try to say. My mouth opens and closes, but only my mind speaks.

Who are you? Her voice, my words, circle slow laps through my head, a song, a prayer, a song, a prayer—*Who are you?*—until I wake up rock hard, confused and somehow refreshed at the same time.

And with a wet face.

The hell? I sit up. It's like someone threw a glass of water at my head while I slept, but no one's here.

I'm on the couch. Once again, didn't make it to the bedroom. A book lies open on the coffee table: *The Iliad*. I'd read it when I was crawling back to life at Mama Esther's and picked up my own copy at a used bookstore that's now a boutique selling $400 T-shirts.

Her face is gone, but that sultry ease remains, left behind like a signature.

I sit up. Plants surround me—some dangly things hanging from the ceiling and palm-tree-looking ones on either side of the couch. A flowerpot on the coffee table with a sunflower poking out. This was at Kia—the Iyawo's insistence. "Your place mad drab," she said the last time she was over. "Looks like a dudely dude's den."

"It *is* a—"

"That's not the point," she snapped. "You gotta liven it up. Don't haveta hang no pink curtains, just bring life in here. You got books and a couch and that exposed brick is nice, but really, man, how you think love gonna come to you if shit looking like you hittin' the mattresses?"

"Hittin' the mattresses? Is that a—"

"Godfather reference. Ask Sasha."

"I don't talk to—"

"And that's another thing."

"Look, I—"

"You need more women in your life. Like, as friends. Not that bar chick you dicked down a few times. *Friends.* As in people you confide in and listen to, ya know?"

"I have—"

"Yes, me, but people your own age too, man. Adults

and whatnot. And don't say Reza—she loves you, but she's solidly in Sasha's column at this point; they're like BFFs along with whatshername."

"Janey."

"And Mama Esther doesn't exactly count either, because she's like all our moms."

"She—"

"And I'm a iyawo, so you gotta do what I say."

And so: plants. She's right, though: the place seems more alive somehow, a little forest to retreat to, away from all the concrete and gray slush of the city outside.

The woman's gentle presence persists. It's one of those fragrant candles, just fills the room with a warm glow and some aromatic awesomeness.

And I'm still hard.

For weeks after Sasha and I got together, she was all I thought about. Then everything went to hell, literally almost, and I stopped that, because nothing kills the joy of an orgasm like breaking down in tears immediately after the fact.

But now . . . whoever that woman was in my dream, she left behind a simmering sense of invincibility, and soon Sasha is riding me like she did once on this very couch (not long before pinning me to it with my own sword, but that moment fades away beneath our grinding and panting). My hands slide up her body, cover her bare breasts as she takes me in deeper, throws her head back, mouth open, hands clutching my wrists as if for dear life, as if she lets go she'll float away, and then I'm standing, holding her against the wall, and I'm deeper than I've ever been before; she's howling and biting my neck and then cumming her brains out, and so am I.

All over these sweatpants.

I don't break down though; I jump up, carefully extricate myself without making a mess, and fifteen minutes later I'm cleaned up and scrambling some eggs, the cafetera burbling happily. And that's when I realize I haven't gotten a transmission.

Generally, when the Council wants to reach me, they blurt some ignorant-ass transmission through my mind with their slick dead-people telepathy. It's a one-way connection, of course. I'm not fully dead, so I don't get their slick technology, and if I want to answer back I gotta leave a message on some doofy little 1990s-era answering machine. Most of the time, it's a mission they trouble me with. Occasionally it'll be some random update they simulblast to the whole soulcatcher force: *Soulcatchers are advised to maintain caution at all times when reporting to assignments and use prudence when approaching unregistered spirits.* Because nothing encourages prudence like a regular reminder blasted through everyone's mind. Bureaucracy is so cute. The worst was when Riley went AWOL: *Soulcatchers are advised that an extremely dangerous traitor to the Council is on the loose and is to be apprehended or destroyed with extreme prejudice.* Appropriate word choice. The transmission kept coming through day after day until they finally gave him up for gone.

Anyway, I should've gotten one by now. Because I don't doubt for a second the Council had an ear to the ground last night, and they'll want to know why (the hell) I was at a Fuck-the-Council organizing shindig.

Unless they've already decided why I was there and just want me dead.

Fully dead.

I scoop the eggs onto a plate, walk over to the window. No ghosts outside. None visible, anyway.

I check the bedroom window and even poke my head out into the hallway. It's clear, but an uneasiness has settled in now, evicting the smooth swagger gifted me by the dream.

And my coffee's burnt.

"Fraang pa Konseeli," I mutter, sitting down to my now-cold breakfast.

Two hours later I sit in a rusted folding chair in a second-floor office at the Council's dim Sunset Park headquarters. The room is empty, which is unusual. Standard nonsensical operating procedures usually have Bartholomew Arsten waiting to greet me with some wildly ignorable bit of chatter and then an inane instruction to go somewhere else to receive my more important instructions.

But now it's just me and these shredded tongues of wallpaper, peeled paint, and a dusty conference table. The far window looks out over the vast warehouse floor— a maze of mist and spirits busy with the business of the Council.

I shouldn't be here.

I have children. Two beautiful babies. I should be with them. With Sasha. Suddenly, the past seems so ridiculous: a fairy-tale soap opera. Another man's life, literally.

She murdered me. And it still stings to think of, even though she was someone else and I was someone else, really. It's all just a movie, a bad movie with a terrible ending. I shake my head. If I leave now, Council be damned, I could be at Sasha's in twenty minutes. And maybe she'd take me in, like she did that night when I showed up all bedraggled and traumatized after watching Dro get consumed by a swarm of ngks. And maybe she'd smile, like she did the night we met, and let out that laugh that's uninhibited as it envelops me, her eyes narrowing to a challenging glare afterward, her lips pouted.

Sasha.

I stand, because I'm tired of this shitshow charade and I know what I want, and then the door flies open and Chairman Botus struts in with a tall, limping soulcatcher beside him. A full cadre of soulcatchers marches in next, swords drawn.

And then a funny thing happens: I panic.

I think that's what this is. I've been scared before, terrified even. I've run for my life on more than one occasion. But this clenching, palpitating, shuddering devastation crawls along my arms, through my heart and lungs, floods my brain. Sweat slicks my spine and palms.

I've been dancing along the thin line of subversion for months, teasing my way toward full rebellion, and now I've offered myself up to them without so much as a battle waged.

It takes a conscious effort not to caress the handle of my blade. How many 'catchers can I take out before I go down? I've imagined leaping across this table and cutting Botus in half so many times, but this time the calculations are real. And Botus knows it: that 'catcher beside him must be a bodyguard of some kind. He carries a broadsword that looks like it's designed to bring things to a close with a quickness.

"Good afternoon, Agent Delacruz," Botus says, unusually formal. He shuffles some translucent papers around on the table.

"Afternoon. I see you've brought some friends."

"Indeed. Treacherous times, treacherous times. Tragedies. War. Betrayals." He looks across the table at me. I've never seen Botus so serious. Even when he's upset there's an air of exaggeration to him, like he's never quite present for the mess around him. For once, Botus isn't performing.

"Speaking of betrayals," I begin. I've been told I can't lie for shit. So I didn't practice the whole story of how I infiltrated the anti-Council forces and retrieved valuable information. I just made sure I know all the details, which isn't so hard considering how close they are to the truth. Still, my heart *gagongs* at an unsteady kilter in my ears, my right hand, under the table, seems to be twitching, and every cell in me wants to run out the goddamn room and never look back. And that's not a good condition to be in when you're lying. I'm about to spit out the whole thing, because fuck it, when Botus puts up a hand.

"I don't care," he says, and means it. He really looks weary.

"But—"

"Not right now. Just listen. I don't know what you've done this time, Carlos Delacruz, and I really don't give a shit anymore. You're questionable as fuck; that much is clear. But I think you're honest, deep down, even if it's an honesty I despise."

I raise my eyebrows. None of this is going how I imagined.

"And I think you want what I want, ultimately."

"What's that, Chairman Botus?" No snark, I really want to know.

"Peace," he says. Then he shakes his head. "We sent a subminister to the Deeper Death last night, Carlos. After all his years with the Council, I just . . . he still saw fit to betray us."

"Arsten?" No end to surprises today. "Wha . . . how?"

"Doesn't matter. What matters, Carlos, is that clearly what we have right now is not peace. Not in the least. And it's only going to get worse. You know it and I know it. These"—he waves a dismissive hand over his head, swatting them away—"Remote Districts rising up. Casual acts of subversion and resistance grow into full-frontal attacks, and then we're destroying each other tooth and nail, brother cuts down brother, a cycle that will go on for who knows how long? Bah!" The chairman slumps, then arches forward, leaning across the table. "I don't want it. Do you hear me? I won't have it."

Behind him, the 'catcher with the broadsword stirs on his feet. I can't make out a face through that visor, but something in his posture tells me this isn't going how he planned either.

"Arsten gave the rebels the location of our CentCom," Botus says, listless again. "Most 'catchers don't even know we have a CentCom."

I know I didn't. I mean, I wondered, but I figured all communications stuff goes on right here in Sunset like everything else. But the ins and outs of ghost technology never interested me much.

"Our ability to send messages to a number of our people," Botus says, "including you, was . . . severed. So to speak."

I sit up very straight. No messages. No wonder.

"I didn't kno—"

"Save it. We know it wasn't you. That's beside the point. We, and by 'we' I mean the Seven, now six, do not want this rebellion. We don't want strife; we don't want war. None of it." He rubs his big forehead, stressed. "And we are, after all, six, not seven like we should be." He looks across the room at me.

And this is how it'll happen? After all that talk of reconciliation and peace, *now* he comes out to accuse me of assassinating Chairman Phoebus two months ago? The bodyguard 'catcher must think so too: I can feel that glare through his helmet; his fingers flex on the handle of that broadsword.

But no. If Botus was about to have me executed, he would be smiling. Even this new, morose Botus would enjoy a spectacle he's been waiting to happen for years now. No, this is another thing entirely. Botus's face remains impassive. And then I get it.

"But I'm . . . I'm . . . alive. Partially."

A faint smiles appears on his massive face; then it's gone. "I know, Delacruz, I know."

"I couldn't . . . are you serious?"

"Dead serious. No pun intended." Another smile, equally short lived.

Behind him, the soulcatcher takes a step back—I think in shock.

"The Seven have always been fully dead," I say. "Haven't they?"

Botus nods. "As I said, treacherous times. I don't like it. In fact, I hate it. But the other five voted, and this is what we've decided. And I can't say I don't see some wisdom in it."

"I . . . I don't know what to say." I don't. I feel filthy,

though. The room becomes suddenly suffocating: all this dust and dimness. I want sunshine, air.

Botus rises. "Don't say anything. Think on it. For a day. Then give me an answer. And make that answer yes. Outside of compromise, some new reforms to the system, I don't see how we can bring this . . . situation . . . to a peaceful resolution."

I'm still trying to find some words when Botus and his entourage leave in a whirlwind. The limping 'catcher is the last to go. He doesn't spare me even a glance as he hauls ass quickly out the door and into the dim corridor.

Outside, the sun still sits high in the pale sky. It shimmers across the dark street streams of melted snow, dances across windshields and the barred warehouse windows around me. I put a Malagueña in my mouth. Take it out again.

Was I just offered a spot amongst the Ignoble Seven?

I believe I was.

The eeriest part is that Botus was quite serious. I'm so used to side-eyeing anything he says, it's unnerving to actually believe him, but I do. The thought is chilling. What would I do? Become some cold arbiter of Remote District complaints? More than likely, they'd use me to drip-drop a few tantalizing reforms over the RD's heads and then blame me when the whole thing comes crashing down.

A year and a half ago, the ancient necromancer Sarco invited me to take part in his deathpocalypse scheme to tear open a gash in the fabric between the living world and Hell. I was meant to be some kind of sacred door-keeper, except the door was Mama Esther, against her will, and Sarco's compadres the ngks had already devoured another friend of mine. I allowed myself a few seconds to taste all that power he was offering. Part of it was curiosity; the rest was because I needed him to think I'd really go along for the ride so I could jump him.

Those were moments I'll never forget, though. Some electric-charge imprint must've seared itself into my bones—I still feel the echo of that power flowing straight out the center of my chest, through my arms, out into the world. The world—it seemed so broken and pliable. Standing there in the gateway between life and death, I was a divine incarnation of my own strange predicament; where I'd always been neither/nor, suddenly I was both and all and so much more. I was the crisis of the universe, the turning point and fulcrum upon which all life and death spun.

Wasn't for me, though. Not my speed, all that mayhem and ferocity at my fingertips. I got the memory to cherish, the echoes still clamoring through me, and that's plenty. Perhaps being one of the Seven would come with similar excitement. I get the sense Botus has never revealed his true abilities, and why would he? Subterfuge is the Council's best friend.

I put the cigar in my mouth again, start to light it, realize it's backward. Then Reza's Crown Vic rolls up. I'm reaching into my pocket to get the letter to the twins, so I can ask her to pass it along to Sasha, when the window rolls down. And Sasha smiles at me from the driver's seat.

"Wanna get the hell outta town for a bit?"

"God, yes," I say. It's the truest words I've spoken in a long time.

Sasha

What I was most looking forward to about seeing Carlos again? That ease we always shared, even from the very beginning. It's a strange and magical thing when two people can simply know how to *be* around each other without having to stop and learn.

What I wasn't ready for: those two words, "God, yes," spoken with zero inhibition, like he even surprised himself when he said them. Caught the whole world off guard with that simplicity. I'm sure it was a long time coming, probably many sleepless nights, knowing Carlos, but it was all worth it for that moment. And just like that I'm stricken again, and all I want is to ride him, feel him all around me, let him take me in every way imaginable and then collapse in a limp, panting heap on his chest and let sleep do its thing.

Dammit.

That wasn't the plan.

He's still got that easy charm—that I expected—but he moves more lightly now. He slides into the passenger seat, completely unable to conceal the huge smile on his face.

"Happy to see me?" I ask.

"You have no idea. I've had the strangest day."

"I can only imagine."

I pull us around to Third Avenue, where traffic trundles along the highway overhead, then catch the nearest on-ramp, and we're cruising on the Brooklyn-Queens Expressway toward the Verrazano Bridge.

"So they told you about the little setback over at Cent-Com?" I ask. Takes everything I got not to let this grin out.

"Yeah, I didn't even realize there was a . . . Wait!"

I let it dawn on him, keep my game face on all the while.

"How did you . . . you . . . you did that?"

Finally, the smile comes loose and my whole face is made out of it.

"I missed that smile," Carlos says.

"Consider it my peace offering."

"What? The smile? Offer accepted."

"No, slick-ass. Fucking up CentCom." I want to punch his shoulder, but if I do it'll turn into a caress; I know it will. My hand will betray me, and if I caress him I'll have to pull over and fuck him. I keep my eyes on the road, hands to myself.

"How did you even . . . Wait." He gets real serious, turns to face me in his seat. I ignore my pounding heart. My heart's not pounding. Why would it?

"Thank you." He doesn't smile when he says it. It's not a play, just the truth.

"I would say, 'My pleasure,'" I tell him. "But it really wasn't. Turns out they keep throng haints out there too. One took out some old spook named Dr. Calloway they had running things."

"Damn, I met him last year. Slipped Riley and me some inside info 'bout a ghost zoo the Council was trying to set up."

"Yeah, well he's part of the masses now. A throng haint ingested him, and then me and Janey shattered it. Took some work, though, believe me."

"Jesus."

"Jesus ain't got nothin' to do with what's going at the Spine Islands."

"*That's* where Council CentCom is?"

"Mmhm." I swerve around a tractor-trailer that's hogging three lanes and zip up onto the bridge. Carlos puts his seatbelt on. "Whatsamatter?" I laugh. "You scared?"

"I'm good," he says through clenched teeth. "Just don't do highways very often."

The bay between Brooklyn and Staten Island stretches out on either side of us, sparkling in the afternoon sun. It almost feels like a spring day, if you can ignore all the snowdrifts and brown sludge.

"Wait," Carlos says, "does the Council know you took out their favorite toy?"

"We didn't take it out, not fully. Wasn't time for that, what with the throng haints. But I made sure to pull your thread. And I don't know if they know it was me. I was actually gonna ask you that."

He shakes his head. "No idea, it was a . . . strange conversation. But the babies . . ."

"They're safe," I say. "Gordo took them to stay with some family he got outside of Boston."

"Are you sure they'll be—"

"I asked Reza and Janey to go with 'em."

Carlos finally sits back, exhales. "Oh. Well, then they're about as safe as two babies can be."

I smile, and for a few seconds we both pretend to ignore the way all that's passed between us wells up like a tidal wave. Staten Island passes, houses and hospitals and hills.

"Where we headed, anyway?" Carlos asks.

I pass him my phone. "Call the Iyawo. She'll be under Recent Calls. Put it on speaker."

He plays with it for a second, then says, "Miguel? Miguel the taxi driver?"

"Carlos." I roll my eyes. "We *just* started talking again after nine months. Don't be that guy. Okay?"

He shrugs. "Fair enough."

The Iyawo's phone rings twice, and then she picks up. "Hello?"

"Kiyawo!" Carlos says. I roll my eyes, and I'm sure she does too.

"Wait . . . this Carlos? But this is . . . y'all hanging out?"

"Long story," Carlos says through a smile.

"I bet it is."

Mama Esther's voice erupts in the background like a loving thunderclap. "Carlos and Sasha? What?"

"That's what I'm sayin'!" the Iyawo squeals. "Mama Esther's all giddy now. It's kinda scary."

"Hush, child," the old house ghost chides.

Carlos and I keep our eyes on the road. "You find what we were looking for?" I ask.

"Girl . . ." The Iyawo sighs. I can imagine her shaking her head. "I found it. You ready?"

I've been getting ready. I thought I was ready; then the thousand could've-beens flocked around my heart again, the best and the worst and the truly absurd. I shake my head. Fuck it, we've arrived. Deep breath. Then, "Yeah, what you got?"

"Turns out there aren't that many Aisha Floreses in the United States and only eighteen in the tristate area. Of the eighteen, one went missing five years ago: Aisha Flores of 729 Coral Lane, Sunport, New Jersey."

"Aisha," Carlos says quietly. The last word he spoke before I murdered him. My name.

My heart thuds along in a slow, frantic march, pounds against my face, my wrists, becomes the whole world.

"That much we knew," the Iyawo goes on. "I just wanted to fill C in."

"I'm already lost," Carlos says. "But keep going; I'll catch up."

"The Sunport Public Library digitized their microfiche four years ago, and you're supposed to have a library card to access it but . . . well, you know."

In the background, Mama Esther snorts.

"Anyway, it checks out. According to the local papers, Ms. Aisha Flores, twenty-seven, disappeared without a trace along with five other Sunport residents, including her brother Darren." *Trevor*. "She leaves behind her husband, Juan Flores, and parents, James and Sarah Raymond."

I know what's next. I don't know how, but I know, and without my permission, tears slide down my cheeks.

"A few weeks later," the Iyawo says, "James and Sarah Raymond died in a car crash. A month after that, James's parents, Jane and Reginald, were killed in an electrical fire. Sarah's were both dead already."

I'm shaking my head, because I know it all; it's all some-where in me, this aching truth: they're all gone. Another bridge takes us out of Staten Island, into New Jersey. It starts snowing as we cross the state line.

"It goes on," the Iyawo says. "But . . ."

"It's okay," I say, even though everyone knows that's a lie. "I know." Carlos's hand is on mine. I don't know when he put it there, but his skin is cool like mine, and his heart, his lifeline is shattered, just like mine.

"What about my . . . husband?" It doesn't feel true, that word, but it must be.

"Juan Flores's body showed up in Prospect Park a few months after you disappeared. He was decomposed pretty bad, and animals had chewed his face off, so they had to ID him from dental records, but it was him. Sounds like he might've ODed. Some kind of bizarre murder, then delayed reaction suicide was suspected, but there was no proof, no witnesses, nothing."

I shudder. That empty face beneath the visor.

"Checked the other names out, the ones that disappeared that same day. It took some work."

"You're amazing," I say through a sniffle.

"You okay? I can stop, we can do this ano—"

"No." Comes out sharper than I meant it. "No." Softer this time. "Keep going."

"So, there's a couple I couldn't track, not yet, anyway. One I think was a drifter, this guy Samuel Bennacourt, another a nurse. Celine St. Martin was apparently a beloved schoolteacher and grandmother. And then we have Andre Salazar, twenty-six."

Carlos sits up very straight. "That me?"

"Seems to be," the Iyawo says. "You worked at Video Hut and were taking adult-ed classes in filmmaking."

Now my hand is on his, and his clutches his thighs.

"Don't got much else, but Carlos . . . the situation with Sasha's family? I'm sorry. It's the same for yours. All within a week or two of your disappearance."

Carlos nods, pulls in his lips, closes his eyes. "Say their names," he says quietly.

"Leandro Reynaldo Salazar and Dulce Maria Aviles. It was a home invasion. I'm sorry, you guys." She's holding back tears. "I'm so sorry."

In the background, I hear Mama Esther make cooing sounds and whisper, "Shhh, child, hush."

Could Sarco take out all those people? That quickly?

Someone certainly did; there are no accidents in ghost world, especially when it comes to massacres.

A few moments of silence pass. Carlos watches factory yards and parking lots slide by, shakes his head. "What are we doing, then? What's this all about?"

"Well." The Iyawo sniffles, clears her throat. "Within the library system, I tracked the other names that had come sniffing 'round the same trees I did."

"And?"

"There's one person: Margery Pham. Works at the very library whose computer I ha—er . . . involved myself in an intimate conversation with. She lives in Sunport, at . . . hold on . . . 2453 Park Lane."

I tell Carlos to put that into the GPS.

"The what now?"

On the other end of the line, the Iyawo sighs. "Good luck, Sasha."

"Thank you, Iyawo."

Mama Esther's voice gets loud, like she's nudged the Iyawo aside and gotten up close to the phone. "Carlos, Sasha: I'm so sorry, so, so sorry. You know, whatever I can do . . . just let me know."

"Thanks, Mama Esther," we both say at the same time. We don't look at each other. Snow drifts down around us, oblivious to the chaos in this car, the bloodbath of our pasts, the sorrow welling up, unstoppable. "I sent you both gifts. Little Damian's bringing them to your places; they'll be there when you get back."

"Gifts?" Carlos says. "You've already lent me most of your entire mystery section and—"

"Hush, child," Mama Esther snaps. "A gift is a gift. All you need to do is accept it. This is important. Now be safe out there, you two. Don't let the tide of the past drag you down. There's too much at stake for the future."

The call ends with a beep. Silence settles in; the snow gathers on the windshield, swooshes away beneath the wipers, gathers again. These people are strangers to me, but they surely loved me and I loved them, once. And they're gone. Caught up in the mire of whatever hell I had gotten involved with. All these new pieces and still: so much nothing. So many impossible questions.

"We're not those people," Carlos says. He's looking away from me, out the window, as Jersey slowly turns white around us. "That man working at a video store while he went to night school? That's not me."

"Andre Salazar," I say, to feel the name on my lips.

"Died." He doesn't say it bitterly; it's just a fact. "And Carlos was born."

"Do you believe that?"

He shrugs, his eyes wet. "I don't know. I have to right now. It's all I got."

He's right. And so is Mama Esther. The past is a hideous mouth, gaping out of the darkness. It will draw us in and never let us go.

"Do you want to turn around?" I ask. The idea feels like defeat somehow, but a relief too.

He shakes his head. "I don't know. No. We're here. Anyway, I want to know how we got here. You got a lead from somewhere. And you can teach me what this GPS thing is on the way."

Whoever named Sunport was either an optimist or high. Or perhaps those were just different times. Today, two-story tenements huddle in disarray along the Jersey shore-line. A bleak beach stretches toward the wealthier end of the world, and the rusted-out skeletons of two abandoned factories clutter up the outskirts of town alongside strip malls, gas stations, and fast-food chains. Park Lane sits squarely in the middle of a slightly happier alcove—the front lawns are trimmed and have trees instead of tires or sun-bleached strollers. Still, it's grim. An unsettled air lingers over the whole town, and I wonder if it's still the fallout of so many untimely deaths.

A tall, well-put-together woman answers the door. Her black hair's pulled back into a ponytail, and she's wearing spandex and a purple hoodie. Her mouth drops open when she sees me. She takes a step back, gasps, then looks behind me at Carlos and screams.

"Ms. Pham, wait!" I jam my foot in the door before it can slam.

She flings it open all the way, now armed with a small pistol. It's pointed at Carlos.

"Get back," she whispers. "I . . . Aisha . . . is it . . . is it you?"

"It's me," I say, and I feel the lie in it as soon as the words leave my mouth. Carlos is right: those people are dead.

"And . . . Dre? You're not . . . I don't understand." She shakes her head, scowls at us. "I was so worried . . . I thought he . . . or someone. My God." Before I can stop her, she's wrapped around my neck, her face in my shoulder. The gun presses uncomfortably against my back as Margery Pham sobs.

"We're not here to hurt you," I say. "I promise."

She steps back, eyeing me again. "My goodness, you're freezing, Aisha. Come inside, warm yourselves.

"The children are with their father," Margery says, leading us into a tidy den with a view of the less-tidy backyard. Toys and gardening tools lay half-buried in the newly fallen snow. "Please, sit. Do you want tea or coffee?"

We both shake our heads. Margery pauses her flurry of hospitality to gaze at us for a few seconds, then shakes her head and says she'll be right back. She scuttles off sniffling.

Carlos puts his hand on my knee. "You okay?"

I nod. Strangely, I am. Together, without even meaning to, we've formed some kind of stable point in the storm of all this tragedy. I know instinctively that Carlos won't let me come unhinged. I know I won't let him. I put my hand on his. If we turn them to face each other, palm to palm, his could close around mine and draw me to him, and if he brought his face near mine I'd kiss it. It wouldn't be a thing I'd think about or deliberate—it would be what happens.

But not in Margery Pham's living room it won't.

"Here." Margery stands in the doorway holding a shoe-box. "These are . . . these are yours." She sits on the plush easy chair, holds it out to me. "It's not much. I . . . I don't want you to get your hopes up. Just some pictures."

I take it. *Pictures.* I want to hug her, collapse in a puddle at her feet, but we've shaken up Margery Pham enough today. The box is light when I take it in my arms like a baby. All that's left of the woman who used to have this body.

"They declared you dead, even though there was never a body, and then your poor parents went and . . . oh, I'm so sorry." She wants to ask what happened—the questions hang all around her, but she shoves them all away.

"I don't remember much," I whisper. "Anything really."

"I remember watching you," Margery says. "You came into the library almost every day after school. When you were little, your mom brought you; then you started coming on your own. First it was the books—Greek mythology was your favorite, and then you moved on to vampires and witches. But your true love was in the Media Department." She's staring past me. If our eyes meet, we'll both collapse, I'm sure of it. Carlos squeezes my hand.

"We couldn't get you out of there. There's a little viewing station in the back, just a wooden table and a TV with a DVD player and VCR. You would rush over to the counter to get the key from me, and if someone else was in there you'd pretend not to mind, but I could see it on your face, that pout. You'd wait patiently doing homework until they left and then grab a movie and disappear. Usually the old ones, Jimmy Cagney and Humphrey Bogart and the like." She shakes her head.

"Then you discovered anime, and oh my goodness, I thought we'd lose you for a while there. You were smitten."

"Something stayed with me." It comes out quietly. Hadn't even meant to let the words slip from my mouth into the world, but there they are. They fill the air for a few seconds of silence.

When I look down, I've taken the lid off the shoebox. It wasn't something I did consciously; my hands made the decision on their own. I hear someone gasp, and then I realize it's me. My fingers tremble, can't get hold of the framed photograph, and when they do they drop it again.

"Saaisha . . . ," Carlos whispers beside me. His cool hand

on my arm, the grip firm—it steadies me. I don't float away in the sea of lava this quiet suburban home has become.

"What's wrong, dear?" Margery says from a million miles away.

"This is . . . this was . . ." A wedding photograph. I am aglow, the woman I once was: fully alive, skin a darker, richer brown, smile resplendent in the sun. The man beside me—my husband—that face.

"Your wedding, Aisha. You don't remember?"

I shake my head. That face. Juan Flores. Terra. The same man that watched over us when we came back around. He knew all along, was part of it all. The Iyawo said he'd been found in the park a few months after we went missing, his face chewed off.

His face.

Juan Flores's smile was once wide and generous. Those big cheeks pushed his eyes almost shut. His close-cut black hair framed a light brown forehead, eyebrows raised high with amusement. His arm wrapped around my waist.

I want to scream, but instead I look up at Margery and say: "I'm sorry—you were telling me about the library."

She shakes her head. "You came less after you were married. In part because you'd seen them all, and part because, well . . . I don't think Juan liked you being there. You told me that once. But he liked you being at the video store even less." She casts an eye toward Carlos.

"Video Hut?" he says.

I blink at Margery. "Andre and I . . . we knew each other?"

For the first time since we've met her, Margery Pham laughs. "Knew each other? You were best friends. Insepa-rable."

It's dark, and the snow comes down in wild, windblown sheets when we leave Margery Pham's house. She gives us directions to the highway, urging us to stay in touch and be careful, and we nod, dazed, and drive off. In the car, neither of us has anything to say for a few minutes. Then Carlos adjusts himself in that way he does when he's about to talk. "I'm sorry."

I shake my head. Not mad, just tired. Vacant: an emptiness that throbs. "You don't have to be. And you've said that already, many times."

"I know, but I mean . . . I mean, I'm sorry I didn't tell you."

"What?"

"When we first met. I didn't tell you about Trevor. That I killed him. I should've. I know I've apologized before but never for that, and that . . . that was fucked up."

I nod, crushing my bottom lip between my teeth. "It was."

"It's always bothered me."

"Me too. But . . . why now?"

"Because I need you, Sasha."

I knew that. I could feel it in the tiny movements of his face, the way his body touches mine, even in passing. He's covered in it. As am I. Still makes me catch my breath to hear him say it out loud.

"I need you, and I don't even understand how or why. But I know that to get through *this*. All this." He flails his hands. What good are words when the truth is so gigantic and sad? "Whatever this is. I know I need you by my side. I tried for so long to pretend I didn't, that I could do it all on my own, but it was bullshit. I was a shell. A lie."

I can barely see the cascading snow, and my eyes keep getting wet no matter how much I rub them.

"And if we're gonna be around each other in any kinda way, it's all gotta be out there, on the table. Starting now. At least from me. I gotta get it all out of me. Otherwise it becomes more of the same, and we can't go back to that."

I nod, wipe my eyes. Laugh in a guttural, sobby kind of way. "I'm sorry I killed you."

He shrugs. "It's alright, I guess. It was another me, another you."

I wonder.

In the parking lot of the Sunport Holiday Inn, snow covers the windshield as I tell Carlos about my first terrifying days alive again.

"So Terra's the . . . that faceless ghost that showed up at your door?"

"My husband." The word feels wrong in my mouth—a sour thing, long past its expiration date.

"Aisha's husband."

I nod.

"And now he's a soulcatcher. A prominent one, apparently. He was at the sit-down with Botus earlier today. Looked none too happy when B offered to make me one of the Seven."

"Of course. He was probably gunning for the spot himself, with whatever treachery he's been plotting." If we were outside, I'd spit.

"Still, giving you the CentCom info was no small blow to the Council. What do you think he's playing at?"

"No idea. All I know is he can't be trusted. And he's gonna catch that Deeper Death."

A sinister smile spreads across Carlos's face. "Of course. The question is, how much can we milk his uncertain allegiance before we end him?"

I hug my arms around myself. The blizzard has reached its icy fingers into the car, sends slivery trembles through my bones. "I'd prefer sooner. But you're right. And there aren't that many people left that know what really happened to us."

Carlos grunts, and then silence stretches long between us. He puts his head in his hands, takes a deep breath.

"Tonight," I say after a few minutes slide past, "I just want you to hold me."

He looks up. Considers me slowly. Smiles. Nods.

Then we're out in the storm, moving through windblown snow and darkness, then the bright lobby lights and sleepy desk clerk, the elevator, a corridor that smells of carpet cleaner and cologne, the stark blessing of an empty bed awaiting our tired bodies. Some clothes are shed, two swords and a few daggers placed on cabinet tops, and outside, snowdrifts reflect the murky, orange glow of streetlights across the New Jersey sky.

CHAPTER SIX

~∽∾∿⊙

Krys

The Iyawo slams her (slender, dark brown, beautiful) hand on the countertop, upsetting a little basket of cowrie shells. "Right? So then I was like, 'No, Giovanni Patrick Lamar Summers, *you* fall back!'"

"And then what happened?"

"I mean . . . we talked it out, and now we cool." The shells make little clicks as she drops them back in the basket. Her bangles jingle their tiny song every time she moves. "That's how my cousin and I do, though: we can't stand each other, and then we cool. I will always love him, but yo: I had to go. Being the third wheel in ya own house fuckin' sucks."

"Iyawo!" Baba Eddie calls from the back.

She rolls her eyes. "Sorry, Baba."

"You can stop rolling your eyes now. And wipe that snarl off your face," he finishes as the Iyawo's top lip curls upward. She fists up her face into a firm pout and then shrugs.

"You miss him?"

"Nah, we Skype all the time. Him and Rigo—that's his boyfriend—are sposta come up to visit next month."

"That's cool," I say. It's not a stupid thing to say, but the words feel clunky and meaningless after her wild adventures in Rio, a canoe paddling behind a yacht.

The Iyawo goes back to clacking away on her laptop, and I do nothing for a few seconds, and the music fills the space between us. It's an orisha song: a woman's voice belts out a raw, joyful staccato over tumbling drums, and then a choir that sounds like the whole world singing at once answers her.

Baba Eddie's gotta be side-eyeing me so hard from the back room. I'm here. I've been here for more than an hour now, in direct disobedience of his strict edict against falling in love with the Iyawo. I mean, I'm not *in* love with her, but if she does that little pout one more time I probably will be.

No. Stop. Shake it off, Krys. She can't get intimate with anyone right now, let alone a dead girl. This is madness.

"Is it all worth it?" I ask.

She says "Hm?" without looking up.

"All these rules and wearing all that white and not being able to go out or nothin'. Is it all worth it?"

"Oh yeah." She clicks something, clicks again, and then tilts her head at me. "More than worth it. I mean, I cop attitude, yeah, but really, this has been the deepest, most intense couple months of my life already, and it's only just begun. I mean, you a spirit already, Krys, so I dunno what that's like, but for me, for us flesh-'n'-blood folk, to enter into such a real relationship with a powerful spiritual force, it's like . . . like nothing I can explain."

If I had a dick, it'd be hard. That's all I know. "I was

like a nonpracticing agnostic when I was alive," I say, instead of *Come ride my face, and then let's find out how deep and intense shit can really get.*

"Yeah, my dad's laid-back Protestant, I guess, but we never really did much more than Christmas. And I never really bought into it or felt it myself. This, though, this a whole other level. It's something I can feel deep inside me. All the bullshi— BS falls away. And the orishas are black like me. And the music . . ." She shuts up and lets the drums and singers speak for themselves. "The music. What's dope is, this stuff still resonating in music today. Like, you can hear it in the old salsa stuff Reza listens to. It's in all ya favorite rappers' flow."

"I don't listen to rap," I say.

"Oh, what you listen to?"

"Like metal and alternative and stuff."

"Rohan's double-parked up the block," Baba Eddie says, walking down an aisle of herbs and statues. "We ready to rock 'n' roll?"

"Yessir," the Iyawo says.

Baba Eddie guffaws. "Right, because a ghost stakeout with potential to spill into an all-out riot amidst possible traitors is exaaactly the type of situation a iyawo should be in."

"I mean!"

For a brief, blessed second, the thunder of this crush is replaced by the thrill of a possible battle. "You really think it could get messy?" I ask.

He shrugs, throwing a puffy winter jacket on over his cardigan. "Who knows? A year ago, I'd say no. But these days are different. These days are of tragedy and war. Blood. Ogun stalks the streets at night, and he's hungry."

"That's the orisha of warfare and iron and technology and stuff," the Iyawo tells me.

"And Iku is never far behind," he goes on.

"And that's death."

Baba Eddie seems to snap out of his reverie. "So, yeah, some bad shit might go down. You got Greta?"

I heft Greta up from where I'd laid her beneath the counter. Even translucent, the shimmering rocket launcher cuts an imposing form there on my shoulder.

Baba Eddie looks at me, then shakes his head. "On second thought, leave her. This is sposta be recon, not all-out war. You'll move faster and be more out of sight without that . . . beast."

I grumble and put Greta back down.

"I still don't get how the Council just lets you play with all this newfangled ghost-tech," the Iyawo says. "Especially considering they prolly don't trust your ass."

"I'm the only one that really knows how to use it." My smile is smug. For once, I have some swagger to my swoosh as I balance Greta and slip over the counter. "And this one, they think she's broken."

"How come?"

"'Cause I told 'em she is. I realized they were starting to get wary of me a few months back. Fucked up a whole nest of whisper wraiths they'd sent me to uproot; then I reported that Greta had malfunctioned and I had to destroy her." I pat Greta. "Now we off the grid."

The Iyawo flashes a wily smile. "That's badass. Be safe out there."

"Oh, we will," Baba Eddie says.

"I was talking to Krys," the Iyawo says. "But yeah, you be safe too, I guess."

For a guy that spent two hundred years wasting away in an underground tomb, Cyrus Langley really has his shit together. Riley's probably his number-one fan, but we're all in awe of the old conjureman, his ancient, wry smile and knowing eyes, his mischief and strategies.

We gather on a snowy hill in Central Park. A few joggers and dog walkers trudge past, braving the cold, but mostly the place is ours. I trade a dap with Jimmy and a nod with Big Cane; Riley says a general "Whaddup?" to the lot of us, and then Cyrus starts pairing us into small groups.

"I told the heads of each Remote District to gather their people and await my signal. Big Cane and Riley, you're with Baba Eddie. Y'all fellas keep an eye on Saeen and her District 4 squad. They'll be at Fiftieth and Fifth Ave."

Big Cane is the only ghost I know that can actually lumber; Riley looks like a child next to him as they cross the circle to stand by Baba Eddie. Eddie grins, exchanges a complicated high five with Riley.

"Each of our smaller groups is to post up nearby, somewhere we can watch from. Damian and Forsyth Charles, you two with Rohan here." Damian's already beside the big happy-faced hitman. One of Cyrus's ghost buddies from the African Burial Ground floats over to them on long legs. He wears a stylish suit, and his hair sits in a big off-center Frederick Douglass fro.

"You three head to Forty-second and Ten. Moco will be gathering his folks nearby. We won't be using our ghost-telepathy shit, as Carlos likes to call it; it's not reliable enough and too easily intercepted by the Council. If soulcatchers make an appearance anywhere near your site, your living member is to call the others. Do not let the Remote District folks know. Do not let them see you. Just stay out the way. Understood?"

We all nod.

"Krys." I meet his eyes, and he smiles into mine. "You and Redd go with young Jimmy here."

"Sweet," Jimmy says. "Who's Redd?"

A lanky light-skinned dude with a fade slides up beside us. "That'd be me." A thin red beard traces the contour of his sharp jawline; freckles dot his round face. He's got big teeth, big lips, and big, laughing eyes behind long lashes. Must've died young—he can't be much older than me and Jimmy. Long, slender arms hang down from his torn tank top. A sword scabbard hangs from his belt, and a dagger's strapped to his leg. "What it do?" Just the hint of a smile creases one side of Redd's mouth. The other side seems to swerve down to compensate, a torqued pout.

"Hey," I say.

"You Negroes head to Columbus Circle down by the corner of the park here," Cyrus says. "Hole up nearby. Father Desmond sposta show with his folks from Starrett City and them."

"Aye," Forsyth Charles says. "Where will you be?"

"Me and Dag Thrummond will glide back and forth between RD 7's meet-up point and Vincent and his Bed-Stuy folk." A massive ghost emerges from the shadows of the park. He's another from the Burial Grounds—wide shoulders, shaved head, an axe in each hand. Cyrus's bodyguard, I take it. It's a comforting thought. "We're shorthanded for living folks tonight, what with Carlos and Gordo out handling some shit, but that's alright. I don't expect trouble from Kaya and Breyla, and Vincent is like a son to me."

The snow started as we stood there talking. First a speckle here and there, then vast, windswept droves of it filled the sky, blitzed through our shimmering forms, and swirled up into the glow of the streetlights.

The cold don't really bother us dead folks, but the wind and snow whipping through us as we work our way through the park makes for slow going. Jimmy's teeth are already chattering, but I've told him a hundred times he gotta layer up beneath that puffy jacket and he don't listen.

Redd and I squint and point our heads into the storm. I don't know if I trust him yet, but if Cyrus does that's good enough for me. Anyway, that cutlass hanging from his belt is not a small piece of metal and something in Redd's cool cockiness tells me he knows what to do with it. You can smell arrogance that's born from fear, and this ain't it. When the wind sweeps through Redd's shirt, I see white bandages hugged tight against his chest.

Jimmy sees it too, I guess, and decides to be an ass. "You ain't really a boy are you?"

I swipe him across the chest, but with all the snow and ice he barely notices.

"Are you?" Redd says. Jimmy stops walking. So does Redd.

"I mean, yeah."

I'm between them. If it comes to blows, I don't know what I'm supposed to do.

"How you know?" Redd's face betrays nothing—no rage, no challenge. The question is sincere.

"That was a fucked-up question," I tell Jimmy.

Redd just stares.

"I mean, I got a dick," Jimmy says with a scowl.

"That it?"

"I mean." He knows he's getting it wrong, that he's losing just by flailing in the face of Redd's stillness. "I mean shit. I dunno, I'm a dude. That's it. It's simple."

When I was alive, my best friend Wendy took me up on a sunny hill near our school one day. *I have something to tell you*, Wendy said in a shaky voice. *I'm not a girl. And I'm not a boy.*

I nodded, and Wendy exhaled. The silence that opened between us was a gentle one, not the treacherous kind. *So you're both and neither*, I said, and Wendy smiled.

Redd isn't both and neither, though; Redd's a boy, through and through. Just has a pussy, is all. I wanna speak up, tell Jimmy all about Wendy, and that ain't nothing simple 'bout gender, but I don't have the words and I don't even think it's my place.

Redd lets him squirm for a few more seconds and then smiles. "God put me in the wrong body, is all. He musta been drinkin' that night."

Jimmy barks a laugh, mostly from relief, I think, and all the tension seems to whisk away on these icy winds.

"Where you from?" I ask.

"Born in Jamaica, but I ain't stay there long." We settle back into our march past the snowfields and shimmering trees. "My mama was part of a slave uprising, she handed me off to maroons the night before an attack. They smuggled me onto a ship, but that got attacked by pirates out in the bay. Hopped from ship to ship mosta my life till I ended up on a schooner outside New York

Harbor. We'd post up like we bouta do here 'n' wait for the ships that'd come collecting fugitive slaves. Then we'd roll up on 'em fast once they made it out to deeper waters and throw the crew overboard, take the slaves back to port."

"Whoa, that's badass," Jimmy says.

Redd shrugs, but you can tell he feels good 'bout who he is and what he's done. We've passed through a line of bushes and now crouch by the low wall dividing Central Park from the chichi avenues of Midtown Manhattan. Across the street, a stone Columbus surveys the snowy traffic circle from atop his pillar. Skyscrapers loom above us.

"So how y'all know each other?" Redd asks.

"So, I was dating this girl Mina, right?" Jimmy says eagerly. "Mina Satorius, and one time she invites me over to her house in Staten Island."

"Man," Redd sighs. "Staten Island. Musta been some grade A pussy."

Jimmy cranes his neck, mouth open to the falling snow. "Bruh."

Twenty minutes later, he's still talking about Mina—how they broke up after all that shit with her grandma went down, but they stayed friends and like, always had that connection, you know? And she had some spiritual magic-type shit going on that Jimmy could never get to the bottom of and she would never talk about, and how this one night, yadda yadda yadda—shit Jimmy and I been over a small mountain of times, none of which has a thing to do with how him and I met, but ay . . . He's craning back again, explaining some weird porn he saw that reminded him of her and ignited the whole relapse, when Redd catches my eye and smiles.

It's just a muted grin—if he unleashes the full glory of those giant teeth, even the obtuse living world would take note. This is a laser beam, though, for my eyes only, and I have to dampen my own fast-expanding giant grin to return the slyness in kind.

Then a tinny electronic voice over a beat blots out the moment: "*I am the riot the riot the mothafuckin' riot!*"

I roll my eyes. "You ain't changed that damn ringtone yet, Jimmy?"

"Or learned when to set it to vibrate?" Redd says. "Shit."

"Sorry!" Jimmy says, fumbling the phone out of his jacket pocket. "Hello?" His breath rises in little cumulus phantoms. He squints. Nods. Says, "Okay. Okay. Shit. Alright. Thanks, Rohan." He stands, repockets the phone. "Well, that's that."

Let me tell you something about ghosts: fucking with the physical world takes effort. Unless you're really, really good, all your physical and mental capacities gotta be laser focused on what you're doing. And it's exhausting, even for a badass like Riley. So when Redd wraps a firm hand around Jimmy's wrist and physically pulls him back down behind the wall, I'm impressed. He does it with an unhesitating certainty, and you can tell from Jimmy's face he's startled.

"What?" Jimmy demands.

"That's never that," Redd says. "Never. What did Rohan say?"

"That the soulcatchers just massed over by the West Side Highway at Forty-second. Him and Damian and the flower guy—"

"Who the fuck is the flower guy?" Redd says.

"I dunno—he's one of yours from the Burial Grounds . . . Magnolia Fred? Hyacinth Bob?"

"Forsyth Charles," I say.

"Oh my God," Redd says. "Your mind is a very strange place, Jimmy."

Jimmy shrugs, undaunted. "Anyway, they're gonna go let Cyrus know, and that's that. Moco the fucking snake."

"Ain't no that's that," Redd says, a whisper of urgency in his voice now. "All we know is soulcatchers are at the West Side. And we don't even know that. We know that Rohan said that. We trust Rohan?"

"I don't know Rohan that well," I say. "But Cyrus and Carlos both trust him entirely, and that alone is enough for me. I get what you're saying, though."

"I mean," Jimmy says. "Wasn't nothing mentioned about all the other possibilities of what could go down. We here tryna smoke out the mole; we found the mole. Now we dip." He frowns. "Right?"

Redd shakes his head. "How you know it was Moco even?"

"Because," Jimmy is saying, but then we all shut up and freeze because there's movement in the park around us. Ghost movement.

"See," Redd hisses. "This the shit I'm talking 'bout. Ain't no that's that."

Translucent shrouds flash through the underbrush. I glimpse the horseshoe-crab helmet of a soulcatcher rush down a hill, then another. Then many more. They emerge from the shadows of the park, converge in long strides on the stone entranceway a few dozen feet further along the wall we crouch at.

Blades are drawn; a cruel wind whips up, the collective

frenzy of so much spiritual activity. It tastes acidy and somehow sweet, and I realize I'm terrified. If they spot us, they'll know who I am instantly—these are my fellow soldiers, and then the jig'll be up, so to speak. I'll have to watch my every step, never knowing when that freaky connection they have to all of us will kick in and I'll be caught.

And then tortured maybe.

Or fed into one of those throng haints people keep talking about.

Or just destroyed.

Suddenly, all that joking around we were doing just a few minutes ago seems utterly insane. We sit in the belly of the beast; at least three Council squads are converging less than thirty feet away. What were we thinking? "What's the move?" I whisper, because anything is better than just sitting here, waiting. Except, there's probably nothing better to do than sit here and wait.

Redd shakes his head. "Ain't shit to do right now."

"Damn," Jimmy sighs. "This probably means there two rats. None of the RD leaders knew about each other's meet-up spots."

"In theory," Redd says. "They coulda told each other."

"But if Father Desmond ratted *and* Moco ratted, what happens to their groups? Like . . . are both those Remote Districts out the game now? Are they on the Council's side? Shit."

"We can't know none of those answers right now," I say, just wanting everyone to shut the fuck up so this moment can be over. It won't end, though, not yet, anyway. The soulcatchers cluster at the entranceway. What few pedestrians had been out and about quickly disperse, probably suddenly nauseous from the burst of annoying

Council energy. Three soulcatchers hold court in the middle of all the rest: one leans on a cane like Carlos; another looks to be a captain of some kind. I can't make out the third at first—too many bodies in the way—and then I see: Botus.

The chairman himself has deigned to make an appearance. They really gunning for us, then, in case that wasn't already clear.

"Rohan," Jimmy whispers into his phone. "We got soulcatchers here too. At least three squads." Rohan's extravagant curse barrage comes over in a tinny thunderstorm; I only make out a couple words, but I get the gist.

"What you wanna do?" Jimmy says. "Where's Cyrus?" He nods, eyes wide, says, "Okay," and hangs up.

Redd and I glare our questions at him.

"He doesn't know," Jimmy reports.

"Doesn't know where Cyrus is, or what we should do?" Redd demands.

"Either. He just said, 'Man, fuck this, fuck everything, shit, sit tight, little tall dude, sit tight, shit.'"

That's probably a word-for-word account too.

"If we make a break for it, they gonna see us," Redd says. "And Krys, you on the inside. You cannot be seen."

I nod and then shake my head. "Yes, but if we stay here we just waitin' for them to stumble on us. They *everywhere*. I know you don't like sitting and waiting, Redd."

Redd smiles with half his face again, this time even wider, his mouth slightly open, one eyebrow raised. "How you already know that 'bout me an' you just met me?"

"I mean—"

"Don't matter. Point is, you right. That's why I'm not gonna. But you are. Me? I'ma divert."

Jimmy scrunches up his face. "Divert?"

I frown. "Redd, no," I say, but it's too late. He's already up, over the wall, and flitting across the street on those long legs. He moves fast to the far side of the traffic circle, cuts hard down an avenue, and then saunters out again, cool as could be. I watch, my eyes wide and mouth hanging open. Even if he survives long enough to make a run for it, I'm not sure they'll send enough 'catchers after him to make a difference.

For a very surreal few moments, Redd stands just outside the huge throng of Council warriors. They're so engrossed in whatever debate Botus is having with the captain and this limping ghost, no one pays any mind.

I shake my head, squinting. "Probably shoulda all just made a run for it. They ain't lookin' anydamnway."

"Nah," Jimmy says. "They'da seen the three of us. My tall living ass scampering off with your fat ass and Redd's pirate ass? They'da seen us."

He's right. I know he's right.

Redd leaps, pirouetting across the open air, and lands on a soulcatcher. The 'catcher stumbles forward, and Redd unsheathes his cutlass. "The fuck, bruh?" Redd yells. "Watch where the fuck you goin'!" A dozen helmets turn to face Redd. "Oh, y'all thirsty? You wanna taste Bitchmaker?"

"Hey!" The captain who had been arguing with Botus shoves his way through the crowd as shiny ghost blades emerge in the haze of falling snow. "Who exactly do you think—"

He doesn't get to finish, because Redd lurches forward, cutlass flashing. The captain steps back, draws his own blade just in time to parry twice, and then the other soulcatchers flush forward.

They're going to kill him. They're going to kill Redd, and I just met Redd. Why would he throw himself into the jaws of certain death for me? What am I supposed to do with all this?

The clang of ghost blades rings out into the night. Redd is retreating, blocking swipe after swipe as the horde of 'catchers tries to flank him on either side, fails, tries again. The rest of the Council start to follow, but Botus calls them back: "Let your brothers handle this, men. Don't get distracted."

Dammit. "That was our chance," I whisper. Now Redd's gonna die *and* we're gonna be stuck still. And then I hear yells from the other end of the circle.

"The hell?" Jimmy hisses.

It's Big Cane. He wades into the thick of the soulcatchers, towering over them, blade slashing to either side, chopping fools indiscriminately. He must've just rolled up smooth, same as Redd, and then come in chopping. The 'catchers are rallying now, translucent steel clashes on either end of the circle. Big Cane is an insider in the Council just like I am. There's . . . there's no reason he should be revealing himself except to . . . save me.

"No," I whisper. "He can't do this." Jimmy must know me pretty well by now, because just as I make to dash out into the fray, his warm, flesh-and-blood hand is on my cool, barely there arm.

"No," Jimmy says. "*You* can't do this. They're doing this for you. Don't make it for nothing."

I shake my head, and tears find their way out my eyes, slide down my face.

Big Cane has never moved this fast. He gets the job done, don't get me wrong—there's no one I'd rather have at my back in a fight—but he gets it done in his own lumbering time. Now, though, Cane fights with a fury I've never seen. He's cutting, slashing, stabbing. Four 'catchers surround him, taking turns advancing, then falling back; he blocks and parries and then sends them all scattering with a lunging slash.

"Take them alive!" Botus hollers over the clang of battle. "I want them alive for questioning!"

"We gotta go," Jimmy says. "This is our chance."

"Ayo, mothafuckas!" Riley stands at the far end of the circle. Soulcatchers stream past Big Cane, their howl reaching out into the night. Riley's been public enemy number one since he defied the Council a few months back. Any 'catcher knows his capture will enshrine them in Council history forever. In seconds the concrete park around Columbus's pillar is almost empty.

"Scatter!" Riley yells. Then he dashes off down a side street.

Big Cane cuts his way out of the throng and then breaks in the opposite direction, a shimmering mountain barging through the snow-covered streets. Redd is already gone.

"Come the fuck on," Jimmy growls.

He's right: it's time to go.

CHAPTER SEVEN

Carlos

"So," the Iyawo says with a mischievous grin, "y'all basically saying you're living a Badu song. Am I right?"

It's midmorning, and Baba Eddie's Botánica is empty but for myself, Sasha, and the Iyawo. Some sad child croons R & B out the speakers; two dozen plaster saints watch us from the aisles.

"I have no idea what you're talking about," I say.

Sasha clearly does, though. She cackles as the Iyawo raises one eyebrow, Rico Suave–style, and leans across the counter at her. "Your whole vibe is . . . you know, I could see myself being with you forever."

Sasha touches her face with exaggerated shock. "Wow, that is really—that's really beautiful. I kinda dig you too; you know that. We . . . but we friends, and I'm in a situation. I'm in a relationship, and you know what that means."

"Well"—the Iyawo drops her voice down to a sultry baritone and squinches her face to hold back laughter—"whatever I gotta do, I'll do it for you."

   "Sure put me in an awkward situation," Sasha says.
Then they both burst into song, perfectly harmonized. I
just smile, partly because I'm clueless and partly because
I want to take it in, this shared moment between these two
amazing women in my life. A flash of joy in the storm.
This morning, Sasha and I woke up holding each other
like one of us would float away if we let go. I'd dreamt
about that woman whispering my name again; she had
honey on her lips and I felt guilty but somehow peaceful
about it. It was warm under the blankets—neither of us
generate much heat, but somehow the collective energy
of our entwined bodies did the trick. Morning wood
throbbed between my legs, and all the sex we could maybe
have danced a ruckus mambo up and down my spine, but
I kept it to myself. This wasn't the time.
   Sasha made coffee and told me about the kids—how
Xiomara talks and talks in the nonchalant gibberish of
toddlers and Jackson just watches, wide eyes taking in the
whole world in gulps. How they both dote on Gordo, curl-
ing up in his huge lap while he tells stories about his delin-
quent years and reads my letters out loud. I listened and
smiled through my aching heart, and then smiled more as
Sasha went on about how her and Janey and Reza had
formed an unlikely trinity of deadly excellence, how they
go around having each other's backs in various supernatural and gangland shenanigans across Brooklyn, how they
took out the Council brain project on the Spine Islands.
   And I'm smiling now, watching Sasha be unbreakable
in the face of past and future traumas. She and the Iyawo
hit a high note, and the song collapses into giggles. For
a second, we're something like a normal family—one
that hasn't killed and died to get here. I think: if after

everything that's happened and all that may yet come, Sasha can still step outside the storm to find hilarity with a teenage girl, then somehow there's a way through all this. Sasha's laughter is a light that will guide the way. And I'll follow that light through Hell if need be.

"Carlos!" the Iyawo yells, waving. "Come back to us, man. Sash, you gotta make him a mixtape or something—how he don't know Mama Erykah?"

Sasha rolls her eyes and pats me on the shoulder. "I'm gonna work on him, Iyawo, but he just found out about GPS yesterday; it's gonna take some time."

I like the sound of that so much that I can't concentrate on a snappy reply. The Iyawo shakes her head. "Get to it, girl."

"I'm on it," Sasha says, pulling on her coat. "But now I gotta handle some shit. C, I'll hit you later on tonight. Iyawo"—she crosses her arms over her chest—"be good."

"Pshaw," the Iyawo says. "Being good overrated as fu—rt."

I raise an eyebrow. "Furt, Iyawo?"

"Shut up, Carlos."

Sasha's still laughing when she kisses my cheek; her breath is warm on my neck. Then she's gone, out the jangly door, into the bright winter morning.

"Well," the Iyawo says, "*that* happened."

"Mmhm."

"Y'all fucked?"

"God, you sound like Riley."

"But did you?"

"Nah. Sometimes it's better to wait. Wasn't the time. So much shit going on . . ."

"Homey, that is *exactly* the time when you gotta lay

pipe. Stress-relief sexy times. Ain't a thing better." She does a little samba behind the counter.

"What you know about . . . You know what? Never mind. What happened in Rio stays in Rio."

"I feel you, though," she says, sobering. "You got long game, and I respect that. For real."

"Thanks. You're peppy this morning."

"The Iyawo has coffee today!" She takes an exaggerated sip from a burgundy ceramic mug and says, "Ah!"

"You don't usually drink coffee."

She shakes her head. "But hey! Hey!"

"Maybe that was a good thing."

"Hey! Oh, I meant to ask you: How well you know Krys the ghost?"

"She's good people," I say. "And a force of nature in battle. Kind of reminds me of you now that I think about it."

"Why, cuz she's a black girl? Fall back, halfie."

"I'm taking your coffee away, Iyawo."

She grips the cup, eyes wide.

"Anyway, why you ask?"

"Just wondering. We were talking yesterday; she seems cool."

"Carlos!" Baba Eddie pokes his head in. "Let's roll out—we're late. Hi, Iyawocita."

The Iyawo smiles, eyes narrowed, brows raised, lips pushed out.

"I'll talk to you later," I say. We trade an air high five, and I follow Baba Eddie into the cold.

"What you know about dreams, Baba?"

Rohan guides his Crown Vic through the crowded

Bushwick streets toward East New York. Baba Eddie sits in the passenger seat, halfway turned around while I catch him up on what's been going on from the back. He'd stopped me outside the botánica, wrapped his arms around me, and held me for a few startling seconds—I guess the Iyawo let him know 'bout her research—and I thanked him, and that was that.

"I mean"—he puts an unlit Pall Mall in his mouth—"plenty. What you got?"

"It's a recurring one: beautiful woman, dark skin, big hair, smiling usually, naked, saying my name."

"Y'all fuck?" Rohan asks from the front.

"You sound like the Iyawo," I say.

Baba Eddie narrows his eyes. "My Iyawo said what now?"

"Never mind. Uh . . . sometimes, yeah. Usually we're just about to; then I wake up."

"Bummer," Rohan mutters. "I'm sure you finish the job, though."

"She say anything besides your name?" Baba asks.

"Not that I can remember, but it's like she knows me really well. And I know her somehow, except I don't."

"Someone from when you were alive before, maybe?" Baba says.

"I've thought that but . . . somehow doesn't feel right. I can't explain it."

He furrows his brow, fiddles with the cigarette. "And she's naked?"

"Always. And last night she had honey on her lips, like dripping."

"Damn, bruh." Rohan adjusts himself in the front seat. "That's the hotness."

"Oh!" Baba Eddie lets out a chortle and then lights his cigarette.

I know better than to interrupt his moment of Zen, so I just wait while he lovingly inhales, eyes closed, and then releases the first stream of smoke out the slightly open window.

"Oh?"

"This one time, Ogun," Baba Eddie starts.

"That's the war and ironworking one," I say. "Right?"

"Bingo. Ogun gets fed up with being a part of the world. He's over it. People, all the little dramas and bullshit, drama with other orishas. Finito. So he's like, 'Ay, fuck this,' and heads to the mountains."

"That's a direct quote?"

"I mean, he probably said it in Yoruba, but you know."

"Right."

"Thing is, Ogun is technology, he's civilization, he's how shit gets done. So what happens when he leaves?"

Rohan chuckles. "Shit don't get done."

"Eso mismo," Baba Eddie says.

"Get the fuck out the way!" Rohan yells out the window. A city bus has clogged both sides of Myrtle Ave, snarling traffic in either direction.

"Anyway, all the orishas try to get him back; none of them can. Even Ogun's hunting brothers Elgeba and Ochosi can't convince him to come back."

Rohan rolls the window up. "Meanwhile, shit still falling apart back in the world, am I right?"

"Exactly. Finally, Oshun says, 'Lemme talk to him.'"

"Oshun is like the sexy mama orisha," Rohan tells me, winking into the rearview mirror.

"But she's so much more than that too," Baba Eddie says. "Oshun is the youngest but one of the most powerful orishas. That mirror she carries will show you all the deepest parts of yourself if you're brave enough to look. She's both lover and fighter, and her rivers run through every single one of us."

"Damn," Rohan says. "She bad."

This is all way over my head, so I mostly nod and try to keep up.

"Anyway," Baba Eddie continues, "she goes to get Ogun. Ogun not tryna hear nobody. Oshun is like, 'Hey,' puts some honey on her lips."

"Like ol' girl in C's dream!" Rohan belts out.

"And she starts dancing, swaying those hips. Ogun is transfixed. He stumbles out the woods toward her, and she keeps leading him further and further from his hideaway, back to the world."

"Does he hit that, though?" Rohan wants to know.

"Rohan, man . . . ," I say.

Baba Eddie nods wisely. "In fact, he does."

"Ay, this is my kind of story!" Rohan does a little jig in the front seat, then swerves the Vic away from an oncoming delivery truck. "Stay the fuck out my lane, then!"

"You were in his," Baba Eddie points out.

"Yuh mother's pussyhole!" Rohan yells out the window as we screech away.

"So wait," I say. "Are you saying the woman's Oshun and I'm Ogun? Or I'm Oshun and the woman is like . . . inside me somehow? Or Sasha's Ogun?"

"Oh look," Baba Eddie says with a wink. "We're here!"

———

El Mar sits along a bustling stretch of Fulton Street in East New York, not far from where Moco's band of rebellious ghosts made their stand against the Council a few months ago. Bakeries, dollar stores, and nail salons surround it; the J train rumbles overhead.

Normally, folks mill about in front of the tall, darkened windows of El Mar, peeking in to see what corny keyboard wizard or random bachata band will entertain the diners. Today, though, the street is empty. Well, empty of the living. About fifty shimmering ghosts on bicycles crowd the block. The bikes are all full size (not the tiny stationary ones those little demons the ngks use), and painted white. The riders look ornery.

"The hell is this all about?" I ask Baba Eddie as we move gingerly past a glowering spandexed ghost with a beard and helmet.

"Things didn't go so well yesterday, as you may have heard."

"Just a little," I say.

"Seems at least two of the Remote District leaders might be compromised, and we don't know if that means the districts themselves are out too. Meaning—"

"We might be even more outnumbered than we thought," Rohan finishes.

"So Cyrus put the word out to a few groups of semi-autonomous ghosts," Baba Eddie says. "Folks that may or may not be on our side."

"Time to find out," I say.

"Indeed. Also"—Baba Eddie holds the wooden door

open as Rohan and I walk in—"we have no idea where Big Cane is."

"What?"

Baba Eddie doesn't bother trying to answer; reggaeton obliterates every other sound as soon as we walk in. Some kind of monstrous, driving beat and excited dude with a fade and wraparound sunglasses, I'm sure. We move toward the back.

The big round table we normally sit around is gone. Instead, Cyrus holds court behind a long wooden bar at the back of the dim room. Jimmy, Krys, and some of the African Burial Ground leaders sit on one side of him, Riley and Damian on the other. Ghosts of all shapes and colors heavy up the air around us, all of them facing the bar.

"Ah, Carlos, Rohan, Baba Eddie!" Cyrus calls when we walk in. Dozens of translucent faces turn to look at us. "Come, join us."

We move through the chilly crowd. Ahead of us, two dead white women in spandex straddle mountain bikes in front of the bar. "This is what I don't understand, Mr. Langley," one of them says. "You cause trouble, lots of trouble, and the Council responds. You've been causing trouble for the Council since you showed up from that Burial Ground. Terrible situation, by the way; we're awfully sorry to hear about that."

Cyrus nods, his face set in a crooked, indiscernible smile. Riley, on the other hand, looks like he's one disingenuous apology away from losing his entire shit.

The other woman furrows her brow.

"Anyway," the first one says, "the Ghost Riders support your cause in theory, but you can't ask us to throw our whole weight behind and possibly die the Deeper Death for a problem that you yourself caused. With all due respect."

The group assembled behind the bar erupts into angry chatter. "Who the fuck are the Ghost Riders?" I whisper to Baba Eddie as we find our seats. "And why the fuck haven't I heard about them before?"

"It's a group of bikers that got killed by motorists. They bike around the city in a big clump. Usually Manhattan, though—that might be why you missed 'em."

"Sharon!" the second woman snaps. "Don't . . . ugh." She steps forward, dragging her bike with her. "Mr. Langley, I apologize for my Ghost Riding sister's disrespect. We are having some organizational . . . conflicts within the leadership and . . . a great many of us in fact support your movement to topple the Council."

Cyrus raises his eyebrows.

"Damnit, Brit!" Sharon yells. "Can't we *even* get along long enough to present a united front? This is unacceptable."

She starts working her way through the crowd of ghosts, pushing her bicycle along beneath her.

Brit cringes. "I'm sorry, everyone. I'm going to speak to her. I will make this right. Sharon!" She turns and heads for the door. "Why did you do that, Sharon?" The room clears out; spirits depart one by one and in small groups, dispersing into the frosty New York afternoon to report back to their districts.

Cyrus shakes his head again, that smile teasing the edge of his lips. "So much changed, so much stayed the same." He turns to Riley. "When I first met you, you would've jumped down that white lady's throat for her disrespect."

"Ay." Riley scowls. "We ain't got time for the small shit these days. She'll learn or she won't."

"What happened to Big Cane?" I ask.

Everyone looks gloomy suddenly. "No idea," Riley says. "We got into a tussle with the 'catchers. They were all converging right where Krys and Jimmy were hiding and—"

"I didn't ask anyone to save me," Krys insists, striding out of the shadows. "We woulda made it outta there." She's holding back tears. I've never seen her this shook.

"It's okay, my child," Cyrus says. "We made a decision. I made a decision. It was worth risking Cane and Riley for the diversion. They knew what they were getting into."

"Damn right," Riley says. "And anyway, there was no stopping Cane once he heard you were hemmed in. I could barely keep up—that's why he got there first."

"But he's an insider too. Why would you—"

Cyrus stands, moves toward Krys. "He's barely in the know these days—they just bring him in for special assignments. And the weapons, child . . ."

"I *knew* this was about the damn weapons!" Krys slides away from Cyrus, over the bar. "We can't make decisions about who lives or dies based on which of us has the coolest guns."

Cyrus furrows his brow. "Coolest, no? But yes, these decisions must be made, and they must be made with strategy in mind."

Krys turns and storms out the door.

"And this is the burden of the general," Cyrus says as he takes his seat. For a few seconds, his eyes stare at some long-lost moment in the distance. Then he shakes it off. "No sign of him?"

Little Damian says, "No, and we've scoured all of Manhattan."

"Think he was caught?"

"Or he turned on us," Riley says.

A few gloomy seconds pass. Then I shake my head. "I don't see it. Not if he threw himself into the fray like that. Not with how close he is with Krys. Doesn't add up to me. He had no way of knowing it would go down like it did, for that to be planned . . ."

A tall ghost with an axe comes in, one of Cyrus's guys. "Some folks from RD 17 are here," he says. "They want to talk."

At a nod from Cyrus, he opens the door wider, and three old women enter. One steps forward, clears her throat. "We have come to apologize on behalf of the Remote District Diecisiete." She gestures to the other two with a tiny, crinkled hand. "These are my hermanas, Rosali and Angelina. They call me La Venganza."

Cyrus's smile grows wide. "An honor to meet you, my dear."

"El honor es mío," she says with a slight bow. Then her face tightens. "We have dealt with the traitor, Moco. He has been destroyed completely and sent to la Muerte Más Profunda, ya."

The two women behind her spit at the mention of Moco's name.

"And we are here to say that because of this man's disgrace, we have spent the day rallying the rest of Diecisiete and we can now proudly add two hundred souls to the cause of destroying the Council of the Dead for once and for all."

A cheer goes up from the bar as La Venganza bows again and then retreats with her sisters.

"Thank you, hermanas," Cyrus calls after them. Then he turns to us. "Father Desmond's district is less assured, unfortunately. He took about half with him when he defected."

"Which puts us at about the same place we left off," Riley says.

I stand. "There's something else . . ." I tell them about my meeting at Sunset Park yesterday, the limping ghost and Botus's offer to make me one of the Seven, and how Sasha took out the CentCom and freed me from the meddlesome reach.

"Excellent," Cyrus says when I'm done. "Excellent."

"What?" I say.

"They're terrified and confused. Right where we want them. Things are about to get very bad, more likely than not. And then they'll get worse. And then we'll have a real fight on our hands."

Sasha

"They're good," Gordo assures me over the phone. I'm in a crowded coffee shop and some gloomy and perfect piano blues fills the air, so it's hard to tell if Gordo's scared or not.

"How 'bout Reza and Janey?"

"The kids love Reza, no matter how much of a tough guy she pretends to be. Janey's been taking a lot of walks. I think she is maybe going through something with Nesto? Yo no sé."

"He needs to marry that ass," I say. "No offense."

"None taken! I told him this myself."

"Alright, Big G. I'm gonna brood in this coffee shop some more. Keep me updated."

"I will and . . . let me know what's going on with the Council situation if you find anything out."

"I will. Thanks for . . . everything."

He chuckles and hangs up.

The guy playing piano has brown skin and locks all the way down his back, just like Trevor's. He wears some big ol' grandma glasses, and a goatee frames his mouth. He closes his eyes and leans into the keys as the song comes to a head, pounding out blue notes that seem to slide in between the melody, and then he lands back on the one with a resounding power chord. The whole coffee shop bursts into applause—no one was ready for such stunning accompaniment to their studying or brooding. I know I wasn't.

He nods his thanks, smiles, and then mumbles something about the next tune in a sultry voice.

And then all I see is Juan Flores's face—the face before it was devoured by rats. He's looking down at me, squinting just slightly. I'm vomiting bile and blood into a bucket, my whole body trembling, the edge of death creeping along my limbs. That squint: it was pain, shame. I knew it then but didn't know why. He never showed any emotions with the others, a complete mask. I had figured it was some creepy guy gaze—here I was destroyed and helpless at his feet. He held my hair away from my face as I retched, his hand on my back.

I shudder and coffee splashes on the table.

"*I could take her to my home,*" the pianist croons, "*and bring her up into my room alone.*"

I was married to that man. We were intimate once. Disgust overwhelms me, and I have to breathe deep to ease my shaking hands.

"We would do what lovers love to do."

For once, I'm grateful my memories are gone. If Juan Flores and I were in love during that first life of mine, I don't want to see it, don't need the images, the echoing emotions. Let it go, all of it.

Carlos is right: those were other people. Aisha is not Sasha.

"And I would wrap her in the soft cocoon. We'd light the night up like two crescent moons."

Carlos. The memory of him clings to me, a welcome phantom to keep watch over this aching heart. His big hands wrapping around me in the hotel room, the weight and length of him, a shelter encompassing me.

"But in the end I'd only break her little heart in twooooo."

Miguel's big hands aren't like Carlos's. Each edge and cuticle trimmed and manicured; the palms are warm and sometimes wet as they glide over my cool skin. I never let myself cum with Miguel, couldn't, but his penis is a thing to behold. He's stockier than Carlos, and shorter. A bad breakup sent him solace-seeking at the gym over the past year, so he's almost perfectly toned and wears the sculpted bulges like a shiny suit of armor. He was gentle at first—too gentle—and I had to teach him how to man-handle me right.

He shows up some nights after his shifts, always texting first to make sure I'm up, always smelling of air freshener and cologne, the air around him bristling with customers' annoyances and petty fare negotiations. We don't talk about our days—he knows better than to ask—just trade quick pleasantries, and then I ease him out of those jeans and unbutton his shirt. He smiles when I take him in my mouth, grunts when I let my bathrobe collapse like a slow splash of water, pool around my feet. He moans when he enters me, fisting his face to hold back the explosion that already shoves its way through him, obliterating the tiny indelicacies of the day. He sighs when he hits his stride, a goofy smile overtaking him, his big, warm hand around my slender, cool neck, squeezing; then the smile peels back, his eyes go wide, and Miguel gasps when he cums, a guttural, unapologetic blast that I fear will wake the kids but never does.

And then Miguel sleeps.

"*Cuz it should be you*," the pianist sings, hitting the chorus at full stride. "*It should be you-ou-ou.*"

It shouldn't be Miguel. It was for a time, in an easy, we-don't-have-to-explain kind of way, but all that is over. Everything is different now.

"*You're the only one I should be giving all my loving to. It should be you.*"

Certainty, that rare and beautiful gem, seeps over me.

"*It should be you-ou-ou.*"

He's having too much fun, the pianist, and I love it. Each word becomes a tiny poem on his lips, emboldened by that rich, molasses voice.

"*You're the only one I'm gonna give all of my lovin' to.*"

I sip coffee, take in the moment.

And then Miguel is there, all puffy in his winter gear, smiling over his scarf.

"Sasha!"

I stand and embrace him. He de-jackets and orders a

coffee and joins me, and the words are forming in me, the gentle letdown, the gift of clarity, however cutting, and then he says, "I'm glad you asked me here today, Sasha. I have something to tell you."

I raise my eyebrows.

"Yes, and it's not easy, so . . . you know, let me just . . . I just want to . . . yes."

"Take your time," I say.

Miguel does things with his face—mouth twisting to one side, then the other as he closes one eye and furrows his brow.

"You okay?"

"Yes!" he assures me. "Sorry, I . . . yes. The thing is, Sasha. I feel that I should, that we should . . . we should stop." He exhales the word and then seems to deflate.

Without meaning to, I brighten. "Really?"

"Yes, and it's not because you aren't amazing, Sasha. You are. And even saying that, I feel its meaning is cheapened because I am telling you now and not then, as we lay together, so it becomes more a thing said in retrospect, a going-away present, and that's not fair, but . . ."

My smile is sincere. "I never doubted you found me amazing, Miguel."

He sighs. "I'm glad. It's just I realized the other day that I'm not really the man I should be, still. I mean, I'm over Vanessa—that's not a question, like, at all. I'm just not ready to do a serious thing yet. I'm still, you know . . . me and I just need to, I need to be me, and not me and someone else, for a little while. Longer. If that makes sense?"

It only half makes sense: Miguel and I never approached anything like couplehood—we barely spoke! But why complicate a simple gift like him taking on the burden of the break? "Makes perfect sense," I say.

"Not that we ever . . . but you know . . . my life has been very strange the past couple months, ever since that whole thing by the river I told you about."

Carlos, Janey, and Gordo helped him fend off some kind of demon, but he got disemboweled in the process and barely survived. We never got into it in detail, but I gather that's why he just accepts all the not-quite-right things about me. He may not understand it, but he's content to not know, and that's its own kind of understanding.

"And I thought I could just go back to being who I was, you know: Miguel. Like, ayyy Miguel!" He cheeses unnecessarily; I know exactly what he means. It's cute, though. "But no." Suddenly despondent. "No."

He sniffles, and I send up a prayer that he won't break down.

"Yeah," he says, rallying. "Anyway, a lot is changing, and you helped me through, like, the worst of that, while I was healing still and everything, so thank you for that. Really."

I swat away his thanks. "I didn't do anything, man." It was my pleasure. Literally.

In the back corner of the coffee shop, a group of rowdy teenagers busts out laughing as one jumps up, swatting a splash of color off her arm. They curse lovingly at each other and settle back down. The pianist find his way out of a labyrinthine solo, sliding back into the gentle strut of the verse.

"And I would make her cry and make her laugh, memorize her like a photograph, kiss her body as the morning drops the dew."

The air between us thickens, no thanks to this obscenely talented man making love to the microphone a few feet away.

"Well, anyway, I should . . . ," Miguel says as I mumble: "Anyway, yeah, thank you." Then we both giggle, stand, embrace, and in that embrace I allow myself to take him in fully—beyond his midlevel Dominican-dude cologne and well-coifed everything. A warmth emanates, a growing, pulsing glow, the soul of a lover, yes, but also a healer. He's moving toward that glow, toward his own core, and when he gets there, it'll be a wonder to behold.

I put my hand on one of Miguel's cheeks and kiss the other. I don't let it linger. He smiles, and then he's gone.

For a few moments, I watch Bedford Avenue out the big coffee-shop window. Across the street, some kids are shoveling in front of a mosque. The city has already mired the once-pristine snow into a gray brown sludge.

"It should be you."

Juan Flores steps in front of the window.

"It should be you-ou-ooooh."

I stand, merging my own reflection across his shimmering form.

"You're the only one I'm gonna give all of my loving to."

Then I walk outside.

I knew he'd come looking for me. Stopped at home this morning after I left the botánica, knowing he'd be watching, waiting. Felt the icy prickle of his glare as I walked in my front door. I showered, already missing the smell and essence of Carlos around me, changed clothes, texted

Miguel, and made it to the coffee shop in time to get a corner table before the lunch rush.

I knew he was coming, and still.

His visor is up. That empty face sends a shiver through me, but I force myself into neutral, illegible.

He'll be curious, I'm sure. Grasping for meaning at the tiny twitches of each muscle, my every move scrutinized. I'll give him nothing and that way, perhaps, learn everything.

Or at least more than the tattered semblance of my life and death I've pieced together.

We head north in silence. Fruit stands and taco joints become kosher supermarkets. Hasids crowd the streets, families and clusters of bearded men talking quietly, laughing. Some shoot me suspicious glares: How dare a black woman intrude on their turf? I ignore them. Somewhere ahead there will be an empty lot or abandoned warehouse—somewhere I can end this motherfucker in peace.

"You received my gift, I see."

I keep my eyes on the street ahead of us. Nod. "Why?"

"Hm?" His voice bemused.

"Why did you help me sabotage the Council? You work for them. And in no small capacity, from what I gather."

"Of course. I'm their minister of war. I stand below only the Seven." A slight growl emerges in his voice.

"So—why?"

He stops. "For you. For us."

Takes everything in me not to scoff and then spit in his face and fill him with holes. I don't, though, I don't. The need for knowledge trumps the need for revenge. At this point, anyway.

"Tell me about my death."

Juan Flores flinches, looks up at the white sky. Exhales.

"It was a Bloody Pentacle—that's what Sarco called it."

I squint, feigning surprise. "You—you knew Sarco?"

"He was like a mentor for a while, when we were alive."

"To . . . to me too?"

"Of sorts. I don't think you ever fully trusted him the way I did—but then you were always the craftier one. He showed up in town one day, the quintessential mysterious stranger, talking big philosophies about the line between life and death and, honestly, making a lot of sense. And one late night in at Gerry's Bar over by the factory, he showed me he had the powers behind all that talk too. It was raining that night, and someone had hit a possum on Route 9. I watched with my mouth hanging open while Sarco chanted something and the tattered mass of blood, bone, and fur lurched to life.

"In retrospect, he probably just shoved some passing spirit into the thing's corpse, but hey, what did I know? I was flabbergasted. And I was in. Life and death? That kind of power? I was a security guard at the time; all I knew of power was kicking someone off the premises."

Anyway, I know all about this side of Sarco. He infiltrated the Survivors back in our early, wary days of existing. Got us all riled up against the Council and had us divided and quarreling amongst ourselves in a few manic weeks. My brother Trevor drank the Sarco Kool-Aid and paid the price for it. Maybe I did too, when I was alive.

"And you . . . Aisha."

"No," I cut him off. "That's not my name anymore. That's not who I am."

A crowd of Hasidic schoolkids swarms past, all yarmulkes and excited Yiddish chatter. A few pass through Juan Flores's icy visage and shudder; the rest flush around him, an unspoken understanding that *something* is very off.

"As you wish. Sasha."

I shudder when he says it. There's no mouth to direct me, but I imagine an ironic, shit-eating grin stretching across his face. I keep walking. If I stand there looking at him any longer, I'll lash out and probably get carted off for causing a disturbance in this well-guarded Williamsburg enclave.

"You were interested too," he continues, catching up with me. "You had a gothic streak in you, all those animations you used to watch, and for a few years in high school you would wear all black, chains and studded neck collars and such."

He says it distastefully, and I smile to myself. "What's this Bloody Pentacle you mentioned?"

We cross the Brooklyn-Queens Expressway. Midday traffic stretches off in either direction. Brick row houses rise and fall on either side, and further along, a synagogue's cement rooftop peeks above the others.

"A parlor game they used to play back in some oldtime European courts he frequented. Five people sit in a dark room with a single candle in the middle. One is the Linchpin, the orchestrator; he plays the other four off each other using various forms of trickery and manipulation. But no one knows who the Linchpin is, and in the course of finding out, the group forges alliances, betrayals, etcetera. Until there are only two players left."

"You and Sarco." My voice is cold.

"I didn't . . . I didn't *know* it was happening! I just . . . I thought . . ."

"Who were the others?"

"Well, you, of course. Andre. Samuel Bennacourt—the one who called himself Gregorio."

The one who tried to feed my children to the roach horde before Reza and Carlos killed him.

"What was the play?"

"You."

"Explain."

"You started getting threatening letters. At the office you temped at first. Graphic, horrible shit . . . rape, dismemberment, whole family killed. All that."

I shudder. At least one part of that came true, though Flores doesn't know I know that.

"Of course, everyone was freaked out—me most of all. I tried to keep you from going in, followed you around everywhere. It drove a wedge between us. I was . . . overprotective."

No shit.

He shrugs, almost sheepishly. It's the first unscripted thing he's done since we've met. "I was convinced Andre was behind the whole thing. I never liked him, and it fit nicely into the twisted image I had of him inserting himself into our marriage. You two were . . . close. Sarco was a genius for letting other people's fantasies convince them of whatever he wanted them to believe. Andre thought it was Bennacourt, a local drifter. I convinced you, somewhat, that Andre was a threat—he'd started acting erratic at the end too. Sarco kept ratcheting up the terror—a shattered window late at night, more notes, a stray dog killed on our doorstep—until one night he arranged it so we'd all end up at Grand Army Plaza along with a few other folks that had gotten involved. Tensions were already so high, it quickly erupted into violence. Andre cut down Bennacourt, who was reaching for you, both thinking they were protecting you. You killed Andre, thinking he meant to kill you."

"And you killed me?"

He shakes his head. "I could never, Ai . . . Sasha. *Never.* I was meant to, though. Sarco had poisoned my thoughts against you, made me believe that you'd been cheating with Andre. He knew I was jealous."

"I hadn't though, had I?"

"No, never. Which made it all the worse. But I didn't do it. I couldn't. I ran, terrified, when the blood started flowing. I . . . I did, I ran. I had figured out there was more at play once Andre showed up in a fury."

"Who, then?"

"Sarco. You were holding Andre's body in your arms, sobbing. He cut your throat. He told me later . . . when everything had come to light."

I rub my throat, shoving away all the images that try to rise in my mind.

Not now.

Not here.

"And then there were two," I say. "You and Sarco."

"I didn't know he was behind it all then." His voice pleading now, a guttural whine. "I didn't know. And even when I figured out it was him, I didn't realize to what extent. Took a few weeks to unravel the whole thing, and by then—"

"You'd already helped him kill us."

"I never killed anyone!" A shriek. The stone synagogue

looms above us now. It's abandoned, pillars desecrated with posters and graffiti, windows shattered and shuttered.

"Not with your hands, no."

"When I found out, I couldn't . . . I couldn't bear it. I'd put most of it together, and then one night outside the safe house, I confronted him and he told me the rest. How he'd studied us, figured out all of our fears and eccentricities, then turned us on each other like pieces on a game board. He'd made it seem like we were helping you, nursing you all back to life. Like everything would be alright."

"You were so mad at Sarco you offed yourself in the park."

"I was ashamed! I'd let it all play out. I . . . I couldn't live with that. You were the only woman I'd ever loved."

I can't stop the shudder that runs through me when he says it.

"And I thought maybe . . . maybe I could make it up somehow, if not in life, then in death. You were . . . you are the light that keeps me going, always. And I'd learned from Sarco, learned mysteries about the line between life and death. I knew how to access power in that realm, what to do with it. And I was half-crazed with guilt and grief; I figured I could strike back somehow, get on the inside."

The implication of what he said creeps slowly up my spine. "You were already inside. You were working with Sarco."

"Not inside Sarco's operation, inside the Council."

There it is. "The Council was—"

"The Council was allied with Sarco from the beginning. They funded his work, sent him soulcatcher support teams, had his back in every way imaginable."

I stare at him, my face stricken. The Council . . .

"Right up until he got what he wanted—a team of inbetweeners to play with at his will. That's what they wanted too; that was why they were helping him, because he promised he could deliver. They needed someone, or someone*s* preferably, to handle that murky borderline, do the shit they couldn't.

"But then Sarco went rogue. He lost track of Andre that night when a Soulcatcher Prime came upon him as Sarco's people were removing the rest. Or perhaps he left him there on purpose, a token to placate the Council. Anyway, three didn't survive. Sarco took the ones he had and started plotting against the Council."

"Along with my brother, Trevor."

"And then the—"

"Council sent Carlos to destroy him. And you?"

"And I—"

"You laid low like you'd done while we were being slaughtered. What? Biding your time? Letting everyone else do the dirty work?" My voice rises above the quiet murmur I'd kept it at. People begin to stare.

"Biding my time, yes. Not everything gets done by being hotheaded and irrational. Sometimes strategy is involved."

This useless piece of shit.

I move us down a side street—less pestering attention, but still I'm outnumbered and outgunned as soon as I present a threat. This area has its own security force, and when the cops do come, they'll shoot a black woman with a sword on sight. I'm sure Flores took all this into consideration when he led me north.

"What do you mean?" I demand.

"I've worked my way through the ranks, from soulcatcher to 'Catcher Prime to minister. I thought I'd be one of the Seven at this point, but that didn't quite work out how I planned."

"To what end?"

"We change the Council from the inside, Sasha. They will never see it coming. I've gained their trust, and I know how to maneuver the politics of it. And they need me, at this point, what with the war coming. They—"

I hold up my hand. He shuts up.

"We?"

"Yes, Sasha. *Sasha.* You and me. There is so much power between us—you don't feel it?" He drops to one knee and still is almost as tall as me. "I know we've come through a bloody corridor to be together again, but we can let that blood be a cleansing, a fortification for the future we have together. I know you don't trust me now, but you did once, and I believe you will again. I believe we will sit side by side and bring peace and balance to the realms of the living and dead. This is our destiny, Sasha, you and I. And all this, all that I've done, I did it for you. I did it for lo—"

I've heard enough. My hand flies back, grips the handle of my blade over my shoulder. I'm fast, but Flores is no slouch. He throws himself to the side as my blade drops. The cut glances off his shoulder guard, shredding a slice off that cloak.

"Aisha, no!" He rolls backward, scrambling for his broadsword.

"My name"—I slash again, up, then down and across, catch him twice but never deep—"is Sasha."

He's fast. My next cut crashes against his sword.

"Hey!" someone yells nearby. "What's going on over there?"

Time is running out.

"You don't understand!" Flores pleads.

I waste no more words. My blade rains down in relentless strikes. He blocks and blocks, refuses to cut back. I
can't get inside his defenses, though, not for more than a
glancing blow.

Car tires screech at the end of the block. Footsteps run
toward us from Bedford. I must look insane. Sweat pours
down my face. "You there! Woman! Hello?"

This has to end, but there's no endgame, and I'm running out of energy already.

From a few blocks away, a siren sounds.

"Hello? Ma'am?"

Figures close in around us. I put my back into the next
hit, crash this blade down hard enough on his to throw
him off-balance. And still his defense holds.

"Hold it right there!" someone yells. No guns have
clicked yet, but still . . . The siren gets louder.

"You disgust me," I whisper. Then I spit into his empty
face, and then I'm gone, down the backstreets of South
Williamsburg and out by the open throughway near the
river.

"You okay?" Carlos says over the phone as I slide into
the back of a black livery cab.

"Yeah," I manage between pants, "but you gotta reach
out to Cyrus, tell him to go on high alert. Council's about
to come out swinging."

CHAPTER EIGHT

◦~◦◦~◦

Caitlin

The Tammany sits a half block from Luther's, but it's a whole other world. Luther's bursts with thundering pop and flashing lights, a half thousand customers blaring their mediocre days into each other's ears and squiggling across the dance floor like so many worms abandoned after the rain. The Tam is a back-roads shotgun shack in comparison. I mean, we're in Midtown Manhattan, so it's not like it's actually a dive—rather, a carefully constructed rendition of one. It does the trick, though. Folks only come here to sulk and soak in their gin and tonics, texting exes or drawing elaborate suicide plans on napkins while a guy with a receding mullet sings Hootie & the Blowfish knockoffs over the PA.

I come to get work done, because it's easier to concentrate here than in an office full of bleating crisis donkeys. And here no one cares when I have unusual visitors. Every once in a while, a ghost shows up. The dead like dives, even the fake-downtrodden ones like this, because hey, these days you gotta take what you can get, am I right?

But that's fine. Whenever one tries to set up shop in a dark corner with all those shimmery tendrils and moans, I just walk up to it real slow and put my face in its face and growl. They're so startled I can not only see them but also don't give a half a fuck about them that they usually beat it right then and there, and then it's just me again.

Well, me and the half dozen fuckups that find solace in this hole. And the bartender. His name is Ennis, but he's alright. And that body . . . Ennis looks like he could bench-press me and not break a sweat.

Probably gay, though. Never met a straight guy named Ennis.

Anyway, tonight I'm nursing my second Guinness and breezing through these transfer documents, feeling pretty good, when Bellamy starts yelling at Ennis to turn the TV up. Bellamy is a self-absorbed human catastrophe that loves to feel important, so I don't pay much mind. Scribble the last signature on the doc I'm on and then glance up and turns out a plane went down in some forgettable Asian country that no one cares about. I'm about to look away when they cut to a shot of the wreckage—charred, smoldering heaps of metal, and then I'm back in front of my childhood home that night almost a year ago, and all that's left are charred, smoldering heaps, and one last fire engine is still there, painting the whole block with its pulsing glare.

Carlos Delacruz set that fire, along with that bull-dyke bitch Reza he started running with.

The Blattodeons had collected my parents' corpses and gave them a proper burial in the underground passageways. And the truth is, I'd never been close to either of them. From a very young age, I knew I was different and bound for a different life. Richard and Evelyn Fern were a means to an end. They knew it and I knew it. And parents are parents, even if only genetically, and then there I am again, the air cluttered with smoke and ash and the only home I've ever known just a blackened pile of embers and melted plastic and charred metal.

"Caitlin?" The man standing over my table is backlit, and I'm still caught up in that smoky Queens night. Sloppy. I stand too quickly, upset some foamy Guinness onto my paperwork, curse, and squint through the lights at my visitor, who's now trying to mop up the foam with my napkins.

"Detective," I say. "Don't trouble yourself, please."

"No, it's fine—I didn't mean to startle you." We're both fumbling with napkins and papers now, and finally I just lift the whole stack and put them on the table next to me. Paramus Jim is too far gone to notice.

"You didn't, really. Sit."

Detective Randall Corvin of the NYPD Special Victims Unit is all sharp angles and brisk, indelicate movements. He takes off his jacket and sits, placing two pointy elbows on the table and leaning in. His weasely little face is pinched into a sour pout, but then a grin appears, which is even more alarming. "Caitlin."

"Detective."

"Please, Caitlin, I'm off duty. Call me Randy. Really."

I'll never understand why someone who could be called detective would voluntarily insist on being called Randy but there it is. "Randy." I make myself smile. "Do you have it?"

"Caitlin, this can't keep happening. It's very, *very* difficult to pull an unauthorized records search like this."

"I know, Randy, believe me, I do. My job requires constant wrangling with arbitrary systems that do nothing more than get in the way of those of us protecting society's least vulnerable members. But we do what we have to, right? And sometimes that means taking risks. I promise I only ask because there are lives at stake. Young lives."

Detective Randy flinches. "I don't like it. Any of it. Technically, if you're concerned about a crime being committed, you should—"

"Call nine-one-one and let the cops handle it—I know, Randy, but you know as well I do, better probably, how many issues there are with that. Don't play naive with me. This has to get done, and it has to get done fast, and it has to get done right. We need to make sure those children are in the safe home the state has entrusted us to put them in, and if they're not, it's my job to find out. And I'll be damned if I'm going to pass that responsibility to an agency that has all the delicacy and investigative skills of an inbred llama."

This is called "bringing it home." Randy and I have talked at length about his own department's failings. He is chronically despondent and in over his head. He'll probably be dead in a year, if not from some pedophile's knife, then the stress will take him out. Either way, he's useful to me now, insofar as I can use his own hatred of the department against him.

"I don't like it," Randy says again, as if him not liking something is a novelty. He puts his briefcase on the table, digs out a file. Doesn't give it to me. "If *anything* goes wrong, you're to call nine-one-one. If you have *any* concerns, doubts, questions, whatever, you're to call me."

"Understood."

He squints, his already-tight face squinching into a crumpled sheet of paper. "Okay." He passes the file.

"Thank you, Detective."

"Randy."

"Thank you, Detective Randy." I smile and he sort of flinches, and then some small talk happens, dwindles, and then he's gone and I'm scanning this list of calls, but really I'm there on that night with the dying embers of my childhood home.

"*Everything is gonna be alright*," the mullet guy howls over and over. I want to punch him in the fucking face.

Ten minutes later, the murmuring bar gets quiet. Everyone has turned to stare at two tall men walking toward me. I get it: to the normal human eye, the Blattodeons just look off somehow. It's an offness you can't name or place; the brain recoils at their slightly arrhythmic gait, their unblinking eyes and fixed pupils. Makes sense. They are, after all, deteriorating human carcasses sheathed in a single layer of large, pink cockroaches, all nestled in close together to form a skin-like cover. But they're designed to blend in, and even if they don't fully do that, it's generally enough not to get the cops called or too many eyebrows raised.

And behold: by the time the two Blattodeons reach my table, everyone's turned back to the bar, their cell phones, their tired, shiftless lives.

"*Brazen!*" the mullet sing-yells. "*Your love was brazen when it rained down on me . . . a-down down down on me-ee-e.*"

"Sit," I say, and they do, in that awkward, Blattodeon way. The file lies open in front of them. "The highlighted lines, you see?"

Nods.

"She will be there. It's far away, so you must leave immediately. Take six more of your own. Scope the place out well before you attack. Don't underestimate the target. She is ruthless and almost unkillable. You must not fail me. There will probably be others with her. Spare none."

More nods. A roach detaches itself from one of their faces, adjusts itself, snuggles back in with the others.

"If the babies are there, bring them to me."

Both widen their dead eyes. The Delacruz twins had been slated to host the Blattodeon Master Hive until Reza and Carlos got in the damn way. What was once a divine trinity with empires of roaches to command was shattered in one night. Now it's down to a single spiritual legacy that lives on in me alone. And I barely know what to do with it, to be honest, except what I've always done, what I did when Jeremy was the High Priest: clean up the messes everyone else has left behind.

"Now go," I tell them. "And report back immediately when it's done. There's a war coming, and you'll be needed here."

They stand, and the bar quiets again as they make their way out into the cold night.

"Paisley, baby, baby paisley hey! Your love was brazen baby paisley hey!"

I'm done here. I collect my papers and am heading for the door, waving vaguely at Ennis and Bellamy and whoever else may care, when I come to a full stop a few feet from the door.

The ghost with no face stands there, leaning on his cane. He looks like shit—more hunched over than usual, and his cloak is tattered. He looks down at me, that shimmering emptiness its own kind of glare.

"Come with me," Juan Flores says in a choked whisper. "I have need of your skills tonight."

"You sure you want to do this?" I say. Flores and I are standing on Franklin Avenue where it meets Eastern Parkway. The winter night has frozen all this gray slush into a solid shiny coating. Down Franklin, new Thai restaurants outshine dusty ghetto Chinese joints, and fancy gluten-free fruit stands edge out the last few bodegas. "She won't go down easy."

Flores shrugs. "She'll go down, though."

"Maybe. And she'll take us with her if we're not careful. It's a suicide mission, Flores."

He turns toward the parkway, where soulcatchers are emerging from the darkness. "That's why I brought backup." There must be four, no, five full squads of them. All decked out in full battle regalia, the 'catchers stride directly through passing traffic toward us.

"We march!" Flores hollers. We launch forward, and the collective momentum of all those single-minded warriors clears Franklin for blocks ahead of us. Some trash tumbles down the street in the icy winds, but otherwise the place is empty. We pass laundromats and bistros, the last dive bar standing, and a Panamanian spot, and three coffee shops.

I like this whole thing less and less the closer we get. Flores seems to be running on some half-crazed impulse, and I'm positive the 'catchers don't know what they're in for. But I told Botus yes, I would join his strange cabal as the first living subminister of war. I would help him squash the resistance if need be, or forge a fragile peace.

Even with Delacruz. At least for now. Because the truth is, right now: I'm no one. An orphan, brotherless. Powerful yes, but to what end? My dwindling dozen of Blattodeons hardly constitutes an army. I live on a wretched, forgotten island in the New York Harbor. The offer caught me off guard but also couldn't have come at a better time.

We'll sort out the details in the next few days, Botus assured me as we strolled through the park two nights back. Ha.

Flores stops us before an abandoned brownstone on a residential block. The 'catchers fan out behind us, and I can feel their uneasiness finally settle in.

"House ghost!" Flores yells. "In accordance with New York Council of the Dead Measure 8-12 Section 5, we are here to notify you that you are in violation of Council protocol. We request that you remo—"

A wide, gigantic face appears at the front of the brownstone. It looms over us like an unimpressed moon. Mama Esther doesn't speak; she just glares.

"Remove yourself from the premises immediately and without delay."

An uncomfortable silence follows. Some cars pass; the wind whips through us; soulcatchers adjust their positions. A block away, the shuttle train rumbles by, screeches to a halt, collects some passengers, and then rumbles on its way.

"House ghost," Flores says again. "You have been advi—"

Mama Esther sighs a monsoon—trees shiver, and plastic bags take flight. She shakes her head. "No more talk."

"On behalf of the Council!" Flores roars.

"No more talk!" The world shudders. All five soul-

catcher squads flinch back a step. Only Flores and I stand firm. "Come get me," Mama Esther says, disconcertingly quiet all of a sudden.

"Very well," Flores mutters. He flicks his hand, and the two squads on either end of the line flush forward, blitz across the street, and bum-rush the front door. They make it to the third step. Mama Esther closes her eyes, and a glistening wall of spirit matter booms forth, decimating them entirely and pushing the rest of us back against the opposite row of buildings.

"Squad 7," Flores growls, recovering himself. There's a pause. Mama Esther stares down at us as the 'catchers stumble around. "Squad 7, I said!"

They're up and then in formation in seconds, and then they move in, and I gotta hand it to them, they're not as shaken as I probably would've been in their shoes.

This time, the front door flies open.

"Where are my manners?" Mama Esther chuckles. "Please, come in."

They flood inside. The door slams shut, and soon the howls of soulcatchers fill the night.

The two squads left are on the brink of scattering. Flores turns to me. "Fix this," he says. No desperation there. I'm sure he knew how this would play, and now he wants to see what I'm made of.

So be it.

I send my mind across the trembling front line of 'catchers—Squad 3. They tense as I reach up inside them, then straighten and draw their blades. They are mine.

I'll tell you something most people don't know about ghosts: they're made up of a fiber that includes particles of many elements. Tiny flashes of water, air, and even earth course through spirit matter, so miniscule as to be virtually inconsequential. Unless you stimulate them. My mental tendrils surge through the phantom DNA of all twelve 'catchers, sort through the water, past the air, beyond the microscopic rocks, and finally coil around that singular flash of light buried deep within their cellular framework: fire.

I clench down. Ignore the swirling sky and gathering hurricane of Mama Esther's ferocity. The force builds inside me, and I send it out through the line of 'catchers, tempering it so it doesn't spill over. My shoulders hunch forward, and Squad 3 takes the first step toward Mama Esther's. Then the next. Even through my closed eyes, I can see the twelve red glares flicker to life as the soldiers break into a run. When I open my eyes, it's still just a warm glow; they're halfway across the street.

Mama Esther's eyes go wide, then narrow to slits. She's reaching toward me, a huge hand crashing out of the sky, when the first soulcatcher bursts into flames. He's fast, and the fire only accelerates him into the brownstone's tattered doorway.

Mama Esther's hand flies back up with surprise. I force the others forward with the last of my energy. Two, then three, then another two flaming soulcatchers crash into the front wall. The flames are real, not spirit flames, and by the time the last four reach the doorway, the whole building has caught.

"I'm impressed," Flores says. And then a horrible, echoing laughter erupts over the flames. Mama Esther's mouth hangs wide open, her giant hands reaching out into the night. "Finish this," Flores says, and the last squad of soulcatchers rushes past us.

The laughter gets louder, and I know something's wrong, and then she looks down at us, suddenly somber. I'm turning to run when the whole world becomes a bright light. Bricks, metal, and stone flash through the air—something glances off my arm; something else nicks my face before I collapse as another blast tears through the night, and then everything is dark and I hear a single voice, laughing and crying at the same time.

And then there is nothing.

CYCLE THREE

❧❦❧

FIREBALL

Ayy, espiritistas inciertos,
Que muchos hay por allá,
Porfiaban con terquedad
Que los del Trío habían muerto.

Ayy, those uncertain conjurers,
Of which there are plenty over there,
Insisted stubbornly
That all of us had died.

"El Trío y el Ciclón"
Trío Matamoros

CHAPTER NINE

〜⊛〜

Carlos

Cyrus Langley shakes his head slowly. "We wait." It seems like everything he's done has been in slow motion since they killed Mama Esther. No one's seen him cry or raise his voice even, but he moves like he's sifting through a swamp.

The room erupts into growls of dissent. We're in a vacant project basement up in Harlem. Since the attack on Mama Esther, we've been switching locations each time we meet, releasing the info at the last minute. Cyrus raises a hand, and gradually the murmurs die out. A week ago, the same motion would've brought instant, rapt silence.

"I know you're upset," Cyrus drawls. "We're all upset, trust. And no one"—he looks up, meeting our eyes for the first time in days—"*no one*, wants revenge more than I do. However . . . this is not the time." He nods, his eyes faraway again. "We wait."

It's been two weeks.

Two weeks and the constant jackhammer of grief against my chest hasn't dulled so much as become the new normal. Some days, rage replaces the sorrow, and I storm through the streets, blade ready, hoping to bump into some passing soulcatcher and exact a cheap mockery of vengeance.

But Cyrus has been very clear: *We wait*. What's less clear is how long the assembled anti-Council forces will continue to care what our broken leader says.

"Now is exactly the time," Saeen says. "The Rebel Districts have reached an unprecedented unity. Calls for the destruction of the Council ring out across New York. We may never be this strong again, Mr. Langley." Her voice slides from ferocious to pleading. "Mama Esther was beloved by everyone. The Council made a grave error in this, and they will pay."

"Did they?" Cyrus says. "Or did they do something very strategic, knowing this is exactly what would happen next? The worst thing we can do right now is be predictable, and launching at the Council full force is *precisely* what they expect us to do. Mark me, they will be ready for us. We are stronger than we've been, yes, but that doesn't mean we're strong enough."

Riley sits stony faced beside Cyrus. His eyes narrow like he's clenching back a scream of pain; his translucent hands grip the bar. Riley knew Mama Esther longer than I did—he's the one who brought me to her place when he found me, and she took care of him after our attack on the ngks went sour. I'm sure that's not the only time she's saved his ass. All our asses. I shake my head. None of this feels right. Nothing feels right.

A bearded ghost in a bike helmet stands. "We've been hitting Council soulcatchers with small, coordinated ambush attacks for the past week," he says to murmurs of surprise and a few cheers. "They started traveling in squads, not pairs like before, because they're expecting an attack. Still, we found that they're not hard to catch off guard, and soulcatchers can be tracked when off duty and dispatched quickly. Now they've cleared the streets almost entirely. Can barely find 'em."

Cyrus squints across the hazy backroom. "You are with the Ghost Riders, no?"

"Aye," the man says.

A woman stands up beside him, one of the ones from last time. They both straddle white bicycles. "We had a change of leadership," the woman explains. "Sharon was . . . handled."

"When we last saw you," Cyrus says, his voice barely above a whisper, "you could barely get consensus on whether to join our movement. Now you've taken it upon yourself to take out Council troops." The room gets very quiet. "Understand that they may be easy targets now, but the next time you hit them, or maybe the next after that, they will be ready for you. And if they have cleared the streets, it's only in preparation for a final attack."

"We'll be ready for them!" the bearded man says.

Cyrus just shakes his head. "The battlefield has changed. A war of attrition will wear us out and destroy us slowly, even with public opinion against the Council. An all-out assault on Sunset will see us broken in a matter of minutes. I want to destroy the Council, not lash out with no plan. When one of you brings us a strategy for winning, not dying, we will move forward."

He stands, his slender arms supporting him on the bar, and glares out at the rebels. "That's all."

The crowd disperses with a resentful mutter, and soon

it's just me, Riley, little Damian, Vincent, and Dag Thrumm-
mond, Cyrus's huge axe-wielding bodyguard from the
Burial Grounds. And Cyrus, who remains frozen with his
hands splayed open on the bartop, eyes fixed on the empty
room.

"Mr. Langley?" Dag says.

Cyrus shakes his head. "I don't know."

"Don't know what?" Riley asks.

"Don't know what the move is. I don't even . . ." He
looks at Riley, then me. "I don't know how to move."

"We're all a mess," I offer. "You're allowed to be a
mess too."

Cyrus offers a gentle smile. It fades fast. "We can't
afford inclarity right now."

Riley nods, his eyes closed. "It's true. But I'll be honest: everything in me wants to strike. I know there's no
endgame for that, but . . . when is there ever? If we keep
waiting for some kind of foolproof plan, the moment will
pass and . . . then what?"

"The moment," Cyrus repeats, back in his faraway
place.

"It's not a foolproof plan we're waiting for," Damian
explains. "We don't have any plan. Hit them and then hit
them again till they hit back and break us is not a strategy."

"Where's Krys?" Cyrus says. We all look around. I
figured she'd been hiding during the general meeting like
she usually does, but she would've shown up by now.
"Has anyone seen her?"

"She's been taking Mama Esther being gone pretty
hard," Riley says. "We spoke the day before yesterday
and . . . I know she's hurt. I mean, of course we all are,
but . . . you know, she's young, in a way."

"We need to keep an eye on her," Cyrus says. "Keep her safe. Krys must be protected at all costs."

Riley and Dag nod.

"What now?" I ask.

Cyrus just puts his head down, doesn't say a word. We leave slowly, sorrow pounding us.

It's a bright early afternoon, and 125th Street is bustling with families, hustlers, cops, and vendors. Here you can get a bucket of shea butter, a DVD of Malcolm X speeches, an unknown rapper's mixtape. There a bearded man sells body oils and incense in front of a fancy clothing store. Some old soul song blasts from an old man's boom box as he struts through the crowd wearing only a puffy jacket and underpants.

"Let's cut off the main drag," Riley says. "Too much going on."

I nod. I hadn't even realized he was beside me, honestly, but I'd been meaning to swing through the park anyway. We hang a right, and immediately the whole world is calmer. Up ahead, patches of snow cluster like filthy, frozen waves on the fields of Marcus Garvey Park. The last time I was here was before they killed Mama Esther. The last time I was most places was before they killed Mama Esther. A simple thought, but the hollowness seems to deepen inside me in response to it. I suppose this'll keep happening until I've been everywhere, and then it'll keep happening anyway.

Riley glances at me as we step through the gate into the park. "I know, man. I know."

I shake my head, holding back an unexpected rush of

tears. "I just want to . . . kill things." My teeth are clenched, my fists too.

"All I can think about doing is war."

"You think the old man's making a mistake?"

Riley scowls. "I'm not sure if it'll matter one way or another pretty soon. The Rebel Districts lookin' like they bouta be fed up with waiting. Hell, those spandexed fucks already started their own little insurrection. Won't be long before there's another hit from one side or the other."

"And then all-out war."

"Which the Council will win."

I nod.

"It's the general's dilemma," Riley says. "We want blood; he wants to win. At the moment, those two wants are incompatible."

"I want blood *and* to win."

"Word. What I'm worried about is, what's the end-game? All the COD really has to do is stay holed up at HQ and wait for either the wrath to die down or the RDs to fuck up and rush in unprepared."

The sky is white and gray. We've strolled across the main field and up a small hill to the edge of the forest. It's darker in there than it should be at this hour of the day—a gloom hangs over the woods that can only be supernatural.

"Park spirits are mourning too," Riley says.

Garvey Park is home to a cluster of particularly old, mellow spirits that mostly hang back amidst the trees and bear witness to the odd comings and goings of the living. One of them is an ancient great-uncle of mine; I don't understand the way-back-when language he speaks, but

I call him Blardly, mostly because pretty much everything he says sounds like *blardly-blardly-blardly-blardly*.

"You going in?" Riley asks.

I nod. I hadn't really known I was coming here for this, but now I'm sure I need it. I've passed through a few times since I learned about my ancestor, usually when I'm all fucked up trying not to think about Sasha and the kids. I always leave a little more intact than I am when I came, cleansed somehow. There's something to that ancestral magic, something reviving. Usually, Blardly shows up and I talk and talk some more and then, occasionally, burst into tears, as the towering, bearded spirit nods sagely and mutters: *Blardly blardly blardly blardly*.

Riley looks around with a frown. "The joint is morbid," he says, then walks in beside me.

It's a warm winter day, but the world cools around us as soon as we enter the shadows. I exhale, and my breath becomes a ghostly little cloud and then disappears. Something glints in between the trees, and then, very suddenly, we're not alone. It's not just Blardly this time; he brought all his friends too. They're all tall and decrepit, folds of wispy, shimmering flesh drooping along their towering frames.

"Whoa," Riley whispers.

The form a cluttered half circle around us, and Blardly steps out into the middle. I lift my hand to him and he reaches out, places his cool, translucent palm against mine. His mouth, usually a little O shape beneath his beard, forms a sad smile.

"*Blardly blardly blardly,*" Blardly says, shaking his old head. Specks of light dance and spin around him like tiny moons.

"They're sorry for our loss," Riley says. He aced the ancient-ghost-languages class in 'Catcher Academy—something about a teacher he was hot for. "At least I think he meant 'they' and 'our.' They don't differentiate plural and singular in their language. That is, everything is plural."

"*Blardy blardly blardly.*" I catch a glint of anger in my forefather's tone, and the other spirits rustle and mutter behind him.

"He says they'll fight with us."

This I hadn't expected. I'd just come for solace, not on a recruiting mission. A little pulse of joy opens up inside me, the first in a long time.

"*Blardly blardly blardly.*"

"Mama Esther was a good friend to them, he says."

"*Blardly!*"

"Says they'll bring down the Council."

"*Blardly.*"

"One way or another."

I sniffle back a sob. "Tell him thank you."

Riley mumbles a *blardly*, and the old spirit nods, touches my face, then squeezes his mouth tight. "*Blardly,*" he says.

"Something else," Riley translates.

Blardly launches into a lengthy speech, complete with head shakes and thoughtful hand gestures. Riley nods, eyebrows creased with concentration. Asks a question, nods again when Blardly explains.

"Apparently," Riley says, "Mama Esther was working on something before the Council killed her."

"What?"

The ancient ghost raises his palm to me one more time. I touch it, and his bleary, old, glowing eyes meet mine. "They . . . ," Blardly groans, squinting with concentration, "woant . . . ad . . . wat . . . yew"—he nods his old wooly head at Riley and then me—"woant."

"They wanted what we want? Mama Esther, you mean?"

Blardly nods with a slight smile, retreats slowly back into the shadows of the forest. The others nod and gradually vanish. I look at Riley, my eyebrows raised, and then we trudge through the underbrush toward the park.

"If she was working on something before she died—" Riley says.

"And she wanted what we want—" I continue.

"Then whatever she was working on has to do with bringing down the Council."

"Even though she's always swearing she'll remain neutral."

I scoff. "Mama Esther knows . . ." Shit. "Knew . . . the neutrality's a myth people use to make themselves comfortable."

"Of course, but she aimed for it. Or she made it look like she did. Remember all those times she told us to fuck off because she didn't want to get involved in no infighting?"

That stops us both in our tracks as the shitty truth settles once again in our bones. Mama Esther's ferocity was matched only by her lovingness. Shit. "But even when she didn't get involved," I say after a moment of silence, "she always had the right . . . Oh shit."

"What?" Riley says.

"Books."

"Speak, man."

We're back out in the park field now, and it's dark, that eerie moment when the sun has set but the streetlights haven't gotten the memo yet. I'm fast-walking toward the street, which'll take me to the train, which'll take me to my place, where there are . . . "Books!" I say again.

Riley's huffing and puffing to keep up with me. "Sentences, dammit!"

"Mama Esther gave me some books before she was killed. Gave some to Sasha too, I think."

"I mean, me too, but I didn't think—"

"Exactly! It was weird, but she shrugged it off with something cryptic about spreading the library around. Lemme find out she was being strategic all along."

"Wouldn't surprise me, knowing her. Where they at now?"

"Mine? My place!"

Riley almost clotheslines me with an icy, damn-near-solid arm. "Hold up."

"What?"

"You just gonna cowboy back in there? You know the Council gonna have that place on watch."

I've been staying at a cheap motel on Atlantic Ave since they killed Mama Esther, on Cyrus Langley's orders. Riley's right, but I'm undeterred. "We'll have to. Sasha will help and . . ." I stop talking because a shiny figure stands at the entranceway to Marcus Garvey Park. Riley follows my gaze, squints.

"Is that . . ."

"Krys!" I yell, breaking into a run. "You are literally *just* the ghost I wanted to see!"

Sasha

Anger flickers across the young ghost beside me like lightning teasing the edge of a dark cloud. Our backs press against a graffiti-splattered brick wall around the corner from Carlos's place. Krys's every move bristles with her loss. I want to offer my condolences, but it's not the time for that. Any moment now, Carlos will text that they're in position and we'll move out. I steal a glance down the block; it's empty. Which is unexpected—maybe bad.

"Carlos says you went off the radar," I say.

Krys nods, eyes scanning the deserted street around us. "I just couldn't listen to old Cyrus tell us to wait one more time. This rage is . . . it's too deep . . . I don't know what to do with it."

"I probably would've done the same thing."

"Hell, you basically did," Krys says, and I know she's talking about when I walked out on Carlos, and I know it's a jab to test my defensiveness, and I know Krys is a teenager and that's what teenagers do, even dead ones, and still I flinch. She catches that flinch and flashes a wry smile and, against my will, I like her. I roll my eyes, let a hint of smile flash so she knows there's no hard feelings, and check my phone.

Nothing from Carlos. An odd uneasiness settles into my gut. All the shit I've seen and done, in the past few months especially—it's strange that a little grab-'n'-go should throw me.

"There are Council goons around," Krys says. "I can feel 'em."

"This is kind of a coming-out party for you, isn't it?"

She shrugs. "Only if one of the soulcatchers lives. Anyway, they been giving me the royal side-eye from jump, so, only kinda."

"But there's a big difference between being under watch and being a full-on rebel. Ask Riley."

"Oh, I have. I'm ready."

"You tell Cyrus?"

Krys scans the rooftops, pouts.

"Oh boy," I mutter.

My phone buzzes: *Unexpected holdup. 'Catchers headin your way from the south. Sorry, tried to get em all.*

Shit. "Heads up," I say, drawing a blade. Krys unholsters two pistols, and I'm reminded momentarily of Reza, who always travels well armed. But where Reza is ice cold, Krys is all fury and hellfire. Either way, folks get dead, but I wonder who would win in a matchup. Hope to never find out.

When no 'catchers round the corner, my unease gets shriller. Worn-down warehouses line the block. An SUV and two taxicabs are parked on one side; on the other, a huge black puddle reflects muddled, technicolor murals from the wall toward the sky. A few blocks away, a car passes.

I text: *Don't see em. Where u?*

I dislike all of this. Carlos should've taken those damn books with him when he left for the hotel.

Something flickers; then two burly soulcatchers sprint across the street at the far end of the block. They don't stop or turn, just beeline out of sight without noticing us.

"Damn," Krys says, taking a cautious step toward where they passed. Carlos and Riley sprint after them, blades drawn. Carlos glimpses Krys and me, waves us away, looks behind him, runs harder. Then they're both gone.

"Krys," I hiss. "Come on! We get the books and—"

She raises both her guns, keeps walking away from me. She opens fire before I even see the 'catchers round the corner.

From what I hear, even the great Council minds can't

really explain ghost ballistics. When the dead want something in their realm, they just keep it with 'em for a while and eventually it goes ghost, so to speak. Death always wins, as Carlos likes to say. But the mechanical transfer remains something of a mystery. Case in point: it's taken them this long to figure out how to get things that shoot when they're in physical form to also shoot when they're in spooky woo-woo form. And even when they did that, it turned out not many ghosts could get the hang of shooting things, the notable exception being Krys.

Guns never made much sense to me until Reza took me to a range out in Long Island and made me shoot till my whole body thrummed, and I got addicted to getting better and better with each squeeze of the trigger. Now I carry an old German Mauser Reza gifted me once she'd deemed me a halfway-decent shot. She said the swords were cute and all but if I was gonna run missions with her, I'd have to roll fully loaded. And she was right.

Krys lets off a steady volley of shots, and I watch as three 'catchers stumble and collapse at the corner. Four more draw their blades and charge; one gets clipped just as she's breaking into a run, crashes heavily into the pavement and fades. By the time Krys is backstepping to give herself time to change clips, I'm flushing forward, both blades out.

One of their blades nicks me as I hurl into the throng. It's a smooth, superficial slice across my shoulder that I barely register except for the eerie blue glow that pulses in the corner of my eye. I block a wild swing from my left and then behead the one that tagged me. Two more shots rings out, and I flinch and then gape as the last two 'catchers fall on either side of me.

Krys isn't smiling. She nods at me, and then we turn

and head back up the block and around the corner just as Carlos and Riley come barreling around the opposite corner. We meet in front of his building. He's panting and smiling; Riley looks annoyed.

"These motherfuckers ain't even putting up a real fight," Riley says. "Gimme a smoke, C."

"You guys alright?" Carlos says as he lights a Malagueña and passes it to Riley.

"Little cut," I say. "I'm cool."

Carlos gives it a concerned frown but doesn't get all gooey, which I appreciate, and then Krys says, "We going in?"

"I need you on the door," Carlos says. "Any ghosts get near, fry their ass." He looks at me and Riley. "You two with me." Being in command comes naturally to him, I notice. He doesn't lord it over anyone or get extra polite; it's his house and his operation, so he calls the shots. We hustle into the front hallway, and I begin thinking of ways to take his mind off all this mess when shit calms down. It's a train of thought that's been showing up on its own these past couple days. I fought it at first—just didn't seem like a good time for all that, but all that doesn't give a damn about timing, I've learned. And anyway: there I am, on my knees in front of Carlos, his hands gripping my hair—he's about to explode.

"We got 'catchers," Carlos whispers, peering around the corridor corner. I snap out of it. We've gone up a flight of stairs while I was lost in my thoughts, and this is *exactly* what I mean about timing. I growl at my slippery mind and dropped guard, draw my sword. "You alright?" Carlos asks.

I nod.

He checks again, holds up three fingers.

"What you wanna do?" Riley asks.

"They just standing there," Carlos says. "Lemme find out how much trust I still have with the Council."

I don't like it and I say so—why put yourself in danger to find out something that doesn't matter much anyway? But Carlos insists. "If it gets hairy, come through and dehairy it." And then he strolls around the corner, whistling like an asshole.

"Ah," I hear one of the 'catchers say, "Agent Delacruz, you're here!" He sounds genuinely surprised.

"It's my home," Carlos says. "Question is really why are you here."

"Orders," the 'catcher says. "What with the unrest, we wanted to make sure your property is secured."

"Thoughtful of you."

"You haven't been home for a bit." Smugness barely concealed.

"Indeed." Carlos's voice gets cold. "What with the unrest."

I hate this.

The lock clicks, and the door squeaks open, then slams closed. Riley and I trade an uneasy glance. A minute passes. Then another.

"I'm going in," Riley says.

I shake my head. "Wait. There'd be a scuffle, something . . . He wouldn't let them take him down without at least a yell."

Riley growls but stays put.

"Think they're somehow onto what we're doing here? If they were gonna let him roll on in there unharassed, why would that squad attack you guys outside?"

"Nah, we started that one," Riley says. "Soon as we saw 'em round the corner Carlos dropped two and I took out a third. Then two more made a break for it, and you saw the rest."

My hit on the communication center must still be fucking with their telepathy. Or the whole thing's a setup.

"None of this is cool," Riley says. "In fact, nothing been cool since we lost Esther."

"I know." I put a hand on his glowing shoulder. "I'm sorry."

He meets my eyes, knows I don't do that kind of thing a lot, acknowledges it with a nod. Then: "Two minutes, then I'm going in there swords out."

I steal a glance around the corner. The fluorescents blink an erratic rhythm of shadow and light along the corridor. One 'catcher still stands outside Carlos's door. He's tall and carries a hatchet; his heavy cloak hovers a few inches above the tiled floor.

I show Riley one finger.

A minute has passed.

"Fuck this," Riley announces. He stands, draws his blade, and strides around the corner in a single, perfectly fluid motion. The 'catcher sees him, raises the hatchet, and then turns suddenly as the door bursts open and Carlos flies out, blade drawn. Carlos doesn't stop, he yells "Run!" and cleaves a good chunk out of the 'catcher's midsection as he blows past him.

"The fuck?" Riley gasps. Then the screech takes over everything. It shreds through all our minds, turns the world into a vicious splattering of pain for a few seconds. The throng haint's long, mouth-covered appendage emerges from the doorway a few seconds behind Carlos. The rest of it soon follows, a hulking, bulbous mass, barely contained within the narrow corridor. This one is about three times larger than the one Janey and I dismantled on Spine Island. For a second, the hugeness of it shocks me to stillness. It crashes into the far wall and then adjusts itself, reaching four, then six long-fingered arms toward us as it breaks into an off-kilter run.

Carlos barrels past, grabbing my arm, and Riley catches up as we take the stairs three at a time, pivot off the landing, and almost hurl down the rest of the way.

Through the window on the front door, I see Krys with her pistol raised at something off to her left. She's talking; her glare promises the Deeper Death.

The throng haint comes crashing down the stairwell, tendrils flailing out to either side, mouths screeching. We run down the front hall and then we're out the door. A soulcatcher stands a few feet away, blade out. He's decorated with imperial medals and armbands, a superior officer of some kind—I never bothered to learn their fucked-up little titles.

"No luck," Krys says. She lets off two shots: one smashes through his breastplate with a clang; the other shatters his face guard and then, presumably, his face. He crumples as we run past.

"Throng haint!" Carlos yells. "Supersized."

Krys catches up running backward, both guns trained on the door. "What's the plan?"

"The plan is to fucking run! I got the books!"

"Dammit," Krys mutters. "I wasn't done killing."

We scatter into the industrial north Brooklyn back alleys, but the throng haint doesn't make another showing. One day, someone will have to do a behavioral study on those

things and why they don't have much chase in 'em, but
for now I'm just happy to be far the hell away from it.
After fifteen minutes of random turns, I find Carlos and
Riley at the small dog-walking park we'd agreed on. They
stand side by side, facing the river, Malagueñas in hand.

"Mission accomplished?" Riley says.

Carlos nods. "Definitively."

"Where's Krys?" I ask.

No one knows.

"If it was anyone else," Carlos says. "I'd be worried. I
mean . . . I'm always a little worried these days, but . . .
Krys has been on that rogue shit for a week now."

"I'm gonna see 'bout the books Mama Esther left me,"
Riley tells us. "Think it was poetry or some shit, didn't
pay it much mind, to be honest. You two stay safe." He
daps Carlos, blows me a kiss, and fades into the dying
light of the afternoon.

Bundled-up dog walkers bustle along behind their
charges, stooping to scoop up droppings in plastic bag-
gies, chatting idly, checking their phones. The night
advances with that winter suddenness: the light purples
fade to dark blues as our breath becomes gray; the city
lights twinkle at us across the river, and a chill enters our
already-cool bones, as if from within.

Carlos is staring at the tome Mama Esther left him,
but I feel his attention cover me in gentle, cautious waves.
And sorrow radiates out of him, punctuates his every
thought and movement.

Finding out the family I have no memories of was
wiped out: that brought its own strange, creeping sadness.
After the first deluge of shock, it's a sadness that made a
home inside me. Sometimes I don't know if it's the mas-

sacre itself or the fact that I don't remember them that hurts more. Trevor's been dead two years and each memory of him is still smudged with his death. I made peace with the ache, but that doesn't stop it from aching.

I look at Carlos very suddenly and realize I've forgiven him. It wasn't a conscious choice. I've tried many times, given up trying many times. I don't know why or what happened, but it feels like a tiny ray of light on a dark, dark day. I wonder if he's forgiven me in this same sudden, inexplicable way, or if he's still just trying to convince himself to.

Even in this hurricane of grief and oncoming war, I'm still the sun he revolves around.

"Hey." I step closer to him, wrap my arm through his. "C'mon. We can have reading time somewhere where it's warm."

He exhales a tense laugh. "Where? I hate my hotel, and my apartment's got a throng haint infestation."

"My hotel."

He cocks his head at me, one eyebrow raised. "You didn't—"

"There's a lot of things I didn't tell you."

"Is it—"

"It's nicer than yours. Not to brag, but . . . it is."

"How do you—"

"Just come with me."

I first started doing runs with Reza a few weeks after everything went down at the lighthouse. Once the dead were buried and I stopped checking on the twins every five minutes, once my slow, slow heart rate returned to its even-slower normal, once the nightmares cooled off, I called Reza and we met for coffee at that diner she likes. She tried to talk me out of it at first, and everything she said was right: joining forces was messy, irresponsible, and ridiculous. I had no business putting my life in danger with two brand-new lives in my hands.

And still.

I wasn't sleeping. Was barely eating. It wasn't fallout from warring with the Blattodeons—it had been going on before all that. I was hungry. That's the only way I could describe it to her, and when I said that, she nodded with a slight smile, her eyes sad.

I didn't have a name for what I craved—it wasn't blood or adrenaline, just . . . movement. Challenge, maybe. After everything that had happened, the only thing that felt really wrong was being still. Anyway, soldiers don't leave the army just because they become parents. Plenty of cops have kids. (Reza rolled her eyes: "My least favorite cop is a mom.") I asked Janey's future father-in-law, Gordo, if he needed some extra cash and was good with kids (an enthusiastic "jes" to both), figuring I'd pay his babysitting fees with whatever little cash I made on the runs.

And then it turned out that the cash was not so little. Reza's organization was at a kind of philosophical turning point when I started coming around, transforming from a gunrunning prostitution ring to a kind of cleanup service for the Underworld—cleaning up shitheads, not messes—so there were plenty of raids, gunfights, assaults, and with them, the cash flowed. In three weeks, I'd made more money than I knew what to do with. Like . . . college tuition for both of the twins kinda money. And I'd gotten used to living off whatever meager cash the combined efforts of the Survivors pulled in—all I knew of money was how to horde it and stretch it and make do without it. And for the most part, I kept up the caution, so when this ghost war came menacing, I had more than enough stashed away to check into a nice—okay, a *really* nice—suite. In a really nice Manhattan hotel.

"What . . . the . . . fuck," Carlos whispers as I lead him into the elegant living room. Night has descended fully on the city outside the floor-to-ceiling windows. Jersey glistens across the river, casts a dazzling light show in the dark waters of the Hudson.

"Long story," I say, peeling off my own coat and then his. "Listen." I place myself in front him, facing the dark sky, the shining city. He wraps his arms around my waist.

"Yes," he says.

"Don't you even want to hear what I was going to say?"

"Yes." I feel his smile against my neck. "After."

The orgasm felt like it had been building in me for months, my whole body a stretched slingshot. It teased the edges of my awareness as Carlos held me open beneath him and jackhammered away. It let itself be known gradually, a cloud on the horizon, faded slightly as he maneuvered into a different position, returned full force as he fell into a new rhythm, faster and fiercer this time. Then it was right there, hovering over both of us, waiting, and then white light covered the world and my neck craned. A howl escaped me that I didn't know I had inside. Somewhere far away, Carlos's whole body spasmed too, and his thrusts got frantic and so did mine, and then stillness took over as he grunted and collapsed, and now stillness is everything, and lying here, with my head draped upside down over the edge of the bed and the city an upside-down masterpiece of darkness and light and the sky its own kind of city, a few straggling stars amidst a few splotchy clouds—now, I know peace.

No thoughts no fears no words: just peace.

His cool body lies entwined with my cool body and between us there's only warmth, somehow, just like we somehow made full life from half-life, and I smile because we defy all the rules of nature, Carlos and I, and every other rule too, and here we are, well fucked and smiling anyway.

I must've drifted off, because a noise startles me awake, and my hand flies to the dagger on the bedside table. A hundred escape routes, entrance points, projectile trajectories splay themselves out across the walls, windows, and doorways, and then Carlos walks out of the bathroom, sees my stricken face, and says, "What?"

Wartime tattoos paranoid maps across the insides of our eyelids, and in a second they're splattered outward over the world. I shake my head, willing my heart rate to slow, my breath to ease. How quickly it can all come crashing down. How fragile this peace. I've been running as long as I've had memory. Running and fighting. The entirety of this new life is struggle, punctuated by a few blessed moments of joy. Carlos climbs into the bed. They could have followed us. They could be watching even now. They could bust through the door, and all our skills, all our combined will, all we've been through wouldn't matter a damn against greater numbers.

He reaches out; his fingers hover just above my naked shoulder, waiting for permission. Smart. He can see how tightly wound I am; the wrong touch might cost him that hand. Instead of just nodding, I nuzzle into him, allow his length and muscle to encase me. I don't have to explain— he already knows. That in itself makes all this worth the wait.

My heart slows to keep time with his. And then I mount him, take him fully inside me, and lean forward, letting my braids cascade around his face.

"The thing?" Carlos asks when we stop panting and the stillness settles and the world returns to some kind of normal.

"You mean what I was going to tell you before you decided to manhandle me?"

"And then you decided to womanhandle me—that thing, yeah."

I look up and he's stroking himself, staring down at my supine and spread body with a holy hunger in his eyes. "Easy, big fella. We got shit to do."

He scrunches up his face, grunts. "I know, I know."

"Put your pants on. Ain't nobody gonna be concentrating on shit with that big ol' thing just hanging out and about." He raises an eyebrow, nods glumly, goes in search of pants. "Get started," I say, somersaulting out the bed. "I'll catch up."

Fifteen minutes later, I emerge from the shower, pulling my long braids into a ponytail, and find Carlos hunched over the book Mama Esther left him, muttering to himself. He's just in pajama pants and a tank top that leaves little to the imagination, and I imagine straddling him from behind, letting this towel slip away as he turns to face me . . . Back in the bathroom, I take a few deep breaths in the mirror, then wrap my hair. He's left a gray T-shirt in here, and that'll do nicely. I pull it on, then hunt down a pair of baggy sweatpants and plop into the easy chair beside the desk he's working at.

He looks up, blows me a kiss, and everything just feels so simple. The brutal world creeps back in—I know that book he has open will lead him into heinous shit, and beyond that, the Council looms, always. Still, in a small way, we're suddenly what it always has felt like we should've been.

"That thing," I say.

He makes a show of sliding the book away, his focus on me full. "Yes."

"Forgiveness." I let my stare stay on him for a solid few seconds, unwavering, so he knows. Then I nod.

He does too. "I had been holding on too. To blaming you, I mean. And . . . yeah. It's gone. I don't know how or why, but it is."

"It might come back," I suggest.

"I know. For either of us."

"Yes."

"And then we'll deal with it."

"Yes."

"Good."

A moment passes. And then I pull the recliner closer to the desk. "Whatchya workin' on?"

"One of the books Mama Esther gave me. Thing is . . . I've read it before. Well, some of it. It's . . ." A moment of hesitation; he lets it pass. "It's one of the ones Trevor was researching. She dug it up for me when I was trying to figure out what he was up to."

"That's especially weird," I say, reaching around him to pull open a desk drawer, "because she did the same thing for me." I pull out the hefty tome I'd found waiting inside my apartment the day we got back from Jersey.

"Oh shit," Carlos says, leafing through the pages. "I remember this one too! And she left in all the Post-it note page markers he had placed." He opens to an elaborate rendering of a man on horseback surrounded by corpses beneath a giant skull. "This was the framework for Sarco's plan to obliterate the boundary between the living world and the dead one. A grounded ghost." He points to the skull. "Mama Esther on the first try." Just a slight flinch as he says her name. "Pasternak at Grand Army on the second. The ngks are hidden in the border motif, see." He points to where a tiny, scrunched-up face peers out from behind twirling, golden leaves. Nearby, another lurks. "And this guy, the halfie."

"There we are."

"Mmhm. All part of the diabolical equation. You remember what it felt like when you were up there and the gate was opening?"

"Barely," I say. Sarco had possessed me and taken a kind of spiritual hacksaw to the inner workings of my soul, so it's all a little blurry. Most of my energy was directed toward not letting him hurt the babies. "Was it awful?"

Carlos shakes his head. "Not at all. That's what was terrifying. Felt amazing. I was already unnerved because that madman was actually making a fair amount of sense, besides the whole thing about reaping mass death on the universe—bridging the gap between the living and the dead has always seemed like a pretty decent idea to me."

"Of course."

"But I was playing along. I knew Sarco had to be taken out. When he had me up there and things started heating up, the ngks had their hooks in Mama Esther and the gateway began opening, well . . . all this gibberish Sarco had been babbling about fulfilling my destiny and how there was more to life than being the Council's cleanup boy suddenly felt so much truer with all that power surging through me. The Divine Gatekeeper, he called it. I felt it. It was . . . like nothing else."

"You walked away, though."

Carlos nods. "Sarco had already killed Dro and Moishe, and I knew he was caught up in how we all got like this. There was no way I'd entrust the balance of life and death to such a madman, massive influx of world-changing power or not."

"I respect that."

"But why would Mama Esther give us the books?"

"You think she's pointing us back to Sarco somehow? He's fully dead, right?" That whole part is pretty hazy in my memory too—I remember tossing the little squirming ngk to Carlos, seeing Carlos raise it up to meet Sarco's blade, and then watching with relief and horror as the ngk split clean in half. Things got blurred right as the other ngks converged on Sarco and began swarmfeasting on his soul.

Carlos shudders a nod. "One of the foulest things I've ever seen but yeah, there's no coming back from that. Trust me."

"Let me see the other book?"

It's considerably smaller, a leather-bound volume with

yellowed pages, which, when he opens it, turn out to be filled with floor plans.

"It's Council headquarters," I say, tracing my finger along an ink line demarcating the outer wall on First Avenue. "But these aren't architect plans."

Carlos shakes his head. "It's a ghost map. See, some of the spiritual defenses they set up are marked. And this." He flips to a bookmarked page. It's the basement. A darkly shaded circle marks one of the corridors. The word ENTRADA is written beside it.

I gape at it. "At Sunset? Think she meant for us to use it as a way in?"

"Or a way out," Carlos says. "It's gotta be heavily guarded, though—both sides. And there's no way we could get an army through there without getting slaughtered one by one."

"So . . . what do we do?"

He smiles up at me. "I have no damn idea."

CHAPTER TEN

Krys

They dipped out a half hour ago, left this place a chilly, gray splatter of steel and concrete and the living and dead. And then darkness ate the sky, the streetlamps blinked on, and the temperature dropped; car headlights and the dull glow of bodega signs and the flicker of lighters and cell-phone screens illuminating faces, reflecting off windows, along the river and still: all those billions of megawatts surging through millions of bulbs, tiny and huge, and they only barely hold back the night.

The empty industrial back alleys of Williamsburg, rat-infested rock piles by the river, frozen puddles and frost-covered trash bags waiting on the curb like fat old men who've given up. Every now and then: a bar. Inside, strangers seek warmth from the weather in half-reckless intimacies and missed connections. And drink. A gaggle of hipsters huddle close to each other, smoke and steam rising from cigarettes and lips, shadows thrown long and wavy into the deserted street.

They don't see me.

No one sees me.

South along the river. Manhattan begs my attention; I keep eyes ahead. Projects loom, Hasidics bustle back and forth; in the distance, a synagogue. Beyond that another glass tower cuts the cityscape.

Bayliss didn't have time to react when I blew him away. He was just there, and then I unleashed and he flew backward. Now he's gone. We must've stood there for a full thirty seconds without saying a word. He'd said my name, his voice choked from the knowledge one of us would soon be dead and one would walk away having killed. I'd been scanning the street. I'd been focused. Don't know how he'd slipped under my radar, snuck close enough to get the drop on me, but it's Bayliss—he was always inscrutable, impossible even.

He was the only academy instructor you could really call a master, a tactician, an artist even, and war was his art. The rest were bored, broken, corrupt old lizards that had landed there either as luxury or punishment, and either way: useless. It's no wonder the 'catcher fighting regimen is mediocre at best. They keep an elite corps stashed away for moments like the one we all know is coming, but . . . the rest: nah. Any acuity they have, any shred of discipline or brilliance, is—was now—because of Bayliss.

So in a way I suppose I just dealt a major blow against the Council.

Still.

He was my teacher. My friend, maybe.

Do I regret it?

The Brooklyn-Queens Expressway stretches like a corroded metal snake through the heart of the borough.

Here it slides belowground, then arches up between brick towers and loops around over the water and shoots off toward Staten Island. If you follow it around that bend and past Red Hook, you can see the dusty warehouse where the Council makes their home. I could show up. I could kill. Be destroyed in a blaze of glory.

It's tempting.

I would be talked about for ages, my memory a banner beneath which the revolution would swell.

But we already have our martyr.

My face tightens. I cut sharply south and blaze through the streets; the gourmet pizza spots and wine bars and hood Chinese spots and nail salons become a blur. The hipsters and homeboys and homeless blend into each other as I whir past.

They don't see me.

No one sees me.

Bitch, I'm a house.

That's how I'll enshrine Mama Esther in my heart: laughing. Laughing at me and herself and all the sadness and survival we shared.

I myself blur into a shining spectral whoosh as I cascade through the Bed-Stuy streets.

Also: I will remember her as a warrior. I've imagined her last ferocious moments a million different ways now; it rips through me every time. The onslaught is relentless, the 'catchers terrified, legion. The air must've been alive with death as the first sparks caught; the night must've tasted like terror.

I can see her last yell. She's laughing, the way I see it. Taking in blow after blow of charging 'catchers, hollering through her pain and approaching end. She must've known how vulnerable she was, felt it coming a mile away. Of course the Council would target the one amongst us who could never hide. Still, there's an undeniable ballsiness to the move—she was easily the most powerful nonaligned spirit around, the most loved. The architect of that hit combined cold calculation with a fiery fury.

I pause on Atlantic. Let the bustling night traffic blast through me. Even now, a couple years into being ethereal and barely there, watching those headlights lurch toward me sends a shock dancing out from my core. I still wait for the screeching brakes, the shrill horn, the cursing driver. Instead the car doesn't even slow, just blasts through with a prickly iciness, and I close my eyes, stabilize, and take in each flashing millisecond of rushing steel and cushion and flesh and bone. And then it's past and another comes and then another, and then Mama Esther laughs as she goes up in flames and somewhere some commander smiles in the ash-strewn night.

I zip up Bedford, giving the monstrous-old-fortress men's shelter a wide berth. I swing right toward Franklin, slow as I approach where the house once was. Try to pull loose from the mire of memories, fail. Mama Esther telling me about the different women who lived in that house over the years, each of whom became a part of her spiritual swirl. Mama Esther reading out loud to me while I sulked after a mission with two new recruits went sour. Mama Esther listening while I talked about the dramas and heartaches from my life, my life when I'd been alive, and the one that bled over into my death: Magdalena.

I round the corner onto Franklin. The night has become crisp; the air whispers of snow. A bodega on the corner; brownstones line the block. And there . . . except no. I pause across the street. Where I expected a pile of rubble hidden by a construction fence, there is a cheerful neon sign on a brand-new brick storefront: JUNIPER'S PET GROOMING AND ORGANIC CUPCAKERY.

Juniper . . . pets . . . cupcakes. How can one even put those two things in the same . . . It doesn't matter. Confusion flattens and disperses beneath the sudden onslaught of rage. It covers me, burns and glistens inside me. I cross the street, oblivious to the passing cars, the passersby. Smiley faces gloat around the words on a sign saying there'll be a grand opening next week, complete with DJ and a "PET COSTUME / CUPCAKE CONTEST." Through the window, I can see the darkened front room, with cartoony arrows pointing to the grooming area and the bakery. Some cans of paint and rollers lie around on the floor, but otherwise the place is pretty much done. Some entrepreneur's lifelong dream, perhaps, or maybe not—you never know what people with extravagant resources will do on a whim.

The rage, somewhat subsided as I took the place in, reignites.

I enter, feel the windowpane's density prickle through me as I breach. Then the stillness surrounds me. This was once the empty front room. Just two weeks ago. How does the world move so fast? I would step in and take a deep breath, like I'd just crossed a border back home. Here I was safe. Now . . .

The sob that comes out doesn't sound like me—it's high pitched and it catches me off guard. I only know it's mine because I feel my whole body heave when another one comes out. Mama Esther was my safe place.

Mama Esther was my safe place, and now we're at war.

We're at war, and I've already killed my own teacher. And ahead there's only more killing. And Mama Esther is gone, my safe place.

The third and fourth and fifth sob come in gulpy hiccups, and there's a precipice—that moment where the deluge will either burst forth or fall back, I'll wipe my eyes and walk away or I'll fall apart. The strength of this rage and sadness is such that I don't know what'll happen if I let go; I feel I may never come back.

I hang there for a good few moments, barely breathing, just a fat flickering shroud in an empty room on a winter night. Tiny flickers erupt within me. Flashes of bright amidst my vast darkness. My safe space gone, I am untethered. Here is where I would've come to cool this hatred.

More flickers. I don't know what they are, what they mean. They register as momentary, condensed unravelings—like slivers of my DNA are coming undone, each sending out little blasts of light as it trembles and then dissolves.

A pause, and then more flickers. Many more. Bombs exploding across a darkened city. Flares in a night sky. Then they catch and spread, unchecked, a million now, blistering and burning across all of who I am, each minuscule spirit cell explodes to life and light.

Finally, I look up from the crouch I've been trembling in. The night has caught fire around me. No—I'm on fire. The flames spit and lash from my shining translucent arms, my belly, my heart. The rage issues forth in bright yellows and purples. It is real, not just a spectral illusion: the quiet lobby glows now with all this rabid heat; I am aflame.

The first thing to catch is one of the drapes they've laid out for painting. Flames tiptoe along the edge, find some flammable bit of chemical along its surface, and then scream to life. Soon one of the walls has caught.

And me? I keep burning, but there's no pain. The fire is me—it can no more burn me than burn itself. We are together: one. I wonder, briefly, if I'll ever be able to put it out, if it'll matter, because maybe I'll be gone soon anyway. And then it doesn't matter, but not because I'm gone, because it's simply what I am. There are no more questions inside me as I tip to one side just so, lighting the reception desk, with its cartoon puppy dog explaining in bubbly letters how to follow them on social media. The desk explodes into a million shards of wood and glass, shattering the front window. From the wreckage, I gather someone had stored a twelve-pack of PBRs and some bottles of Captain Morgan in one of the cabinets, probably for the grand opening.

From not too far away: sirens.

Then more—they're coming from all sides now, and an irrational panic wells up within me. Cops. Firemen. They'll find me. Destroy me, somehow, but no . . . no. It's not just that I'm invisible: I'm fire. There is no finding me; there's no catching me. These flames keep up their steady dance along my shoulders and up my back, the crown of my head.

As the engines screech up, I walk forward, as slow as I feel to, arms outstretched, out of the flaming wreckage and into the street. Their eyes sway past me; there's too much going on to bother with glints of flame sparkling in the air in front of a massive four-alarm fire.

The first pressure blast from the hoses rises into the night sky as I turn my back on all that carnage and stroll slowly down Franklin Avenue.

———————

The tiny lights are still glinting across my body when Jimmy, the Iyawo, and Redd find me around the corner from the wreckage. I look up from the ball I'm curled in, and there they are: two full-flesh-and-blood humans, one shining in her white puffy jacket against the night, and a ghost. They've become friends over the past weeks—we all have. The coming war gave us common cause, Baba Eddie's a place to meet. And then losing Mama Esther cemented the bond. I still want to slide all the way up on the Iyawo when I see her, and every time Redd flashes that huge grin I want to take all of him in my mouth, but somehow I manage to put all that to the side and just be cool with them anyway.

The Iyawo is the first to speak. "Did you—" She nods to where the pulsing emergency lights beat against the sky.

I nod.

"You've still got some on you," Redd says. He smiles, hugely. "Like, right *there*." He points at a random spot on himself. "No wait, now there."

"Actually over there," Jimmy says, pointing at his knee.

I roll my eyes. "Y'all found me for the purpose of annoying me, or what?"

"How did you even do it, though?" the Iyawo asks. "I mean . . . what happened?"

"I . . . I'm not sure."

"You okay?" She looks more concerned than I've ever seen her, that big ol' forehead of hers—the only thing big on her—creased with worry.

"I dunno," I say. "No."

"Neither are we," Redd says. "That's why we found you. We figured you'd be as fucked up as we are."

"Solid basis for a friendship," Jimmy muses.

"It'll do," I say.

Redd spits a gooey, translucent loogie into the ether. "Ay, fuck a cupcakery, though. The fuck is that? And how I look eating baked goods out a spot where they clean a dog's anus? Gonna get some literally ass-flavored-ass cupcakes, is what."

Jimmy's laughing uncontrollably. "You sure got twenty-first-century Brooklynized real quick for someone who just walked out of slavery era a couple months ago."

Redd shrugs. "Been hanging out with the Black Hoodies since I showed up. Guess you could say they initiated me into the ways of today."

"Let's get out of here," the Iyawo says. "Council prolly gonna have some goons out soon enough to see whatsup, and anyway I'm not even supposed to be out at night."

"Uno!" the Iyawo yells. Then she giggles. She never giggles. Again I imagine an imaginary phallus rising through my translucent pants. As it is, I'm soaked.

"Bitch," Redd says without looking up from his cards. "You always on Uno. How is this even— Jimmy, your go, man."

"Jimmy out," I say.

"What? He had like eighty cards a second a—oh." He finally looks up, sees Jimmy leaning against the Iyawo's bed with his head slumped over, a little gob of drool dangling from his open mouth. "Well, damn. Then it's my go." He drops a "Draw 4." "What's good now, son?"

"Fuck." I add four more cards to my already-mountainous hand. "This some bullshit."

"Whoa," Redd says. "You know you're still kinda lit up? And it flared again just now when you cursed."

I shrug. I don't know what's going on with me, don't know what these flames mean. Truth is, though: I like them. It's like a moving fire tattoo, reminding me that I brought hell to the establishment that tried to replace Mama Esther. I hope it never goes away.

The Iyawo taps, which brings it back to Redd, who drops a "Draw 2."

"Shit!" I say, laughing now, and sure enough, the tiny flames dance to life along my arms and down my chest.

She gapes at me. "That's amazing. Does it hurt?"

"Not exactly. It prickles, I guess. But I like it."

"Me too."

"It's pretty badass," Redd agrees.

"Lemme feel," the Iyawo says.

Redd and I lock eyes. We've talked about the Iyawo before, chewed over and over whether it's the forbidden thing, or the curve of her spine, or the full picture of her fineness ("Many hot parts," Redd said, "and an even hotter whole"), or how she doesn't take any shit, whatsoever, from anyone. We never came up with one answer, but it was fun trying, and a relief to be able to talk about it with someone who agreed but, magically, doesn't feel like competition. Maybe it's because I want to grind up on Redd too. And yeah, at first I got glints of jealousy when I'd see them talk together, but pretty quickly those got swallowed up by how much fun we all have.

She's wearing bright-white gym shorts and a wife-beater, which reveals a generous portion of sideboob.

Very slowly, I place my shimmery hand on her knee. She watches, then meets my eyes. "Now swear or something," she says with a mischievous grin.

That grin. I don't have to swear—the lights sparkle on their own, a direct response to the gap in her teeth, the sideboob, the warmth of my translucence on her brown knee, the possibility of closing the gap between us, sliding along her skin, and letting these lights light her up too.

And then, as Redd watches with wide eyes and an open mouth, I do. The Iyawo's head falls back; her spine arches, receiving my shimmering girth in the space behind her; my other hand finds her other knee and a million explosions erupt across me, sparkle and flit across the blurry boundary where my skin meets and merges with hers.

She lets out a sigh; her hands slide along my arms, land on my hands, guide them up to her shoulders. The lights flicker fiercer, and for a second I wonder if the pillows we're sitting on will catch fire. "Ow!" she whisper-yelps, and I'm about to apologize when she laughs. "Don't stop."

I don't. My hands slide down her sides, brush that sideboob, send minibursts of light firecrackering from my gut to my crown. When I look up, Redd is kneeling before her, the Uno game scattered beneath him. She reaches up and draws him in; his lips find mine in the muddled place that is the Iyawo and is me, and we all catch fire. The whole world seems to light up at once, but really it's just me. That is: I am the source, the fountain, the burning heart of the flame inside this burning room, and they are the leaves, also aflame—one dead, one alive—curled and curved and writhing around me. My hand slides along the Iyawo's thigh; hers caresses my face;

Redd's open mouth is still pressed to mine, his tongue entwined with mine, his hips rocking forward toward me, his fingers tracing a slow pilgrimage along her spine.

The sorrow doesn't go away. These flames don't singe it. It stays; it is fuel; it burns through all of us. I embrace it, with the same embrace I hold them in, and I let it bristle and crackle amidst us.

And then we're rising. Heat rises, and we are the embodiment of heat in flesh and soul. The Iyawo gasps—she's close to tipping point, and I'm afraid for a second she'll get hurt, this light will consume her. But these aren't the enraged fires from before; this is a whole different flame. Her eyes closed, she opens her mouth slowly and lets out the illest moan, curls forward suddenly, shoulders hunched, and nods, nods again. Then she stands, steps away, cracks a smile, and shakes her head, rubbing her eyes.

"Yo," she gasps. "Yo."

Redd reaches for her, but she steps back again.

"I ain't even sposta mess around with anyone if we ain't a thing, let alone two mothafuckas at once."

"Let alone two dead mothafuckas," Redd says, mostly I think, to assure her we don't take it personally.

She smiles at him, nods, steps back. "But there's nothing that says I can't watch." She plops onto the bed, slides a hand into her shorts. I want to ask if she's going to be okay, what breaking the rules might mean: Does she have to clean off somehow? Is she in trouble? But the questions sizzle and pop out of existence when Redd turns back to me, his eyes alive and sly. There's nothing between us now, no flesh and bone, and I feel naked, even amidst my wildfires.

It is terrifying; it is thrilling.

Normally now, the terror would win. I'd try to shrivel inside myself somehow, become small, vanish, maybe. All this bulk, all these layers of me, I'd wish them gone. Even ghostly, my flesh is mountainous; I am girth.

But instead the terror and excitement combine into something brand-new, a wild cocktail I have no name for. These fires have birthed bravery in me. Redd steps forward, whispers "May I?" through his smile, and when I nod—because truly, whatever it is, he may, he may—he slides the straps of my shirt down my shoulders and then pulls it down my body entirely till I shimmy out of it. He struts a slow circle around me, taking me in, and I am glorious, a revelation. His hungry eyes say so, his pursed lips too. From behind me, his hands slide along each curve and fold of my torso, lift my breasts, tease my nipples.

Then he eases forward and enters me, all of him slides within all of me, and he begins anew, teasing and caressing, but this time from inside. I gasp, almost scream, glance at the Iyawo, and laugh because she, like Jimmy, has passed entirely the fuck out. From within me, Redd snickers, and I close my eyes and give myself over entirely to pleasure.

Day hasn't broken yet when I rise, but it must be close. Jimmy's still knocked out at the foot of the bed. I almost feel bad he slept through what may have been the most epic night of his life, but the way it was is the way it had to be. The Iyawo is curled like a bug in her white comforter, snoring with a slight grin. Redd lays spread out across the floor, mouth wide open to the ceiling, chest rising and falling.

I barely slept. Joy and sadness were making too much noise as they battled it out over my mood. The hundred fires still leap and fizzle across me, but they're subdued now, the gentle glow of coals.

The Iyawo's room is a damn mess: comic books lie scattered around the floor and desk, along with various balled-up socks and panties (all white). There's an empty bag of Doritos and a half-finished Sprite on the window-sill beside an ashtray with the plastic tip of a Black & Mild sticking out. Magazine cutouts decorate the wall, various black and brown models with natural hair being fabulous and unapologetic. A postcard from Rio I can only imagine is from her cousin Giovanni. A record sleeve for an album called *Red-Handed Royalty* by King Impervious, with a black-and-white photo of the King herself spitting frantic verses into an adoring crowd.

I push some of the comic books to the side and take out the gigantic tome Mama Esther left with me before she died. I been lugging it around in my pack for weeks now—hadn't worked up the courage to look at it, to be honest. But now I'm something new, somehow unstoppable, and so I ease it open on the Iyawo's desk.

Mama Esther told me something about her library once, and it's always stayed with me. The books, much like Carlos, are both of the dead and of the living. That gentle ethereal glow they got? It's because yes, they're spirit books. They're easy for us to touch and carry and all that. But they're not, like most spirit stuff, invisible to the living. They're really there, full and physical, for even those non-ghost-seeing folks.

For a terrible few moments, my mind tries to wrap itself around all the wisdom we lost in that fire, all those hundreds of thousands of pages of truth and art. I shake my head to clear it—there's enough loss to be consumed by without going into all that. It's gone. That's it. Now we have to see about bringing hell to those who did it.

Perhaps literally, I think, sliding my glowing fingers along the elegant lithographed words on the title page: *An Atlas of Hell.*

CHAPTER ELEVEN

❦

Carlos

A tense giddiness crackles through the war room when Sasha and I walk in. Could be the location—this morning Cyrus has called us to the back room of an event hall in the Bronx, where about two dozen little Mexican kids are running wild. It's a birthday party or something—their shouts and laughter reach us through the thin walls, and it's somehow easy to forget why we're there.

But then young Damian calls everyone to order. He's unnervingly deadpan for a kid, even a dead kid, and the room shuts up quick. "Thank you for coming. Cyrus would like to say a few words before we get into the nitty-gritty."

I hadn't even noticed Cyrus. He sits on a bright red plastic chair beneath posters of cartoon animals and a big banner that says FELIZ CUMPLEAÑOS JESUS in balloony letters. I'm wondering which of the little guys playing in the other room is Jesus when I realize it's fucking Christmas. "Thank you, Damian." The old ghost stands, strolls

into the middle of the circle of foldout tables we set up.
"I feel your frustration, friends and comrades. It's been
a difficult two weeks." He pauses so long, I wonder if he
may take a nap. "For all of us."

Mutters of agreement.

"And I know the general sentiment is toward action,
attack. And I have asked for restraint, and you, for the
most part, have heard and respected my call." He looks
up, locks his eyes with various ghosts around the room,
then me. "And I am thankful." I suppress a twinge of guilt
about starting shit yesterday over the book, but I know it
had to happen. Cyrus would understand. "For me, it's
been the most difficult two weeks since I've risen from
that Burial Grounds. Mama Esther's murder hit me harder
than I ever could've imagined it would." Another excru-
ciating pause. Only Cyrus could command this undivided
attention amidst such silences. "And I admit, I didn't
know which path was right, so clouded was my mind with
grief. I believe that now the time has come for action."

A burst of nausea rises up in me as sighs of relief erupt
around the room. So much hinges on what happens in the
next few moments. But then, so much will hinge on the
moments after that too, and the ones after that. All there
is to do is get used to the new norm. Across the room,
Riley catches my gaze, nods. Good.

"I've divided up command responsibilities," Cyrus
says. "It's very unfortunate that both Krys and Big Cane
are still MIA."

Shit. With Krys already being so erratic, it's impossible
to tell whether her absence is more of that or something
far worse.

"Each soul in this room has a role to play," Cyrus continues. "You are what they call the inner circle now. The battle begins and ends with us."

This was unexpected. Sasha shifts in her seat beside me. She'd come to pledge her support to the cause, not get caught up in any leadership role.

"Damian, who as you all know is my only known descendent and the carrier of this family's spiritual legacy, will be running logistics and supplies. I'll let him speak to you." He looks around once more, lands his warm, wrinkled gaze on each of us, then returns to his seat beneath the festive posters and steeples his fingers.

"Each of you commands a battalion of spirits," Damian says, launching into the air as a flickering collection of tiny images comes into view around him. They're the Remote District forces, I realize; numbers appear beside the shimmering ghost clusters. "In the past two weeks, five Remote Districts have gone rebel, swelling our ranks to well over a thousand. We estimate the Council forces have bolstered too, to at least fifteen hundred. They are currently holed up inside Sunset, trying to wait out this revolutionary fervor they've stoked. The newly joined Rebel Districts, because we're not calling them 'remote' anymore, are RDs 8, 9, 10, 14, and 16. The first three are in Harlem; the last rep parts of Queens and, shockingly, Staten Island."

"Ay," a burly ghost in the corner grumbles. Everyone laughs.

"Plus we have Vincent Jackson's Black Hoodie Squad, Cyrus's African Burial Ground Crew, the Ghost Riders, a full battalion of dead construction workers, and about three dozen homeless ghosts, repped by the esteemed Mr. Trant." An older ghost nods with a genial smile. "And Sergeant

Milford will head up the squad of veteran ghosts." A young man stands at attention, snaps a salute, sits. "Everyone in this room right now," Damian continues, "will be functioning as captains in the field."

"Even half-dead guy?" the Staten Island ghost says. "He ain't even rea—"

Cyrus and about two-thirds of the room stand, cutting him off midword. "Delacruz has done more for this movement and risked more than most of the spirits in this room," Cyrus says. "He is an excellent tactician and a skilled fighter. We need him."

"And he didn't wait till it was cool to join up, like some people, Talbot," Riley adds.

Talbot mumbles something and shrugs.

I wonder if it's true, though, what Cyrus said about me risking more than most of the spirits in the room. Folks here have lost loved ones already; my own loss feels so far away, literally another life. Sasha places a hand on my leg, brings me back with a smile and a whispered "You okay?"

I nod. Things are happening fast, though. Already, little Damian is handing the floor over to Riley and explaining that he'll be the lead commander of the allied revolutionary forces in the field.

"Sweet," I whisper as the room explodes with cheers.

"Thank you, thank you," Riley says. His grin is subdued, though, by Riley standards. He knows there's only Hell ahead. "Talbot, any wiseass comments?"

Talbot waves him off. "I'm good, Commander."

"That remains to be seen." Everyone laughs, even Talbot. Then Riley signals to the far side of the room, where a squad of ghosts is rapidly emerging into view.

"My friends," Riley says, "I present to you the much-rumored and sought-after Squad 9, formerly of the Council of the Dead, here to pledge to the Revolutionary Dead."

Sylvia Bell steps forward at the head of her squad and says, "Greetings." She's a squat, middle-aged white woman, who also happens to be one of the most ruthless soulcatchers the Council ever trained. She went renegade after the Blattodeon wars, took her whole team with her, and they've been underground ever since. And now they're here, and ready to fight.

"Welcome back, Captain Bell," Riley says, but his smile says, *Hello, beautiful woman of my life.* I never quite got the full rundown on what all went down between them—Riley was uncharacteristically quiet about it—but it seemed serious.

Sylvia nods, salutes, and walks up and plants a kiss right on his shocked face. The whole room says "Whoa!" at the same time.

"Missed ya, babyboy," she says, walking back to her squad.

"I . . . missed you too . . . ," Riley says.

"So," little Damian says, floating up into the center of the room. "If you're quite finished, Commander Babyboy?"

Riley fake sneezes an *Ahh, fuck off* and then says, "The floor is yours."

"I have another special . . . er . . . surprise guest." I've known Damian for a few months now, and it still unnerves me how old and young he is at the same time. His little translucent child's body turns a slow circle, staring each of us down with those big haunted eyes. "You will not like this one. It doesn't matter. It's a piece of the puzzle. This is where shit, as Carlos says, gets real."

"We sure we trust everyone in this room, D?" Riley says, glaring at Talbot.

"You have something to say, Commander," Talbot rumbles, "then say it."

"I just did."

"*Everyone*," Damian says, "in this room has my trust. We've done our homework, Commander. There are no leaks, no rats here. We don't have to like each other, but if you trust me, and you better, then you trust everyone here. You have my word."

"And mine," Cyrus croaks from the back. Then he says again, quietly, as if to himself: "And mine."

Riley nods curtly. "Alright. I'm with it. Talbot, you good by me."

Talbot allows a slight smile.

"Ya borough trash though."

Damian sighs and holds a hand up to preempt Talbot's clapback. "Gentlemen, I'd like to continue. Time is short. Now, many of you received what we've come to call farewell gifts from Mama Esther. Commander Riley alerted us last night that the Garvey Park spirits believe Mama Esther was working on some kind of plan of attack, a way to take out the Council, when she was killed, and that she passed on the pieces of what she was working on to each of us, with the hope that'd we'd assemble them into a full picture—one that may or may not be complete—and make our move."

"What'd she give you?" Saeen asks. Then someone coughs, and someone else grunts, and a general murmur of discomfort rises. I look around, but nothing has changed in the room; no one has walked in, although the walls seem somehow drab now. The FELIZ CUMPLEAÑOS sign glares off the wall, a suddenly vicious shade of red. I shake my head. Sasha's hand wraps around my wrist, and I see from her face she feels it too, this deep-down wrenching of soul.

"I believe our guest has arrived," Damian says through gritted teeth. He's diminished—all the spirits are. Their shrouds flicker and fade as they rub their eyes and scowl. "Let the telemon through."

"Oh hell fuckin' no!" Riley yells. And then I remember when I've felt this way before and why it would upset Riley. The door opens, and an immense figure walks in. His solemn, pale face peers out evenly from beneath a hood. He carries a large duffel bag to the table, places it with the utmost care, and then retreats to the corner of the room.

The first time I saw an ngk, it was posted up in a house near Mama Esther's, puffing away on its fucked-up little stationary bike, as they do, and chuckling to itself like a maniac, as they do, and making the air utterly unbearable all around it. As they fucking do. They're tiny, come a little higher than my ankle, and absurdly powerful—basically a rat-sized chemical grenade for spirits. On a stationary bike. And if you kill one, which everyone always wants to do because they're so horrible, all the rest materialize with a quickness and eat your entire essence. Like, they will feast on your body, mind, and soul. I've never seen a feeding frenzy like when the ngks swarmed Dro, and then Sarco. I still have nightmares.

The one that emerges from the duffel bag has brought its stationary bike along, but it isn't riding it—which I presume is why all the spirits in the room haven't run out screaming yet. The ngk rests one creepy little hand on

the handlebar as it passes an eager gaze around the room.
It has little tufts of hair sprouting along its wrinkled body
and row after row of perfectly aligned, razor-sharp teeth,
all the better to shred your entire fucking soul with.

"I . . . This is a bad idea," Riley says. "With all due
respect. Whatever the idea is, it's bad."

The ngk bows its head slightly at Riley, turns to Damian.

"Hold on," Damian says. "First off, Baba Eddie, you
there?"

Baba Eddie and Rohan enter, each carrying a huge
bowl of blueberries and shaking their heads with distaste
at the wretchedness pulsing through the room in brutal
waves.

"Thank you," Damian says.

"Yeah, yeah, yeah," Baba Eddie grumbles, leaving
quickly with Rohan.

"We've discovered that blueberries contain certain
properties that counteract the effect of that special . . .
ngk sensation we're all . . . feeling."

Everyone dives for the blueberries at once, and for a
few seconds a rabid feast ensues.

"Still say whatever it is is a bad idea," Riley says
through mouthfuls of blueberries. "I only feel slightly
better."

"It is," Damian says. "But it's the only one we got. We
can't assault Sunset head-on. The Council forces won't
leave. So we have to give them a reason to leave. We've
smuggled out their evacuation plans—they can't mass such
a huge army in the crowded Sunset Park streets, so the
route leads directly up the hill to Green-Wood Cemetery."

"Where we'll be waiting for them," Cyrus says through
a strained grin.

"And Riley," Damian continues, "you of all people, who was nearly killed by the ngks and lost a partner to them, has cause to enter into this with trepidation."

"I'm not entering it with trepidation," Riley says, shoving another handful of blueberries into his mouth. "I'm just not entering it. You shoulda let me in on it before you put me in charge, so I could let you know. This is fucked up to the nth degree." He looks at the ngk. "No offense."

"Hear me out," Damian says. "Hear the play, Commander. We have no other options."

And then something clicks in my head. And I can see it. I can see it all.

I stand. "I'll do it."

"The hell you will," Riley says. "Do what?"

I rustle through my bag, retrieve the book of floor plans Mama Esther gave me, drop it on the table. Grab some berries while I'm up. The ngk regards me with an unnerving grin, then nods sagely. The vile fuck.

"What is it?" Damian asks. He's better at hiding it than everyone else, but I see the way he squints through the discomfort.

"The Sunset floor plans. Which will help me place the ngk in Council headquarters and get out quickly—here." I flap some pages forward and point to the entrada we found.

"They got an entrada at Council HQ?" Riley says.

"Why don't we just bring the army in through there?" Talbot says. "No ngks necessary."

Riley shakes his head. "We'd bottleneck and be slaughtered. They'd hem us in and come cutting from both sides. No room to maneuver. Anyway, you're gonna do what, Carlos?"

"I'm going with you," Sasha says, standing and stepping beside me.

I start to object. My whole body is a volcano of objec-
tions, about to overflow, but somehow I cap it. We just
found each other again, finally, and we just started making sense, and somehow, still, our bodies fit together just
right, our minds just right. And now she's going to run
into Hell at my side? Truth is, I'd rather go alone, die
alone, keep shit simple. What if they take her? What if
they make me watch her die? What if—I shudder, then
look her in the eye and nod.

She's right: everything she would say if I tried to object
would be right anyway. If I go down, who will get it done?
A ghost wouldn't be able to hold the ngk long enough to
make it inside even with a mountain of blueberries. Rohan
hasn't been inside HQ, and he's still kind of fresh in the
whole chopping-spirits department. Sasha's the best warrior I know. There's no one I'd rather have my back.
There's no one I'd like less to have my back.

I turn and look her full in the face, catch my breath. Try
not to think about how her eyes get wide when I enter, the
contour of her naked back; it's all I think about, though,
all I see. Her whole, exquisite form lies painted across the
inside of my eyes, and I'm helpless.

Sasha narrows her eyes. It was only a flicker, a momentary lapse, all those thoughts, but she caught it—saw my
gaze drift back to the hotel room, the night on fire around
us, her thighs embracing me. "C, it's decided."

I close my eyes. Accept it. Turn to the group.

"We're gonna bust up in there," I say, "drop the ngk
off, and then be out, through the entrada, into Hell, and
up to the surface again."

"*Sssssssssssss.*" The hiss comes from the center of the table, and everyone takes a wary step back. The ngk is smiling that unacceptable smile, gazing at us sublimely.

"¿Qué, motherfucker?" Riley growls.

"Easy, Riley," Damian says. "He's our ally now."

"I don't—" Riley starts, but he's cut off by another appalling hiss from the ngk.

"*Ngk,*" it croaks. "*Sssssssssssss.*"

"Oh," I say, squinching my face. "Plural. Ngk*s.*"

"Fuckin' great," Riley sighs.

Sasha

"Why don't they just bust down to Hell through the Prospect Park entrada," the Staten Island ghost they call Talbot says. "And then get in through the secret Sunset Park entrada in HQ?"

"No dice," Riley says.

"Why not?"

"It'll be heavily guarded, for one thing," I say. "Especially right now. Probably both sides of it."

We're standing on the highest point of Green-Wood Cemetery, a tombstone-speckled hill: Riley, Talbot, Sylvia Bell, Vincent of the Black Hoodies, Damian the child ghost, and Carlos and I. Spread out behind us, the combined forces of the Revolutionary Dead gathers and waits amidst the trees and graves, their sullen, glistening faces turned toward us. Ghostlings run messages back and forth between Riley and Cyrus, who sits at the cemetery entrance taking account of every new battalion that joins.

From this hill, we gaze out across the rising and falling row houses and church steeples of Sunset Park. The Brooklyn-Queens Expressway cuts like an unruly metal worm through the neighborhood; just beyond it the warehouses loom in their industrial wasteland; beyond that is the bay.

"Plus," Riley points out, "it's called a secret entrada for a reason. Just 'cause we know it exists don't mean it'll be easy to find. And we don't have time for C and Sasha here to waste rooting around the back corners and weed holes of the Hell looking for an entrada that may or may not even be visible to the naked eye."

"All while fending off attacks from who knows how many 'catchers," Carlos adds.

"And then however many more show up when they sound the alarm," I put in. "No thanks."

"Okay, fair point," Talbot mutters.

"Y'all could go in under the guise of a diplomatic mission," Riley says. "I'm pretty sure Botus is aching to have a meeting with you at this point, find out what's what and feel out the mood for our surrender."

Carlos and I exchange dubious glances. I shake my head. "Not my style," he says.

"Is getting skewered by a hundred 'catcher blades while the entire rebellion collapses in on itself more your style?" Talbot sneers. "Cuz that's what's—"

My outstretched arm slows Carlos's lunge. "Fall back," I say just to him. "Not worth it."

C's eyes narrow on the ghost, and there's death in them, the Deep kind. But he relents, stomping off to brood for a bit.

"Where does that leave us, then?" Riley asks. It's a

fair question, genuinely meant. He'll be a good commander, provided we give him the chance to command.

"I used to coach the football team at Bellington High, where I taught," Sylvia Bell says.

Riley shakes his head. "You fulla surprises, Sylvia."

"Yeah, yeah, I know. We had a move we'd do in a bind—the Plowman's Plunge, the kids called it. Last down and you're just a few yards from the touchdown line, you run it, right?"

"Depends who the QB is," Riley says.

Sylvia wisely ignores him. "The offensive line forms a moving fortress around the quarterback, right? Then they just plow through the defense as one, blocking any tackles as they go."

"Hardcore," Talbot says.

"The front entrance to Council headquarters will be the most heavily guarded. But the side door where Carlos goes in? Less so. We run the Plowman's Plunge on them, C and Sasha will be able to get inside, drop the ngks, and then escape in the confusion."

Vincent lowers his hood and smiles. "I like it." I hadn't realized how young he is; that goatee is just a wisp on his wide, friendly face, his eyes a child's. He must've been just fifteen or sixteen when the cops blew him away.

"But who—" Riley starts; then he stops.

"Squad 9, of course," Sylvia says.

"It's a suicide mission."

"Squad 9," Sylvia says again. "It's what we do."

"Besides," Talbot points out, "they got the 'catcher uniforms. That oughta send just enough confusion through the ranks to give 'em some element of surprise."

Riley rocks back and forth once, making up his face.
I can tell he doesn't like it—it's the same face Carlos
made when I told him I'd be going along on the mission.
We all wait for Riley to get over it, and, to his credit, he
quickly does. "Bet," he says with a grimace. "We'll begin
assembling in the hills. Your team is ready to roll?"

Sylvia smiles like she's been waiting her whole life to
roll up on the Council in a burly crew of renegade 'catchers running interference for two halfies carrying tiny
spirit-annihilating freaks in duffel bags. "At your command, sir."

The sight of the four telemons marching through the field
toward us sends a chill through me. Carlos and I stand at
the cemetery gate. A gray haze encroaches on the pale
sky; the air tastes of snow. Around us, Squad 9 stands at
attention, their flowing capes fluttering in the icy wind.

"Are the telemons like you guys?" Sylvia asks.

Carlos shakes his head. "I don't think so. There's something about those guys that's not of here. Or was never
really alive."

The wave of nausea and generalized bitterness hits like
a hangover typhoon. I squint through the first blast of it.
Beside me, Carlos rubs his face and scowls. A murmur of
discontent roils through Squad 9.

"Not a shred of humanity," I say. "More like an exten-
sion of the ngks themselves. Or just a vehicle—a man-
shaped taxi." Which makes me think of Reza. And the
twins. Who I may never see again. Which is why I'd been
trying not to think too much about them. The last conversation with the cabin folks was strained and confusing.

They don't even let Gordo talk to me anymore because he can't lie for shit, so it's Reza who brushes off all my attempts to find out what the hell is going on out there. Xiomara and Jackson happily gurgle and chatter into the phone whenever I call, though, and I guess that's about all I can ask for right now.

"It would be too much to ask for the man-taxis to deliver the packages, huh?" Sylvia mutters as the telemon spread in a line before us and gently lower the four matching duffel bags. "I mean, it's like, their job, you know?"

The towering, stone-faced men unzip their bags and we all shove the blueberry gum Baba Eddie got us into our mouths and start chewing ferociously. It's working, I'm sure, but the whole world still ripples with despair, and unease bristles from my gut to my forehead.

"The rule is," Reza told me when we were staking out one of our first runs, "when you on the prowl, everyone you love in life is already gone. Not even dead, just gone. They never existed. You're alone in the world, a beacon. You feel me?"

I nodded, but my face told her I was unconvinced.

"What?"

"Easy to say when you don't have kids," I said.

Reza raised an eyebrow. "How you know I don't have kids?"

It took practice, but I got the swing of it. There's a drawer I put them in, sits in the far reaches of my mind, and that's where they stay.

But this chilly afternoon, as that early winter darkness menaces the edge of the sky, Xiomara's and Jackson's little faces won't leave me alone. That foul ngk magic must've upturned my file cabinet, because I imagine Carlos the way he looked in my vision of his death, my blade entering, the fury and fear etched on his face, my name— my old name—on his lips.

God, I hate ngks.

"Let's do this," I say. The little pale monsters writhe and chuckle from their duffel bags, small heads poking out like newly hatched fetus demons. "Zip them back in please."

The telemons' dead eyes register nothing. After a pause, they lean over and close the ngks back in the bags. Then they turn around and walk back into the gathering darkness.

As Squad 9 falls into formation around us, I turn to Carlos, put my hand on his chest. "Be careful," I say. His heart slams against my palm, and he takes in my face with a strange mix of hunger and desperation. Then he blinks and it's gone: the warrior mask slides into place, clicks, and he's unflappable. He smiles, a true, arrogant kind of smirk, and then kisses me hard.

"You too. After all this, it'd suck to lose you again."

I roll my eyes, close them, fight off the image of those tiny, beautiful faces staring back at me. When I look back up at Carlos, my own mask is on, and I'm ready.

The ngks are heavier than they look. I have a duffel bag slung over each shoulder; Carlos has two on one shoulder, three on the other. "They can't fucking bike their little asses up in there?" he grumbles.

"They're stationary bikes, man," I hiss. "Leave it."

The feeling of that squishy flesh and the occasional poke of a handlebar against my back is some kind of sickening, but I manage to get used to it pretty quickly. Chewing extra hard on the blueberry gum, we find our stride, this monster made of many, moving as one out the cemetery gate and across the street.

The wide avenues of Sunset Park bustle with Mexican families and random hipsters. Through the haze of Squad 9, I can make out the bakeries and barbershops lining the block, a fruit stand, a nightclub, a pseudo-botánica. I wonder how the Iyawo's doing, and Baba Eddie, who saved my life, and then I think about the twins, and then I stop, return to the present, the sacks of tiny, hideous monsters pressed against my back, the throng of badass spirits around me.

Carlos.

We angle down a residential block, brick row houses glistening with Christmas decorations and a snow-covered Virgin Mary gazing serenely at the parked SUVs and telephone poles.

The renegade soulcatchers bristle as we approach the wide throughway beneath the BQE. An early-evening traffic snarl rumbles along above us; porn shops, a uniform store, and a busted little Dominican place glare from across the street. The trilling anxiety of ngkness simmers along with us, occasionally blasting to fever pitch and then fading like some hellish tide. Any second now, we'll see the front guard. Surely. They can't all be holed up in there, right?

But no 'catchers step in our path as we sweep down the cobbled industrial streets between two massive warehouses. Carlos and I trade a sideways glance; he shrugs.

"Forward to the side door as planned?" Sylvia Bell asks from her position directly in front of us.

"Aye," Carlos says.

The bay is a gray splash at the end of the block, almost indistinguishable from the graying sky. The street is deserted. The shuttered windows and gloomy, rotting facade of the Council headquarters tower over us. Up ahead, cement steps lead to a rusted, graffiti-splattered door.

"Squad 9," Sylvia growls. "Battle formation. Blades out!"

A rustle of movement erupts around us, and the renegade 'catchers tighten their huddle as their blades emerge. Carlos and I are inside a bristling, sharp-edged cloud of walking death. One of the ngks adjusts its position in the pack, and I shudder. Then the door flies open, and a battalion of Council soulcatchers pours out.

"Blitz!" Sylvia yells, and Sqaud 9 flushes forward. Carlos and I stumble along, nearly carried off our feet by the rush of spirit. The soldiers smash into each other with a whoosh and the clang of ghost steel. One of our entourage drops immediately, and two more stumble backward into Carlos, clutching their blade arms. But the Council 'catchers scatter to either side, unable to hold off the sustained forward motion of Squad 9. We push through the last few holdouts, crushing one beneath us, and suddenly the world becomes much, much darker.

We are inside.

The last time I entered Council headquarters it was to receive my official pardon for existing, and my whole body was heavy with the brand-new knowledge that I'd killed Carlos. It overshadowed the shallow joy of being able to come out of hiding (I was barely hiding anyway) and tainted the greater relief of having helped eradicate the

Blattodeons. The twins were safe—that was the most important thing—but the pain of what I knew was about to happen still cast its shadow as Botus grinned across the table at me. I would tell Carlos—worse: I would show him, allow him into the unearthed memory. And he would understand that his last word was my name and it was a prayer, one for mercy, not love. And that all of this hell that he lived now, this lifeless life, this ongoing death— that's because of me. I did that. And then he would walk away. And I'd be left alone, standing beneath that gray sky by the bay, broken and twisted inside, and maybe I'd never feel whole again, having found this man I love and then lost him, again and again, by my own hand.

Botus closed the meeting with a nod and a grin and a chilly handshake, and I walked outside and there was Carlos, and I let him in on our ghastly secret, and he walked away, and I stood there beneath that gray sky by the bay, broken and twisted inside, and hated him and hated myself and hated the Council and hated the sky.

Now Carlos draws his blade as we move side by side down an open, misty corridor, and I draw mine. Squad 9 has widened its berth, and it looks like we have a moment to breathe before the next wave of 'catchers shows.

"Gonna drop one here," C says, slowing as the squad fans out around us. He lowers the bag and gingerly unzips it. Immediately, the aggravated ethereal buzz heightens around us. The ngk's ugly little head emerges. It adjusts itself beneath the bag and then brushes itself free, emerging already mounted on the rickety little stationary bike and pedaling away.

I have to yawn to clear my ears as some kind of slow-crawling death dirge erupts through me. "Just make sure you don't touch 'em when you're opening the bag," Carlos says. "We wanna get em as spread out as possible so—"

"We split up," I say. "You go that way; I go this way. We each take half of Squad 9 and meet up back on the battlefield."

Carlos flashes a grim smile. "Indeed."

"I love you," I say, surprising even myself as I pull him close for a kiss.

"I love you too," Carlos says, then blinks a few thousand times.

"Alright, go."

"Incoming!" Sylvia yells.

"Go," I say. "Don't die."

He smiles, turns, and then he's gone.

"Again," I whisper. And cringe.

CHAPTER TWELVE

~⁖⁖⁖~

Caitlin

Yeah, it's been a shitty week.

Two weeks.

Whatever: I've been in the hole.

First of all, worst of all: there's a tiny modulating loop of sound that won't stop cycling through my left ear. The doctors say it's tinnitus, but I'm not stupid. That's the last sound Mama Esther made, that final, triumphant cackle as she exploded outward in a million smithereens and rained fire, metal, and stone on all of us. My fire. My men's fire. Rained it right back on us as she died.

And that laugh.

It was a winning laugh, not the desperate final howl of the doomed.

And some shard of her laugh must've lodged in my earhole. That's all I can figure, because it was there waiting for me, looping endlessly, when I woke up at the New York Presbyterian Burn Center. And it's there still, today, two weeks later, as I walk up the chilly, misty stairwell in Council headquarters.

Fuck ghosts; I can see my fucking breath in this place.
And I'm small—circulation gridlocks in all those tiny
rivulets and vesicles. HQ needs central heating, is what
I'm saying, but I get it: it wasn't built for me.

Still: fuck ghosts.

They came to collect me three days into my hospital
stay. I was just starting to enjoy myself too. Got one of
the orderlies to show me how to disable the limiter on my
morphine doser, so life was, you know, *good*. As good as
it can be when one's holed up at the recovery unit. My
burns weren't even that bad, not really. All superficial,
but everywhere—that supersonic boom Esther went out
with was no kinda joke—so they brought me to the burn
center as a precaution. A chunk of rock nearly brained
me though, and mainly I'm on bleed watch.

Plus that laughter. That put a damper on everything.

The 'catcher squad showed up while a nurse was taking my blood pressure. Materialized in the shadowy part
of the room in that awful ghost way that reminds you that
you have no privacy whatsoever when it comes to the
dead. I rolled my eyes, sent the nurse away, and snarled
a "What?" at them.

"Subminister Fern," the squad leader said with a bow,
"we have orders to bring you in."

"In?" For a second, my pulse sped up. Mama Esther's
cackle ratcheted up a notch.

"For protection. It's a Council-wide security measure.
There've been . . . attacks. Small bands of rebels have
targeted various Council entities."

"Terrorists."

"Excuse me?"

"Call them terrorists," I said. "If you call them rebels, they've already won. Never mind. Where do they want me?"

"Council headquarters, ma'am. They've prepared some very accommo—"

"Hell no."

Except hell yes, as it turned out. A whole squad of 'catchers can be very persuasive if they need to be, and I didn't have it in me to try and mindmeld them.

So here I fucking am, and here the fuck I've been in this dank, breezy, death-filled trash hole, this extra-strength abortion of industrial proportions with its drip-drops and creaks and groans, shattered, boarded-up windows, and rusted file cabinets, rusted table tops, rusted light fixtures, skittering rats, and random, greenish puddles.

I haven't been to the place that ghosts call Hell, but this, right here, is Hell.

I walk up another flight, pause at the landing, panting. More from irritation than exhaustion, though my energy's been flagging since the blowup. And Mama Esther keeps cackling. A 'catcher squad bustles past, barely slowing to salute. I give them the finger. Somewhere a few floors down, there's yelling.

Something's happening, maybe. Or maybe it's just more phantasmagoric fuckshit.

Worst part is, I actually miss those people that could loosely be described as my "friends." Samantha, Gillian, Brittany. I'm sure they're at Luther's *right now*, maybe raising a toast to me. Or maybe forgetting I ever existed, like the tawdry bitches they probably are.

I even miss Raj. Esther cackles louder. I wonder if I could slip out of this rotten anus of a building and secure

a one-off. He texted me a few times in the days before
the blowup. I'm sure I could wrangle back into his bed
and ride him till this cackling stops and I remember what
peace feels like.

"Subminister Fern." Seems a 'catcher has rolled up on
me while I dawdled in this puddle of self-pity. I look up
from the mire and cast her a withering glance. She is
undaunted. "The chairman has requested your presence
in the boardroom."

"Do you think if the chairman hadn't requested my
presence I'd be on this stairwell? I am coming."

"Due respect, ma'am: you've been standing still for
ten minutes."

If that's all the respect that's due, I must not be worth
much. "Get out of my way." I scowl, shoving past the
'catcher and storming—slowly, achingly—up the next
flight of stairs.

What the hell do you want? I'm about to shout when I
finally make it to the top-floor boardroom, but there's
such a flurry of excitement when I walk in, the words get
lost. Ministers and 'catchers alike flutter and fuss in a
frenzy across the full length of the room. I notice a few
of the High Seven in the mix, clucking and muttering
about strategy with the rest of 'em. They've removed the
massive table, and maps of various boroughs and parks
cover the walls. At the far end, Botus sits in his worn
leather executive chair, conferring with Juan Flores.

I'll be honest: few things shake me, but I still get a
chill every time I see that faceless fuck. There is something very wrong with him. More wrong than the average,

wrong-type creep that I deal with. Being near him is like drinking a whole glass of milk and realizing there was a dead mouse at the bottom. And then the dead mouse looks up at you and smiles.

And it's only gotten worse since the blowup.

"Subminister Fern," Botus says, smizing luxuriously. "So nice of you to join us."

"Yeah, yeah, yeah," I grunt, making my way down the long room toward him.

"Something seems to be happening."

"So I gather." It's not just the urgency of the ghosts around me: a foulness beyond the normal Council gloom has seeped into the air. I can't put my finger on it, but it's not good. The bustling ministers and 'catchers seem to feel it too—I catch short, snappy snippets of their strained conversations. Dissonance permeates the room, the whole building probably.

"The rebels are gathering, but our eyes don't know where yet," Flores says.

"Terrorists," I mutter. And then, "But how do you know—"

"Because they're gone," he snaps. Then he lets out a heavy sigh. Whatever it is is getting to him too. "None of them are in their usual spots. Entire Remote Districts have emptied out. They're massing for an attack, somewhere."

"Plus our communication's still fucocked," Botus adds. "As you may have noticed."

"So the usual incompetence of the Council is exacerbating a potentially catastrophic situation. Behold my face of shock."

Botus levels an icy glare my way, and for a half second

I wonder if I finally treaded too far. Then Flores leans in. "The . . . uprising, Chairman. We have to find them. Now."

Botus rounds on Flores. Flores is the most solidly built phantom I've seen—his broad shoulders push out the edge of that cloak like Darth Vader in his years as a linebacker. Botus is a whole other kind of huge and imposing, though—he's almost as tall, with huge hands and thick arms. You wouldn't call him fat; he's just got that ungainly dadbod with random blobs of bulk bulging out in different places. If it wasn't for that broadsword Flores rolls with, it'd be a close fight. "You've been whining about making a move for *two weeks*, Flores. Ease up on the Bustelo and *think* for a second, you faceless fop!"

Silence snaps across the room as two dozen ghostly faces turn toward the chairman. I know I, for one, am riveted.

"Every new day we huddle behind these walls," Flores seethes, "like *cowards*, the rebels ha—"

"The *terrorists*," Botus cuts in, winking at me with a morbid grimace.

Flores looks about to snap. "The *terrorists* have more time to plot, plan, and prepare for our destruction. And what is *our* plan, Chairman Botus? What is *your* plan to defeat the rebellion, besides rotting in this warehouse while our enemy grows stronger?" He's barely whispering, but the room is so quiet we feel each word in our guts, and I know I'm not the only one whose truth he's speaking.

"Stronger?" Botus chuckles. That faux confidence is transparent as hell though; no one is fooled. "Have you not listened to report after report of their stagnation? Their infighting? Their broken spirit? No . . . *you* got us into this position with your overaggressive rushing into that hit on Mama Esther, Speedy Gonzalez. Now *you're* going to fall back and watch me clean up your mess. With tactics. Their little movement can't hold without any victories, without any movement! They'll splinter and disintegrate within the week. Soon, an emissary will show up at our door, meekly begging to treat on peace terms." He turns to the room. "Do you hear me? Mark my words."

No one speaks.

"Meanwhile, Flores here would have us campaign out into the ether, with no target, no clear strategy, no escape. We don't even have a full grasp of their numbers, but you want—"

"With our reinforcements from the Jersey outpost, we are sure to outnumber them," Flores growls over the chairman. "Even a high estimation puts them at twelve hundred, tops. We're close to two thousand. We can sweep them off any field of battle—"

"To walk into the maw of the insurgency, never to be seen again. Is that what you want?" Botus looks up as a commotion erupts from the far side of the room.

"Make way," a gruff soulcatcher hollers, barging through at the head of a tattered, sorry-looking squad. "Chairman, we captured an intruder. It's ah . . . one you'll want to speak with, I think."

An open aisle clears through the center of the room as the 'catchers bustle through, cluttered tightly around their prisoner.

"You see?" Botus crows. "Even as I was speaking, the rebels sent their emissary for peace. Watch."

The whole room gasps when the 'catchers step away and flesh-and-blood-ass Carlos Delafuckingcruz stands there with the slightest of grins on his face.

"Well, well, well," Botus drawls as his elite protective detail of 'Catcher Primes moves into position around him. "Look what the proverbial cat dragged in, so to speak."

Unlike the chairman's forced bravado, nothing about Delacruz suggests he's anything but utterly at ease, happy even. Despite the dozen 'catcher blades hovering inches from his face, the half-dead traitor's body is relaxed, his head cocked just so and that one lock of black hair covering half his face. But it's his smile that gets me: it's only barely there, and I think that's what's so wrong about it. He's not cheesing for the camera; there's no false bravado. He just seems mildly, genuinely amused. Like Mona Lisa, if Mona Lisa was a half-dead Puerto Rican dickhead.

"It's fantastic to see you, Carlos," Botus says. "What's it been? A month since we last met? Three weeks? So much has happened since then. The world keeps turning, I suppose. And to think I offered you a position on the Council. And look at us now. Ooh, baby, it's a wild world, am I right?"

All at once, I remember the moment just a few months back when Delacruz made a move to take me out in my brother's underground roach temple. Murder didn't just flash in his eyes; it was all over him—the man was made of it. And I won't lie: I almost shat myself. I had prepared myself for death. Had been preparing myself for death for years leading up to that moment. I was ready. I told myself I was ready. It was my role in this world, this cycle of life and death, and I had accepted that and stepped into my role, my destiny, amidst the Blattodeon pantheon, and *still*, still the sight of that man swinging toward me with the full fury of a protective father nearly broke my resolve.

Instead, that bitch Kia showed up screaming and fucked

up everything by saving my life, and I buried the relief I felt beneath a mountain of shame as I dove into the murky waters beneath Bushwick and saved myself while the Blattodeon legacy crumbled.

"It's good to see you too." Delacruz's calm voice sends a chill through me, and I realize I'm fucking terrified of that man. He killed my parents, my brother, decimated our legacy. By all rights, I should be burning for the righteous comeuppance he's about to get. Surely he'll be tortured for information. And surely I'll be given a chance to exact my pound of flesh.

But that small smile. It does not lie.

Botus leans forward in his chair, his ghostly form stretching a few extra feet toward Delacruz. "To what do we owe the extreme pleasure of this visit?"

"I came here to kill you." He looks around serenely. "All of you." For a split second, our eyes meet and I have to stop myself from running full speed the hell out of this room. It's like staring down a python. But I'm the hunter, not the hunted—this is absurd! I try to rally myself, but that growing, hissing sense of desolation that'd been sliding through me since I walked in here only heightens.

"We found these on him," one of the 'catchers says, gingerly laying an assortment of daggers on the dusty ground in front of Botus. "And, of course, this." He holds up the halfie's infamous blade, sheathed in its elegant wooden cane.

"Surely you wouldn't deprive an old man of his walking stick," Delacruz says.

"Cut the Gandalf shit," Botus snaps, his fake cool suddenly spent. "You're not the only one that knows how to read, jackass. Now, whatever you think you've come for, here's what'll happen instead. You'll be tortured, first for fun, then for information. Then you'll be tortured some more. Then the information you give up will be used to capture, torture, and kill all your little friends. Any questions?"

There's a play here. I can't see it. Can't map it. But it's there. There's no way Delacruz rolls up in here fully armed, gets himself captured with no play.

Carlos says, "I do have a question, actually."

"Sir," the head 'catcher interrupts. "We believe a few other squads are pursuing another halfie through the building."

"Oh?" Botus perks up. So does Flores, I notice. "A female, by any chance?"

For the first time since he arrived, Delacruz's smile falters. It's only for a moment—he paints it back on quickly, but it dimmed slightly now. I wonder if Botus caught it.

"We think so. Communication's still somewhat—"

"Yes, yes, yes," Botus cuts in. "Anything else?"

"We believe they may have deposited some . . . items in the corridors when they entered, but we're not sure yet. They led us on a hell of a runaround."

"I said I had a question," Delacruz snarls, still smiling.

What did they drop off? Death suddenly feels quite certain.

"The items," Juan Flores growls, his voice silencing the rising commotion in the room. "What were the items?"

I'm glad somewhat else recognizes the urgency of this situation, even if that someone is DeadMouse Milk.

"We don't know," the 'catcher admits.

"You're saying you have reason to believe two enemy entities infiltrated our headquarters and dropped something off and you *don't know what it is*?" Flores steps forward, towering over the soulcatcher. "Did you not check?" His voice a cannon shot on a quiet night.

"Flores." Botus's voice is sober, a warning.

"We couldn't, sir. We tried. There was something wrong in the area where they placed them. It was like . . . I can't explain it. It was wrong."

I can relate. That's how everything's been feeling for the past twenty minutes: unexplainable and wrong. Flores looks like he's about to backhand the 'catcher into the Deeper Death. Botus must see it too, because he stands and moves quickly out of the protective circle around him and between the two ghosts. "Deploy a team, Deputy Chamberlain. Get the packages, find out what they are, and handle them. If you can't get any of your men to go, you go. Otherwise I'll feed you to this guy. Understood?"

Chamberlain bows and scurries off. Flores returns to his seat, unsatisfied. Botus grins at Delacruz, who stares him down. "Now, Mr. Delacruz, you had a question."

"Was it you, or was it Sarco?"

Botus's forced grin fades fast. "Excuse me?"

"My family. Sasha's family. Before . . . everything. They were wiped out."

"I . . ."

"You know," Delacruz says thoughtfully, "it's not really a fair question. I know the answer; I just want to hear you say it. I want to see your face when those words leave your translucent-ass lips, so I can remember that image when I put my blade through your heart."

"Bawdy words from an unarmed man on the wrong end of so many blades."

Delacruz shrugs. "I'm a bawdy motherfucker. Answer.

Answer and I'll tell you whatever you want to know. Don't answer and I swear on the memories of all my loved ones you can torture me until I'm just a trembling pile of fleshless limbs and my lips will stay shut."

Botus smirks, doesn't have a reply. The halfie has danced circles around him already. None of this is going to go well for us. Flores shifts back and forth on his feet, looking, I think, at me, and then back at the prisoner. I'm guessing he wants to just kill him as much as I do and end this nightmare, but we both know that would only be the beginning.

"What's in the package?" Botus snarls.

"A gift," Delacruz says simply. "That's all you get to know until I get my answer."

"Let me—" Flores starts.

Botus holds him back with a raised hand. "What makes you so sure you know the answer?"

"Sarco was a performer. He was a killer too, sure, but he loved the theater of it all. The act of it, with all eyes on him. That time he felled a soulcatcher and Moishe, the real estate agent in the Prospect Heights basement, made sure a whole squad of us was around him before he began the slaughter. He relished it."

"Fascinating," Botus says. Far away, there's a tiny buzzing noise. It's barely audible beneath the endless loop of Mama Esther's cackle, but once I notice it, it won't go away. "Do go on."

"Even when he orchestrated deaths and had us do the dirty work for him, it was right there in public: Grand Army Plaza on a rainy night in March. My parents, Leandro Reynaldo Salazar and Dulce Maria Aviles, were killed in a home invasion. James and Sarah Raymond,

Sasha's parents, were killed in a car accident. Their parents, an electrical fire. That's not how Sarco rolls. That's Council style. That's you, Botus. *You* created a monster, thinking, I'm sure, the Council would get some fancy new foot soldiers from Sarco's halfie project, but Sarco played you—got Council backing and used it to do whatever he needed to do, leaving you to clean up his messes. His messes were our families. And then after massacring *my* family, you brought me in as the cleanup man and sent me to kill *my* best friend, who I didn't remember."

Carlos's subtle smile has blossomed into a full-grown, shiny grin. It bursts off his face, unstoppable. It's terrifying.

"Isn't that right?" he says slowly, like he and Botus are in on some huge joke.

The buzz gets louder, shriller, like it's bursting out of Carlos's suddenly wide smile, but maybe I'm the only one who hears it. Residual trauma from the attack on Mama Esther's? I shake my head, but it stays, droning on amidst the old house ghost's endless laughter.

"That's exactly right," Botus says.

Delacruz laughs, shaking his head, and pushes the lock of hair out of his face. "Oh man . . . you guys."

"What I think you, and others, fail to understand, Carlos, is—"

"No!" His voice is like a gunshot, his smile gone. I want to run I want to run I want to run. "I didn't ask for an explanation. I simply wanted to hear you say you did it."

"But—" Botus is clearly not used to being interrupted.

"I have no interest in how you rationalize your massacres. That's your business. What you've done—that's my business."

Botus, finally fed up, looms over Delacruz, leering. "What makes *you* think you, my prisoner, have the right to tell me what I get to explain and what I don't get to explain?"

It was rhetorical—I'm sure it was rhetorical—but Delacruz chooses to answer it anyway: "Because this is a moment I've been waiting a very long time for." His smile is back. It's still not forced; it's incandescent, unstoppable. I want to run I want to run I want to run. "This is *my* moment. And I want it to be *just* right. Do you understand?"

"Do *I*—" Botus begins, indignant.

The buzz surges into a scream, blasting from everywhere at once like a thousand trains careening toward us. The 'catchers and ministers around me cover their ears and stumble, their faces contorted with pain. The whole room seems to fall to its knees at once. Delacruz and I are the only ones left standing. I don't know how long I'll last—everything's gone shaky, and I feel like several organs have ruptured and are leaking various poisons into my bloodstream. I backstep toward the wall, keeping a wary eye on Delacruz.

He pulls something out of his pocket, a stick of gum, I think. Unwraps it and shoves it in his mouth. Then he moves quickly, snatching up his weapons as the soulcatchers writhe on the floor around him.

"They dropped an ngk on us!" Botus screams, clawing his way back to the leather chair.

"Evacuate the base!" Flores yells. He's doubled over, clutching his stomach and stumbling toward the back of the room.

Delacruz is methodical: with a half dozen slashes, he's

cleared the area around him, cutting down soulcatchers one by one. *Slash* with the long blade, *stab* with the short one. The elite guard has formed a desperate, sloppy ring around Botus, but they keep collapsing over themselves. A few simply flicker out as the earsplitting devastation barges on.

Slash, *stab*, *slash*, *stab*. Delacruz works his way toward Botus, smiling that cemetery smile of his. There's an exit somewhere in the shadows back there. The chairman is crawling toward it, screaming at his bodyguards to hold their positions as they're enveloped in the oncoming tidal wave of those blades. Around me, ghosts are trying to stand up and bolt out of the room, tripping over themselves, clobbering and stampeding each other into a mushy ethereal goo.

Me? I'm frozen. My entire body abjectly refuses to respond as my mind cries out in terror. My eyes stay glued to Delacruz as he cleaves his blade through one elite 'catcher, then another; then he turns, panting, and stares at me.

I can't breathe. Can't move.

He raises one of his daggers, his fingers poised around the point, and is about to release when a huge shape rumbles between us: Juan Flores. I exhale, and the world seems to return to me. Flores swings that broadsword in a reckless arc. He doesn't have much in him—by all rights, I should be the one saving him. I'm sure whatever this ngk thing is is poisoning the air; it's worse for spirits than the living. Delacruz steps easily out of the way and swings his own blade down, but Flores is quicker than he looks. He deflects the blow, almost collapsing with the effort, and shoves Delacruz back a step.

"With me!" Botus yells to his guards.

Delacruz steals a glance back, sees the chairman ducking into that shadowy doorway, growls. He hurls a few fast blows at Flores, nicking him twice, and then spartan kicks him in the chest, sending him hurling back toward me. Then his eyes meet mine. "Today, you die, Fern."

I almost shit myself again, but I don't—somehow I don't.

Then he turns and barrels after the chairman and his shattered entourage.

"Come on," Flores groans, heaving his flickering mass off the floor. "We have to rally the 'catchers."

"You . . . you saved me," I said.

"Don't get misty eyed about it. I made a strategic choice. You're worth more to us in a fight than the chairman, that's all." I help him to his feet, and we stumble toward the corridor, where mayhem reigns. Soulcatchers run wild, screaming, vanishing, collapsing. Some of them cut each other down in a frantic bid to escape the endless howling.

Flores shakes his head, and we launch into the madness. "And we're about to be in a hell of a fight."

CYCLE FOUR

❦

WAR

Sólo dejar desolación, gemido,
El imperio macabró de la muerte,
Sobre el pueblo entero destruido.

Cada vez que me acuerdo del ciclón,
Se me enferma el corazón.

But all that remained was desolation, groans,
The macabre empire of death,
Over the entire destroyed nation.

Every time I remember the cyclone,
Suffering overtakes my heart.

"El Trío y el Ciclón"
Trío Matamoros

CHAPTER THIRTEEN

Sasha

Things have gotten pretty dire when that satanic screech rips through all of us.

For a flickering second, I think I'm going to pass out—the world gets murky, and the floor seems to veer toward me. I hang on, though, come around with one hand pressed against the filthy warehouse wall, the other on my face, both blades on the floor.

Never let go your weapons, Sasha. Reza's voice, like some dapper, gunslinging Yoda with infinite more game and a Crown Vic. It brings me back to myself.

I drop to one knee, retrieve them, glance up and down the corridor. The soulcatchers that had been cornered are shrieking, collapsing, fading. We'd already lost half the dozen or so Squad 9ers we came in with, and two more shimmer into nothingness when the ngk screech peaks.

We have to get out of here.

I grab Captain Bell and help her up, her ghostly luminescence quivering in the half-light of the hallway. "We leave the way we come in," she says.

"And now's our chance."

"Carlos?"

I shake my head. "The plan is to meet at the battlefield, so that's what we do." Bell nods and gathers the troops. Carlos knows what he's doing, but that smile he flashed as we parted spoke of some devious plan, and a few of the Squad 9ers that left with him met back up with us, saying they'd been separated and Carlos had all but vanished . . . I can't think about it now. I start out ahead of the squad, cutting down the scattered 'catchers that haven't fled yet.

A few round the corner behind us and come tearing up the corridor. I don't think they pose much threat, but I'm relieved to see Squad 9 achingly gear up anyway. The renegade 'catchers collect their dropped blades and stumble into a loose formation around Bell. I think it's more instinct than protocol at this point; I've never seen a squad so attached to their leader. Bell gives a hoarse cry and charges. The Council 'catchers hesitate, and that's probably what does them in. Squad 9 barrels into them like a tattered stampede, massacring the 'catchers where they stand.

They turn their weary eyes to me.

"This way," I say. "And kill anything that moves."

The winter night air is life. It's the sudden silence after what felt like a million years of earsplitting wretchedness. It's peace in the thick of battle. We barrel out the door, these four renegade soulcatchers and I, and stumble-run down the block like sprinting drunks on a binge. A few scattered Council 'catchers lay recovering on the cobblestones, but they're too stunned to care about our ragtag group. Behind us, the mass exodus has begun. I glimpse back when we reach the wide expanse of Third Avenue beneath the BQE. 'Catchers, ministers, and bureaucrats flood out of the Council's windows, walls, and doors. Their tattered shrouds flutter down from the upper floors, some already fading into nothingness.

There are so many of them. Hundreds, still alive and recuperating.

A bellow erupts from somewhere in the building, and I cringe. It's one I've heard before: the throng haints are loose. And they're pissed. One emerges from the front wall of the Council, those long, mouth-covered arms stretching all the way across the street as its eyeless head lurches from side to side in agony. Another begins breaching the wall behind it, and I've seen enough. Captain Bell's sharp intake of breath lets me know she has too.

"It's beginning," I say. "We gotta let the others know."

I throw up a silent prayer that Carlos is okay, wherever the hell he is, and then the five us turn our backs on all that festering destruction and run.

Riley's voice booms out across the open field as we enter the cemetery. Even from here, I can hear the urgency in his call.

I'm guessing the Council knows what they're about to walk into, one way or another. They're incompetent on many levels, but generally it's an incompetence born from the inability to wield such a colossal, corrupt mass of dead bureaucrats. And anyway: trying to regulate the line between life and death would bring out the useless fuck in even the most organized desk maven. But they're not stupid. And when it comes to protecting their power to define, they become suddenly ruthlessly efficient. They'll walk into our little trap alright, but they won't be caught unaware.

"And no more." Riley's words echo along the hillside and seem to cover the whole sky. Some ghost voice-projection trick. I'm guessing he's made the same calculation as I just did and said *Fuck the element of surprise* in favor of the terror of his Godlike voice ruling the battlefield before the fight has even begun. *"I said, no more!"* he thunders. And then I hear it: a reply so gigantic and unwavering even the throng haints must flinch: *"No more!"* a thousand ghosts rage at once.

"Tonight, we say no more!"

"NO MORE!" Their voices become one. I feel it in my knees, my gut, as the surviving Squad 9ers and I dash up the hill toward the Gothic spires of Green-Wood's inner gate.

A burly groundsman stands next to a wheelbarrow, gazing uneasily at the hill above him. He has no idea, I'm sure, that hundreds of angry spirits lay in wait, their translucent fingers clutching axes, long blades, daggers, rapiers. But he knows something's up, and he's not thrilled. He shakes his head, mutters, "Fuck this." Then he drops the wheelbarrow and starts closing up for the night.

"For as long as we've known death, we've known the weight of this Council on our back, directing our every move, their long fingers reaching into our hearts and minds!" Riley hollers.

"NO MORE!"

"For as long as we've known death, we've tasted the

bitterness of overregulation, corruption, brutality, murder. Massacres!"

"NO MORE!"

The last few tourists make a hasty exit. I walk through the gate without being seen and disappear into the shadows of the cemetery.

"We have been beaten down, held back, kept from our loved ones, burnt, tortured, broken, silenced."

"NO MORE!"

"They have torn us from our loved ones, killed our families."

"NO MORE!"

Up ahead, something glints in the darkness beneath a copse of trees. Squad 9 and I move up a sloping field between elaborate crypts and weeping angels.

"We have played by their rules, but tonight . . ." He's relishing this moment. Joy and rage pulse through every word. *"Tonight we say NO."*

"NO MORE!"

"We say no!"

"NO MORE!"

"No fucking more!"

"NO MORE!"

Swishes of movement flicker along the tree line ahead. We've reached the outer rim of this magnificent ghost army, and I feel their combined power rattle through me. The commanders of each legion stand out front—I see Saeen, Kaya Doxtator, Vincent Jackson and his Black Hoodies. Further along, La Venganza and Talbot head up their troops. In the distance, some gangly, elongated heads poke out over the trees: the river giants. The whole army faces a pillared mausoleum. Riley's on the roof of it, his back to us, his soldiers spread out before him. Damian hovers on one side; Cyrus Langley stands solemnly at the other.

"*We are many, and we spring from many sources.*" Riley's voice is hoarse with strain and emotion. "*But tonight we form one river, one tide. In life, we were felled by cancer, murder, tragedy, accident. Tonight, we are murder; we are tragedy. Blood and mayhem is our name. They are damaged, and their cause is weak, but they have the numbers. That means we must be the destroyers. No peace, no negotiation, no mercy. We strike once, and that's to kill.*"

An eerie silence fills the air—the first hesitation I've felt from them. I glance over at Bell, and she has all love in her eyes. Riley is doing her proud.

"*Are ya with me?*" Riley yells into the silence. He sounds suddenly like he's working the crowd at Summer Jam.

"*Yaaaaaaaaah!*" The revolution screams back. The battle cry lasts several moments. Behind us, the Council army has begun gathering at the cemetery gate. I see Damian glance back, then nudge Riley, who turns to look. A scowl crosses his face, a flash of fear maybe. I wonder what he sees. He turns back to his troops.

"*Tonight,*" Riley rasps, "*we rise as one and change the world. Say it!*"

"*Tonight we rise as one and change the world!*"

"*Tonight we rise as one and change the world!*"

"*Tonight we rise as one and change the world!*"

From somewhere in the masses, another group of voices rises: "*No! More! No! More! No! More!*" The chant becomes a relentless, driving beat as the rest of the army repeats: "*Tonight we rise as one and change the world!*"

I need to see whatever it was that threw Riley. Bell and I exchange a glance and then make our way through the tombstones to higher ground.

"Tonight we rise as one and change the world!"

"NO! MORE! NO! MORE! NO! MORE!"

I step up on a headstone and climb to the roof of a crypt. Sylvia Bell is beside me.

"Tonight we rise as one and change the world!"

"NO! MORE! NO! MORE! NO! MORE!"

Another mass of voices rises. It's high pitched, like many, many children, and then I realize that's exactly what it is: the ghostlings have formed their own contingent—fed up, I'm sure, with doing the Council's menial dirty work and annoying little errands, fed up with endless dead-lives of perpetual servitude and aimlessness. They have come. Their song is a haunting coo, familiar somehow; it stretches beneath the other two chants, threading them together, punctuating the breaks, a relentless *ooooooh* that chills my bones.

"Tonight we rise as one and change the world!"

"NO! MORE! NO! MORE! NO! MORE!"

"Ooooooooooooooooooooooooooooooooooohhhh!"

And then I recognize it: the song I played for Carlos so many months ago, that first night we spent in each other's arms. The one I'm told he couldn't stop humming the whole time we were apart. The ghostlings must've picked it up from him and made it their own.

For a moment, I just let the whole thundering war song sweep over me, let it rise inside me. Then I turn, and my breath catches. The Council ranks have swelled, almost doubled from what we thought they'd be. Hundreds and hundreds and hundreds of soulcatcher helmets stretch out across the field below us and clutter the dark streets along the cemetery. Throng haints stomp amongst them—at least a half dozen, including that one gigantic one.

"*Tonight!*" Riley's voice rings out over the others. "*For all our lost loved ones! For our own survival! For Mama Esther! Tonight!*"

The chant comes even louder at the mention of her name: "*NO! MORE! NO! MORE!*"

"*We rise as one and change the world!*"

"*NO! MORE! NO! MORE!*"

"*It begins now!*"

Riley draws his blade, turns toward the enemy, and hurls into the air.

Carlos

I can't stop grinning.

There are more 'catchers up in here than any of us had imagined. It may be what crushes the revolution.

Still: the grin stretches unabated, undimmed, across my face.

The ngk call has faded finally, but their relentless ick still sullies up the air; even with stick after stick of this blueberry gum, their ethereal hell burns through me.

And yet . . . this smile won't stop.

It's not that I'm happy, I realize as I race down another corridor and round a corner. Three 'catchers help each other along toward me, one flickering in a way that means he won't last long. I cut through them before the first can raise his sword, leaving them in fading ruins behind me.

Collapse against a wall. Shove some more gum in my mouth. Press forward.

Where was I?

Up ahead, Botus's retinue shimmers around another corner, just out of reach.

But I know where they're going.

It's not that I'm happy. I burn down this corridor quickly—there's no one to stop me, and I'm bolstered by the fresh gum.

I've been happy, and it's not this. This is a skull's rictus more than any expression of joy. You could call it, perhaps, satisfaction.

Not even the satisfaction of the win—not yet. This is the satisfaction of a plan well carried out. Botus couldn't kill me, not yet—I have too much valuable information. And I knew those ngks would sing soon enough. It was just a matter of waiting. Potentially very painful waiting, but what's pain in the face of delicious revenge? It's nothing, that's what it is. It's temporary. Revenge is forever. A closed loop, after so much openness.

The stairwell is a ghastly ruin: no banister, trash strewn about everywhere, missing steps. A 'catcher is halfway down from the floor above where I stand; she sees me, turns around, and disappears back where she came from. I hurl down two flights, almost tripping several times, pause on a landing to catch my breath.

Below, Botus is cursing out his retinue: "Stay tighter, maggots. Don't you dare lapse in your duties. We join the battle soon enough, and you'll have your chance to die gloriously if that's what you seek. For now, you stay alive and by my side."

Can't. Stop. Smiling.

The muscles in my face ache with this perpetual, stupid grin. If I wasn't me, I'd probably punch myself in the face just to wipe the damn thing off. Down another flight, then another; then the world gets even darker: the basement level. A few scattered wall lights flicker here and there, but mostly it's shadow. Botus's men flicker up ahead, an accidental beacon. From the floor plans Mama Esther provided, I have a pretty clear idea how this all works: like the other floors, the basement has a single corridor wrapping around its perimeter that crosses to the far side at three different places. The rest of it is a cavernous supply room and some electrical and heating closets tucked away in various corners. The entrada should be at the far end of the corridor we're currently hurtling down.

The air is stank down here, but by the grace of whatever creepy physics applies to ngks, their presence seems concentrated above them: the roiling degradation is almost entirely absent. I jump over a trashed office desk and come down in a full sprint. I can make out the flapping, translucent capes of Botus's escort.

We can't be far from the entrada now. If they make it, there'll be an entire swarming army of ancient, dilapidated ghosts waiting for them on the other side: Hell's lost-soul welcoming committee. Those geriatrics mean sanctuary for Botus and his men; sliding amongst them and disappearing will be no thing, and I'll have to hack my way through just to survive. They love a fresh body, and they'll swarm me in seconds.

I run harder, trying not to think of the last time I was racing someone to an entrada, the blade leaving my hand, the sound of it renting Trevor's flesh, his body collapsing on the cold December ground of Prospect Park.

I draw, closing on the rear guard, slide my bad leg to the side, and pivot off my good one, launching forward with a roar. The first meets my blade with his but doesn't see the dagger coming from my other hand. I catch him across the neck with a long slice, nearly decapitating him, and parry a thrust from one of his companions as I stumble forward, catching my balance. The second 'catcher swings again; I barely have time to deflect his blade away when another comes at me from the other side.

"Finish him!" Botus yells, breathless and not even trying to conceal his terror. "The rest of you, with me!"

He's making a dash for it. The downside of the ngks' foulness being antigravity is these 'catchers have recovered some too. I throw my back against a wall, swatting away jabs as I move. They're underestimating me because of this limp—I can feel it in their casual attacks. Considering how dire this is for their boss, they shouldn't be this cool. Fine. I feint back a half step, then launch forward, kicking one in the chest with my bad leg—yes, it hurts—and brushing the other blade aside with mine. He staggers, and I catch him full in the face with this dagger.

I behead his buddy as he's stumbling to stand and then run, harder this time, sweat coating me, both blades drawn, down the corridor toward Hell, knowing all the while that I'm too late—Botus is gone.

The infinite emptiness of Hell lies ahead. I don't slow my roll as I approach, don't have time to get existential or cute about this shit. I run full speed, point first into the entrada, fully ready to slash my way through whatever old fogies get between me and Botus.

Instead, I find nothing.

An empty field stretches around me. I make it for about the size of Council HQ. Beyond the field, twisted towers and half-melted row houses reach toward the broken, purplish sky. The air is sharp and tinged with that acidy scent of endless death.

But where are the dead?

There should be hordes and hordes of those lost souls clambering around me like obsessive fans, their fragile, ghostly fingers clawing for some scrap of life. A glint in the distance catches my eye: Botus and his men. I run, try to ignore the icky, warm kiss of Hell's heavy breeze, run harder.

The shimmering forms disappear behind a building. In the far distance, I see the Underworld's ghosty answer to the Brooklyn Clocktower, and, closer, the malformed trees of Prospect Park.

And I know where they're headed. My smile remains. I try to pace myself—don't want to be winded while I cut them down—but everything in me is a relentless engine pushing forward to the kill.

The Prospect Park entrada is a smudge of empty space beneath a copse of sorry-looking trees. The air around it crackles and simmers; I'm sure they've just gone through. I barrel toward it so unthinkingly, stupidly, you could even say, I almost miss the 'catcher they've stationed behind it.

Almost.

He swings out, battle-axe first, from the edge of the entrada just as I'm stepping through. I don't bother cutting my momentum, just adjust my body slightly as I enter and raise the blade to meet his attack. Solid steel clangs against ghost steel at the exact point of neither-here-nor-there, the point that is, essentially, me.

Something shoves my whole body backward, and I land in a snowbank a few feet away from the entrada. I'm up; my hands still clutch these blades, and after a wary glance at the shimmering gateway, I'm out. The soulcatcher seems to have opted to stay safely on the other side, and I don't have time to work out whatever necromantic reaction we ignited back there. The fresh, chilly air of the living world fills me, and I remember how badly I want to keep living, how beautiful life is even amidst death, ongoing, relentless death. Icicles dangle from snow-covered branches, catch the winking shine of street lamps. Galaxies stretch above us, beyond the great gray clouds. The air tastes like oncoming snow.

Kill, rages the engine within. *End this.*

I cross the park, an unstoppable blur of motion, crooked and fluid and perfect and deadly. Launch myself over the fence, because walking out through the regular park entrance is for losers, and sprint through the roundabout, dodge passing cars, ignore memories of passing near here with Sasha once upon a time—not thinking about the babies, not thinking about the babies—then hurl down Prospect Park South, past cozy little shops and bakeries and the cheerful sparkle of holiday decorations.

There. At the end of the block. I've reduced the chairman's retinue to two.

Something booms through the air: my best friend's voice, rising above the thunder of a thousand spirits chanting as one, concussing the winter sky with their rage.

I can't make out what they're saying, but I sing along anyway as I run.

Botus is heading for the battlefield—a wise calculation: with me after him, he'll be safer in a war zone. He won't make it, though.

The three spirits cut a hard right down a quiet block. A few dots of white speckle the murky sky. Then hundreds more. A fine sheet of it already covers the street by the time they reach the cemetery wall and launch into the air. My blade leaves my hand with a whisper. Before it finds its mark, I hurl the dagger.

"*NO! MORE!*" the rebel armies chant. "*NO! MORE!*"

The first 'catcher collapses, and I'm on him, retrieving my blade as the second lands, clutching his arm and scrambling to draw his blade. I finish him with a single downward thrust, then climb onto the roof of an SUV and hurdle the cemetery fence.

I land on a snowy, tombstone-strewn hillside. Botus scrambles toward the summit, twenty feet ahead of me. Desperate cries and the clang of ghost blades fill the air, and all the while the chant churns on: "*NO! MORE! NO! MORE!*" Another melody laces through it now, rising up from some other part of the battlefield.

Botus pauses at the top of the hill, panting.

He turns, blade drawn, then hurls out of the way as my dagger whizzes past him. He rises, deflecting my downswing and shoving me away from him. "You don't want this, Delacruz. Your men need you right now. Would be a shame to die in sight of your own army's defeat."

"Indeed it would." I fall on him, swinging wildly, and savor the panic in his eyes. "James and Sarah Raymond." My blade slices his forearm, and Botus hollers, blocks my next few cuts, and then counterattacks with an off-balance upswing.

"Jane and Reginald Raymond." I carve a nice chunk from his thigh as he stumbles past me. Riley's voice rises over the approaching din of warfare, but I can't make out what he's saying. Something about a lock. Lock them?

"Don't do this, Carlos," Botus rasps, his breath coming heavy now.

My smile goes on, but a tremendous sob wells up in my throat.

"Darren Raymond. Aisha Flores." He blocks the first cut and catches my dagger swipe across his belly, drops to his knees.

"NO! MORE! NO! MORE!" the night sings around me. I'm vaguely aware of a battle raging at the foot of the hill. More yells and clanging. Not my concern at the moment.

"Leandro Reynaldo Salazar." My blade enters his shoulder, and he screams. I pull it out. Ram it into the other side. "Dulce Maria Aviles." Tears pour down my face.

"Carlos! No!"

"NO! MORE! NO! MORE!"

"Andre Salazar." I slice his face as he crumbles. "Trevor Brass."

"Carlos!"

"Mama Esther."

His moans become gurgles; his body flickers. Then he's gone.

Below me, the battle rages on amidst tombstones and crypts. It stretches for miles and miles around me, an ongoing melee that's impossible to decipher at a glance. And a glance is all I have: the clashing troops at the foot of the hill clamber closer and closer. It wasn't "Lock them!" Riley was yelling; it was "Block them!" An interception command. The Council must've had a squad heading my way, and Riley deployed these guys—it looks like some of those bicycle ghosts, judging by their gear—to rush over and hold them off so I could do what I had to do.

It's not going well for them now, from the look of things. The Council goons outnumber them two to one, and the cycle ghosts are hemmed into a tight circle, lashing out as they retreat up the hill toward me. Beyond the throng of 'catchers, though, it's anyone's guess who controls the battlefield, but one thing is clear: there are way more of them than there are of us. The snow is coming down in earnest now, great sweeping heaps of it lashing across the hillside and through the grappling foes.

"Your chairman is dead!" I holler. "Your forces are being routed." I move a few steps down the slope. The 'catchers eye me, their blades leveled at the cyclists. We need to pull back, hold the higher ground, and try to get reinforced, and I'm about to get up in the cyclists' midst and tell them when one yells "Charge!" and rushes forward. The rest follow, and, cursing, so do I.

The 'catchers cut down three outright—it's not even a fight, just slaughter. The rest of us end up, more by chance and sheer terror than any strategy, bum-rushing the center of their line in one desperate burst and breaking it. Four or five 'catchers get trampled and sliced as we clutter through. The rest close in, and then our diminishing squad stands back to back with each other, cutting outward to hold them off.

Two more cyclists drop before a group of Black Hoodies falls on the 'catchers en masse, shredding them. I didn't even see them coming—the cats just seemed to drop out of the sky, blades cleaving away as they smashed the

Council line from the side and swept them away. Before we can thank them, they're gone. The cyclists, to their credit, dive back into the battle, untrained and shattered.

I shove toward the thick of things, blocking, swiping, dodging as I move. There's too much chaos for anyone to bother targeting me specifically—everyone around is just trying to stay alive. A tall, lanky 'catcher gets up in my face, swinging wildly. I parry twice, and then she's clobbered from behind by some phantom from 17. The 17ers rush past and then scatter as a throng haint emerges from the shadows of an old willow tree. It bellows with all those goddamn mouths and shreds two of our guys in seconds.

At first I think it's that huge one from my apartment, but then I realize they're all huge now. They've been feeding. The throng haint hurls its chain out, entangling three 17ers and dragging them slowly back to its heaving girth. The rest swarm in to fight it off, but those chains won't be broken, and four are clobbered trying to unwrap their buddies. Some troops from 4 come up behind it, and I join them. We carve away as the thing howls and swings around. Two of the captured 17ers manage to free themselves in the melee, and then a squad of 'catchers shows up and we're all clanging steel to steel and trying to stay out of the way of those chains and claws.

"*SOLDIERS OF THE REVOLUTION!*" Riley's voice is hoarse but firm. "*PULL BACK! CONVERGE AT THE SUMMIT OF BATTLE!*"

The 'catchers give a collective whoop of joy and press their offense harder. Cleaving two of ours as they rush our ranks. It's made them sloppy, though, and when Saeen appears with a battle-axe already swinging, she and I drop six of them before they can regroup and pull back.

"You heard the commander!" Saeen hollers. "Uphill. Retreat is not defeat!"

"*Retreat is not defeat!*" the 4s scream. "*Retreat is not defeat!*"

It's an awkward kind of rallying cry, but pretty soon it's spread, and I get it—these troops face atrocious odds and have barely been a full army for an hour. Anything that will keep us from shattering will do, any form of loose unity. Unity is really all we got.

Saeen and I put the top of the hill behind us and work our way backward. Her troops spread out around us, a few 17ers mixed in, and hold back the last lackluster assaults from the 'catchers. In front of us, the whole Council army begins to congeal as our troops pull back from its ranks.

It's a terrifying sight.

CHAPTER FOURTEEN

Krys

Don't get me wrong: Hell is hell.

And it's dank and stank and corroded by decay and the endless, dizzying sense of spiraling forever downward. Endlessly, all those torqued-up buildings and trees and hills just seem to seep toward some impossible inner heart of the world. Nothing ever stays perfectly still—that fuckass ethereal wind blows forever—but the stillness of death pervades everything.

It's annoying.

But!

There's something to be said for being in a place that's for you, about you, of you, after all this physical, living-people-world shit. I lean down and pick up a rock. It's a dead rock, a rock of the Underworld, and it fits easily into my hand. It feels right. No concentration required, no skill. I don't have to throw my entire attention into the edges of my being, don't have to think about it at all, in fact. The rock is dead like me. We one.

I look at Redd, and Redd unleashes that wily smile,

and I feel it in my gut—it's a smile I could live off for several days, a full meal. Then I hurl the rock as hard as I can.

It bounces off the back of one of the mangy hounds that's turned away from us, harassing a pathetic, trembling group of very old, very decayed spirits. It yelps, skittering forward, then turns. Snarls. The others turn too.

We run.

Yelps and growls rise up around us as we hurl back to the pen we'd freed the hounds from—what was it, an hour ago? Three? Time gets fuzzy downstairs—whenever we first breached through to Hell.

Mama Esther's books seemed to chart a pretty clear path at first. There were the hellhounds, explicitly described, anatomized, charted, and explained. There they were on the map, penned off from the rest of the dead in a little fenced-in area in a far corner of what in the living world is Prospect Park, and in the Underworld is a vast expanse of eerie wasteland, punctuated by some jacked-up helltrees and populated by thousands of equally jacked-up old lost souls, gargling and gagging along endlessly.

At least, it was until Redd and I showed up an unknown amount of time ago and released the hellhounds. I mean, in retrospect, we coulda thought harder about that decision, but everything Mama Esther left seemed to point us right to that gate, and it's like, when you get to a gate and it's closed: open it. Right? So we did, laughing all along. Don't even know what we were laughing about; everything has just felt so beautiful and terrible since we found fire in each other's arms last night. At dawn, I slung Greta across my back and loaded up a full clip in my pistol, handed some explosives to Redd, and together we strolled out of the Iyawo's room (both she and Jimmy snoring contentedly) and straight to the park and through the entrada.

The hellhounds blew out the gate like they'd been waiting all their ghostly lives for that moment. They made straight for the lost souls, and within a few minutes they'd corralled those sad, drooping motherfuckers off to the far edge of the wastelands. There's only about two dozen of the little monsters, so this whole sheepdog shit is impressive as hell, to be honest. Plus they're all misshapen by tumors and open wounds and extra limbs. As Redd pointed out, it's easy to see how some mortal mighta wandered down here a few millennia ago, gotten snarled at by a few of these guys, and left talking about a three-headed dog guarding the Underworld.

And now they're on our heels, but it's like a game. It's not that they couldn't hurt us. Those phantom teeth and claws will do real damage if they catch up, but . . . the combined cocktail of rage, grief, and whatever this is I feel with Redd has endowed us with a kind of dizzy invincibility. I feel like I could take on a full squad of soulcatchers right now and walk away unbothered. Which reminds me: Where the hell are the soulcatchers? On a normal day, we'da seen at least a few patrolling around this opening area by now. Certainly there'd be a few minding the gate to the hellhound pen, so no one does exactly what we just did.

Redd and I zip through the gate and slam it behind us as the hellhounds clamor against it, slobbering and gasping.

"Now what?" Redd pants, and I want to tackle him and make love here in the den, because why the fuck not? But there's work to do. It's moving through me, eclipsing all the bliss of this hot new thing and the wild freedom of a 'catcherless Hell.

"We gotta find the battlefield, I think. They've probably started fighting."

Redd nods, all business now. "You think they'd come direct at the HQ?"

I think for a moment, trying to picture the assault. "Doubt it, unless they've gotten hold of some kind of siege technology we don't know about. Nah. More likely they lured them out somewhere."

"And dem?" Redd nods at the hounds, who've given up trying to bust back into their own den and are instead chasing each other playfully, pouncing and nipping at each other's ears. They look like puppies. Mangled, mutant, hell puppies.

"We gotta make friends with 'em. Whatever they're for, Mama Esther seemed to have a plan for 'em. So they come with us, wherever we end up."

Redd squints in thought, moves his mouth around his face like he's chewing something sour and delicious. "Ay. Surely they gotta have some food 'round here, right? Nothing makes a dog a friend like feeding his ass."

The hellhound pen is just an enclosed area of the wasteland, the ground a spongy expanse of pebbles and dirt. At the far end, a small structure juts out from the fence, a guardhouse of some kind, I figure. We head for it, bust in, weapons drawn, but it's unguarded like the rest of Hell. There's feed, though, bags and bags and bags of it. We return, a heavy sack on each shoulder. The hounds have stopped playing and stand fully alert when we stroll in, mangled ears perked up, noises pointed. Redd pops the lock and swings the gate open, and we empty the bags into a mountain of feed as the monsters swarm.

Twenty minutes later, or whatever that would be in helltime, we move as one, vicious pack, through the wilds of the Underworld, unchecked and unstoppable. I lead us toward Sunset Park, because we might as well start there, plus I've heard rumors about a secret entrada in the basement of Council headquarters and I wanna know if it's true.

About halfway there, the hellhounds break out into a gallop ahead of us, howling and barking at the empty sky. The whole world feels like it's rising in pitch, like so many moments have led to this one, like we're sliding through an unstoppable sieve straight into the maw of history. Or maybe it's all in my head. All I know is, this beautiful man struts beside me and together we can do anything, shatter the planet, unravel these years of hate, build something brand-new in each other's arms and between each other's thighs.

The hellhounds erupt into a chorus of furious barking; they're downright losing their little mutant minds over something just past the next hill. I swing Greta into position and flick off the safety. Redd heaves his axe onto his shoulder. It's then that I realize where we must be: Green-Wood Cemetery, in the living-world Brooklyn. Nowhere else I know of is this hilly.

A few things click in my mind at once, but I don't have time to think any of them through, because something huge rises over the horizon in front of us, and I'm trying to aim at it through the sudden glint of light and all I hear is laughter.

CHAPTER FIFTEEN

Sasha

Yes, "Retreat is not defeat" sounds pretty, but if we're not careful that is exactly what the hell retreat will turn into. I'd been wondering when Riley was gonna pull us back. He was smart to ride the momentum of that semi-surprise into a head-on attack, even with those abysmal numbers. But we also held the upper ground, and it soon became clear that was about all we had going for us, besides the wily ruggedness of a ragtag rebellion. And that's not quite enough to win.

I've been fighting alongside Kaya Doxtator, of the Oneida Nation, for the past hour. Her partner, Breyla Phan, had fallen in the initial assault. The troops of RD 7 fought with unbridled ferocity after losing one of their captains. With Vincent Jackson's Black Hoodies at our side, we pushed deep into the Council lines, crushing wave after wave of 'catcher squads that threw themselves in our path. But eventually we'd pushed too hard, and lost a third of our numbers along the way. As the momentum and wrath waned, we found ourselves deep in the thick of the enemy, surrounded and with no path back—the Council had closed ranks behind us.

It was Vincent and Kaya who rallied us. The 'catchers were moving through our ranks, cutting 7s down at will and darting back to their Squads or getting slaughtered on the way. Vincent pulled everyone into a tight, outward-facing circle; then Kaya gave the command to push back toward the rebel lines.

I heard Riley's voice bristle across the sky: "East New York, Remote District 5, river giants, push hard on the eastern front." He was trying to link them to us, a bridge through the 'catcher ranks. Bless him. A Council goon slashed out at Kaya while she pressed her attack on another; I parried and slashed his neck open. We inched along, fighting for every step. Exhaustion crept along my muscles. At some point, the adrenaline would run out and that heaviness would take over. I cut down another 'catcher, retreated into our ranks slightly to catch my breath as Kaya covered for me.

"You okay?" she muttered, fending off an attack.

"Yeah, I'ma make it. Don't worry 'bout me."

And then the whole Council squad in front of us crumbled as a huge appendage swept across their ranks.

River giants.

Never thought I'd be happy to see one.

"*Fraang pa Konseeli!*" they howled as they laid waste to a few more 'catchers. The path opened up around them, even as more 'catchers cleaved at their legs. Through the fighting, we could see the troops of Rebel District 5 pushing through the gap.

And that's when Riley's voice echoed across the battlefield again, urging us to pull back to the summit of

Battle Hill. The 'catchers roared forward, finally toppling one of the river giants, but their press was sloppy. With Kaya on one side and Vincent on the other, we shoved through and brought the surviving river giant with us.

Now we've flattened our circle into a single line combined with the 5s. Our backs to Battle Hill, we fend off an ongoing Council assault as we retreat step by step up the slope.

"Push!" Kaya hollers suddenly, and we flush forward in a single, vicious blitz, crushing the front line of 'catchers. "Back!" It's bought us a few steps of untroubled retreat—cold comfort, but my aching muscles are grateful. From this higher ground, I can see the Council troops churn at the feet of several enormous throng haints. The 'catchers regroup and charge, but we're already beneath the trees of Battle Hill and the rest of the rebellion swirls around us; the 'catcher attack autoaborts before they reach us.

We have reached a fragile kind of pause.

My whole body almost gives up when the 'catchers fall back. As the 5ers and 7s disperse into the crowd, I find a tree and collapse against it, letting myself slide slowly down to the snow-covered earth. My breath slows to my normal slow, and I slip inside myself to see what's what. Mostly cuts and bruises. Nothing fatal. Only mild bleeding, no nasty ghost poison seeping through my veins.

Excellent.

It must be late, but I have no way of knowing. The moon hangs in a crisp crescent above the trees and gravestones. The snow sends its luminous glow back up toward the sky. Around me, hundreds of spirits ready for whatever round two may bring as the rebellion licks its wounds and gears up for more.

———————

"Come here often?"

I wake up from a tiny nap wanting to punch Carlos in the neck for being so cheesy and cover him in kisses for being alive still. I settle on a wry smile and accept the hand he's holding out to me.

"You survived," I say, and then we're kissing full on, and even though it's wartime and we're all about to die, the moon is a sliver and the snow a lantern and his lips my home and my slow slow heart is still alive; my slow heart is still very alive.

"I toldya I would," he says once we extract ourselves from each other.

"Botus?"

"Not so much."

I nod my approval. "Figured you were up to no good when you flashed that smile when we went our separate ways earlier."

"Mmhm."

"You did it, right?"

"Oh yes."

"Reminded him of our names?"

"All of 'em. Both of our families. I did it right."

I have to catch myself, the tears welled up so suddenly. I blink them away as I thank him with another kiss. "You're a keeper, I think."

"I'm fond of you as well. Good times on the field?"

"Still alive. Your buddy ain't half-bad in the commander chair."

Carlos wiggles his eyebrows. "I've always known he had it in him to fuck shit up on a massive scale. Speaking of which, there's a war council—he asked me to come find you."

"Oh?"

"Oh indeed."

"Well, let's go, then, shall we?" I offer him my arm, and together we promenade through the snow and the rebel camp to the summit of Battle Hill.

"They'll retreat," Talbot the Staten Island captain snaps as we walk up. "And bleed us out over the next five months." We've set up shop around a tombstone by the Civil War memorial. Snow-covered statues gaze out in either direction around a stone pillar.

"No," Cyrus Langley says calmly. "They'll press their advantage. Botus would've retreated, maybe, but Carlos here has dealt with him." Cyrus winks at us as the whole war council rises to applaud Carlos.

He waves them off. "Y'all were here doing the hard work. I just offed one bureaucrat we've all been wanting to murk for ages. Any word on the other five Ignobles?"

Riley shakes his head. "That faceless guy, Flores, seems to have taken over as commander. He's holed up somewhere in the back, running things. We think Caitlin Fern's with him."

"That'd make sense," Carlos says. "He blocked for her when I massacred the High Council meeting at HQ earlier. We gotta keep an eye on that one; she's a helluva necromancer."

Little Damian grunts. "From what our spies say, Flores has been choking at the bit for a chance to come at us head-on. Botus was the only thing standing in his way."

"He'll attack," I say, and then the whole table turns their questioning glares to me. "We, uh, knew each other in life. Not that I remember life." I hate words. My fingers itch for my blade, an easier way out of difficult situations than talking. I sigh. "We were married when we were fully alive. It's complicated. But I do believe he'll throw everything he's got at us, from what I've seen of him recently."

Everyone nods and turns back to Damian.

"Thank you, Sasha. So, given all that, I'm guessing we'll have a full-on assault coming our direction once they've had a chance to regroup."

"Good," Riley says. "We move into guerilla warfare now."

"My favorite," Cyrus whispers. It's good to see him smiling again.

Riley looks less excited. "We probably can't wipe them out, but we can bring them to their knees, especially once they're on our turf. Mass confusion will be the game. We strike and fade back into the darkness. Hit 'em quick, get out fast. At a certain point, they'll have to give. Then we step up to the negotiating table with the upper hand."

A few murmurs of dissent rise around the table.

"I don't like it either," Riley says. "But we have to be clear about what we can and can't do. And look: that all stays at this table. As far as the troops are concerned, we're wiping the Council off the map tonight. Any word on how bad our losses are?"

"Significant," Damian reports. "But no worse than we'd imagined. And we inflicted some serious damage on their numbers. Unfortunately—"

"They can afford the damage," Riley grumbles. "I know."

Vincent Jackson raises his hand. Riley nods at him.

"There's something else. They're not giving it their all. Like . . . they're demoralized. I dunno if it's the ngk shit working on 'em still or what, but they not coming at us like they have in the past. And they dropping quicker."

He's right. I had noticed it but wasn't sure if my own view was somehow skewed in the thick of battle.

"It's true," Saeen says. "A whole squad melted away when La Venganza and I came at them, even with our reduced numbers."

La Venganza just grunts her agreement.

"I mean, I'd run if I saw you two coming at me too," Talbot says.

"Related to that," Damian says, "there were some unconfirmed—and I stress *unconfirmed*—reports that a sizable group of the Council army has defected."

"*Already?*" Riley blurts out. "We haven't even really begun demoralizing them."

"Multiple scouts reported seeing 'catchers wandering off the battlefield, looking defeated, and vanishing into the night. Getting mixed signals about the numbers, but some say up to a quarter of their forces."

Riley shakes his head. "Can't be."

"Don't underestimate the combined power of being ngked and hating your bosses," Sylvia Bell points out. She would know.

"Touché," Riley says. "Either way, we gotta act like it ain't real till we get confirmation. Don't change much one way or the other. Are all our captains accounted for?"

"Breyla was killed in the initial charge," Kaya reports. In my head, her screams still echo as she fell to the onslaught of 'catchers rushing to hold us off.

"You alright?" Riley asks.

Kaya nods curtly, looks away.

"Two leaders from RD 8 were killed as well," Talbot says. "Delano Fritz and Juan Alvarez. Most of the 8s were scattered and cut down early on. A few fell in with us, and they let us know. They got separated somehow. Sounds like a horror show."

Riley shakes his head. "Alright, so we—"

A trumpet blast cuts him off. The warning call. The whole table rises at once. My pulse thunders in my ears— I haven't recouped fully; my body still burns from the first half of the night.

The message gets relayed up the hill to us from soldier to soldier: "Throng haints. Several of them."

"How many, dammit?" Damian spits.

"We'll find out," Riley says. "In the meantime, get to your troops."

Damian growls. "This is bad. They're sending those haints in because they can inflict maximum damage without any toll on their own troops. Plus they get bigger every time they—"

"We know, Dr. Sunshine," Riley snarls. "Now all of you, get!" The captains scatter in all directions, their troops melting back into the darkness of the cemetery. Carlos and I duck behind some trees. Riley's roar covers the sky—"*BATTLE STATIONS!*"—just as the first throng haint barrels up the hill. It hurls that massive chain forward, crushing a few scattered soldiers who didn't flee in time, and begins hauling them in.

We emerge from the shadows in one whispered rush, the snow crunching beneath my boots, beneath Carlos's boots, everyone else just a silent swoosh of motion as we converge on the throng haint. It swings those massive arms, smashing whole squads out of its path, but more leap forward, weapons drawn, and hack away at its core.

The thing bellows, a hundred mouths releasing the same, piteous, earthshaking scream as we duck and dodge around it, chopping and cutting all the while. The troops caught up in its chain are sprung loose, and the haint is looking like it's ready to collapse when another hurdles up the hill, then another. They're greeted with yells and curses, then swinging blades. Further off, I see three more clambering up toward our troops on adjacent hilltops.

Carlos

Sasha flings herself at the second throng haint with such brutal abandon I'm almost offended. Doesn't she realize we have to make it through this alive so we can go off and be in love, I catch myself wondering. But this is war, and there's no room for such self-absorption in battle. Plus, I remember, watching her deftly swoop out of the way of one of its swinging arms, she's a fucking assassin at heart. Sasha was born, or reborn maybe, for this. All the exhaustion she was covered in just moments ago has receded beneath the rush of life and death.

I chop the dying throng haint at my feet a few more times, then join Kaya's squad of 7s as they rally around Sasha. The gigantic thing won't budge, though. It lashes those chains out, clobbering two 7s who strayed too close, and pulls them in before anyone can save them. The throng haint howls with all its mouths and trembles, growing a few inches taller from the meal.

Another cry comes from down the hill: "Incoming!"

Vague as hell, but there's no time to be annoyed: yet another throng haint comes charging up the hill, this one bigger than the other two. In fact, this one looks familiar, I think, leaving Sasha and the 7s to handle theirs and heading directly into this new one's path. Vincent's Black Hoodies move in with me, and soon we're directly in front of it as it scrabbles up toward us through the snow.

This is the motherfucker that was waiting in my apartment. I don't know how to explain what makes one throng haint stand out from another. To the untrained eye, they really all do just look like humongous voids of rotting Jell-O with long, ungainly arms and chains slung over them in reams. This one, though, besides being even more humongous than the rest, just has a certain bulk to it, wider shoulders and thicker arms, that make it stand out in a hellish crowd.

The Black Hoodies and I stand, blades drawn, bracing for impact, but the damn thing hurls to one side at the last second and bustles past us before anyone can get a hit off it, beelining for the summit. "Heads up!" I yell to the group battling the other throng haint. They turn just as the giant one reaches the top. It runs head-on into its comrade, thrashing it with both arms and sending it sliding across the snow.

For a moment, we all just stand there gaping. The bigger one doesn't stop: it closes the distance on its fellow haint in seconds and proceeds to pummel the ever-loving hell out of it, sending entrapped ghosts skittering into the night sky around it.

"Two more!" the sentry yells from below. "Coming in fast!"

We turn, our mouths still wide open, just in time to

see the two new throng haints charge past us at the larger one. It doesn't miss a beat clobbering the first one before taking a heavy blow to the face from the second. The renegade haint staggers, then hurtles forward into its attacker, clawing at it as they both tumble in a colossal phantom tangle over the side of Battle Hill.

The Black Hoodies move first. Blades drawn, they pounce on the Council haint as it rears up from the fray. It clobbers one, but then the larger haint throttles it, pulling it into the snow and rising over it, smashing it again and again as we cheer in disbelief.

Victorious, the throng haint bellows at the night sky, then reaches into its own face and pulls at either side. All those mouths open together. An ear-shattering scream fills the air, then the throng haint literally tears itself into pieces as tattered ghosts stagger to either side. In the middle, Big Cane stands panting. He drops to his knees. Another cheer erupts from our ranks. The Black Hoodies swoop in to help him as he collapses fully across the snow.

"What the fuck?" I hear Sasha whisper behind me.

I shake my head. "That's where the fuck he was, I guess."

Cane is up again by the time I reach him. And he's smiling, the bastard. "Carlos, my brother."

"You . . . you did that shit," I said. "Did you plan it all along or . . . ?"

"I won't say I gave myself up thinking I was gonna bust out of a throng haint three weeks later. But I figured if I did get caught, this kinda shit might happen, so I trained for the possibility. Always be prepared, the Council taught me." He winks warily.

"How does one even—you know what? Never mind. You're a fucking hero, man."

Cane straightens slowly. "Eh, we still got a long night ahead. I seen their ranks. Even with most of their throng haints gone, we still have a problem, C."

Alice, one of the Black Hoodies, helps Big Cane stand. "Commander Riley's sent word along to expect another wave of 'catchers at any moment. Tolula, you see anyone coming out there?"

A tiny ghost in a child-sized hoodie gazes out into the darkness, then turns back to us and shakes her head.

"Good," Alice says. "Let's get you out of here." We're helping Cane back toward the rebel camp when the alarm horn rings again.

"Something's going on with the eastern flank," comes the call.

"The hell does that mean?" Alice scowls.

"Not a goddamn thing," Cane says. "You see anything?"

Tolula rolls up out of the darkness gesturing frantically.

"Fire," Alice says. "She says they're on fire."

"What?" Cane and I say together.

"Our whole flank?" Vincent asks, running up next to us.

Tolula looks, then gestures again.

Alice takes a step back. "And they're heading this way."

"Caitlin Fern," I say. "Shit."

CHAPTER SIXTEEN

❧

Caitlin

I can admit it: the sight of the enemy troops catching fire, the splash of terror that reaches through me as they struggle against my grip, realize they're trapped, they're mine, and then hurl toward their own comrades . . . It's chilling.

Even to a heart as fallen as mine.

What is wrong with me?

Who have I become?

Mama Esther's never-ending laugh still cycles on and on through me; it has become me, encrypted in my DNA, which means she's won. Somehow, she's won, even dead and gone, ether, nothing more than ether, even as I set fire to her troops and smash them into each other, my helpless puppets; still, somehow, she has won.

I scream, rising from my crouch behind the tombstone. Pant. Mama Esther is everywhere, but the night is empty. Snow. Monuments. Angels. Trees and the dark sky. Empty. She is nowhere.

The troops have faltered as my focus fell away. They

scream amidst the flames I've lit inside them, begin to scramble.

There is no time for this bullshit. I swing back into control.

Ahead, the rebels, *my* troops now, sling back into position, erect. Mine. I push forward with my mind, stepping out from behind the headstone. Push.

The troops burn forward, push toward their own again. Screams cut the cool night.

Never held this many at a time before. Must be at least three dozen. It doesn't matter. I could release some now—even a small group will have the desired effect. But I want them all. I need . . . I need to outdo myself in this moment. That's the only way I can get a grip again. This will bring me back to life, one way or another. The 'catcher protection squad emerges around me out of the darkness, and together we move up the hill, slipping deeper into the woods as the rebels fall back in turmoil.

"Are they fighting them?" the squad leader asks.

I shake my head. The first line of enemy troops just melts away as my flaming assault sweeps through; the second comes thundering in swords out, cutting down half of them as they run. Chaos erupts in the camp; it almost overwhelms me, being so many places at once. More jolts of terror, screams of pain echo down the thoughtlines of my control as my flaming puppets are chopped down by their own friends.

Push.

A dozen remain. As I stride up the hill with my soul-catcher entourage, I grunt and thrust out all their blades at once, shoving back the confused attackers. I will push them straight into the heart of the camp, I'll destroy each captain and bring the whole trembling rebellion down in flames. I'll end this single-handedly and then . . .

Something moves in the shadows of the hill to our left.

Something solid. A full-flesh-and-blood something. Not an animal. My attention surrounds it, and three of my puppets are shredded in a matter of seconds.

"See what that is," I gasp at the squad leader, returning to my duties. He nods, sends two 'catchers into the gloom. "Gonna need more than that," I mutter, but no one hears me, because the sound of the 'catchers being slaughtered fills the air.

I'm down to six puppet soldiers now, and the enemy has coalesced around them. Their worried faces gaze into the flames; their comrades scream. One of the 'catchers beside me shrieks, then falls. The squad leader whirls around, blade drawn, but the night reveals nothing.

Emptiness.

Mama Esther's laugh echoes through me, becomes me.

The last of my fiery puppets falls, struck down by her own friends. The night reveals nothing.

Three 'catchers remain by my side.

He's out there. Carlos.

I can feel him. My fire is nothing next to his. I am barely solid, a fetus, beside his fury. Mama Esther keeps laughing, lodged inside me, and her minion stalks me, moves silently from gravestone to gravestone. My 'catchers all have their blades out; they mutter to each other, but none of it matters—it's just games to him. He will butcher them, then butcher me. He'll kill me slow, war be damned, and make me pay for each death I've caused, double for Mama Esther, even though she still cackles on and on through me, unabated, undaunted, the freak.

To think I once *arranged* for my own death at his hands. Not so long ago either, but a whole different lifetime. Before Siberia. Before Monica fucking Tannenbaum's empty fucking eyes. Before Raj. Before Mama Esther's infinite laugh.

"Caitlin Fern!" he yells into the night. The 'catchers spin and gasp, surprised, pathetic. Incompetent and twelve steps behind as usual. A pinecone cracks against one of the headstones. The 'catchers glance at it, like fucking assholes, and another one gets dropped.

To hell with this. I've done my piece for the Council. Those platoons that snuck off to outflank the rebellion will be swinging in from the rear any time now. And anyway, I won't be slaughtered where I stand.

I turn around and run like hell.

Athletically, I am pathetic. But I'm small, so I can move fast, at least for a short sprint.

And Carlos, I believe, is wounded, probably quite a bit. Plus he's a fucking gimp. So by all rights, I should get away. But I hear his boots pound the snowy gravel behind me. He's not within striking distance, but he's pacing himself. He wants this kill. He won't return to battle till he has it. Fine. I'll draw off the vengeful halfie, for all the good it does me.

I hop down a small embankment, slide, and almost lose my balance and collapse into a snowfield, but I stay up, and once I'm on flat ground, I find the path again and sprint ahead toward . . . toward what? I don't know the full layout of this ghastly place, but somewhere it has to end. It has to.

I wind around an elegant lake, all glistening with moonlight and romance, the grandiose crypt beside it shimmering in its windblown eddies. A quick glance back: he's gaining. Still not close enough to hurl that blade of his, but it won't be long now.

I have a gun. A stupid weapon, really, but there are no ghosts nearby to set fire to and hurl at him.

A gunshot will bring police maybe, and police will believe me when I say a crazed Puerto Rican has been chasing me through a graveyard. I mean, it's true.

Down another slope. I'm winded, losing momentum, but the fear of Carlos, even greater than the fear of death, pushes me forward. A stitch opens up in my side.

I dig through my Lands' End jacket pockets for the pistol as if it hadn't been slapping up against me while I ran all this time. Try to still my trembling fingers.

It's snowing again. I hadn't even realized it had stopped, but now it's on again and coming down hard, so when I turn to point, trying not to hyperventilate, I have to squint through the spiraling flakes.

Mama Esther cackles through me, relentless.

He's gone.

A flash of movement, and the gun explodes in my hand without warning. I pulled the trigger? Carlos, just a dark splotch against the snow, dove as the shot echoed through the night. Or did he fall? Could I have hit him, by blind luck? My arm is shaking; the shot reverberates through me like Mama Esther's cackle, a continuous earthquake. The gun is in the snow, little plumes of steam rising from it.

Carlos rises.

Fuck the gun. Still shaking, I bolt.

The enemy's voice rings out across the cemetery again,

some indistinct gibberish. Up ahead, my salvation: the gate. Beyond that: the street. Snow soaked and slushy and shining. I hurl over the crest of the hill, slip, then slide onto my ass and crumple, turning over and over in the snow, the whole sky spinning above me.

Land in a heap, but I'm that much closer to the edge, to the world, to safety. Rise in a panic. Where is he?

Nowhere.

Everywhere. I scramble up the fence, then over it, shredding my Lands' End jacket in the process.

Come down in a heap once again, my whole body on fire with exertion. He crests the hill, comes burning toward me. He can't keep chasing through the streets. He won't. There are people out, even at this late hour. He can't stay away from the battle this long, surely. He's needed. Surely.

My God.

He's not even slowing. I watch through the gate, long enough to feel the wind of his fury blow over me, my certain death.

I want to live!

I turn, tears flooding down my face. A city bus rushes along Fifth Avenue toward where I stand. It doesn't slow— it's late and there's no stop nearby. Just barrels forward.

I turn again, catch Carlos's eye.

Smile.

Then, as the roar of the bus drowns out even Mama Esther's endless cackle, I step backward.

CYCLE FIVE

~∽◈∽~

REQUIEM

Ay, aquí termina la historia
De tan tremendo ciclón . . .
Aquí termina la historia
De tan tremendo ciclón:
Los muertos van a la gloria,
Y los vivos a bailar el son.

Ay, and here ends the story
Of this tremendous cyclone . . .
Here ends the story
Of this tremendous cyclone:
The dead go on to glory,
And the living dance the son.

"El Trío y el Ciclón"
Trío Matamoros

CHAPTER SEVENTEEN

~ᕲᕣ᠖ᕤᕳ~

Sasha

We're on top of Battle Hill, huddled around the war table once again, when the message comes in: our spies have spotted about three hundred enemy troops moving into position further into the cemetery. So those deserters weren't deserters after all, and now we've been outflanked. The camp is still in mass confusion over those fire attacks, and this won't help. News travels fast, though, and soon we hear the murmur of fear and contention rise around us.

"What's the play, Commander?" Talbot asks, showing Riley a respect he hadn't bothered with before the first battle.

Riley keeps his head down, eyes fixed on the table.

"We have about six hundred troops left," Damian says. "But they're not in great shape, overall."

"We could charge the flankers while they're still lying in wait," Vincent offers. "Leave a smaller group to hold the hill from the frontal attack, then—"

Riley shakes his head. "They'll throw everything they

have at us from the front. We'll lose the hill and the defenders and be caught between two armies."

"We launch a full-frontal charge on these guys in the field," Talbot suggests. "Before the flankers have a chance to attack."

Riley scowls.

Cyrus raises his hand slowly. Riley nods at him. "We split in three," the old ghost says. "The small group pushes hard and sharp into the center of the army up front. Then the two larger groups attack from opposite sides. The Council will be cut in half and fighting on four fronts."

"The middle group will be crushed," Saeen says. "They're the smallest, *and* they'll be instantly surrounded."

"And that's *if* they don't simply get obliterated outright when they try to charge through," Talbot points out.

Kaya grunts, and everyone looks at her. "The Council won't be expecting a push like that. If that middle group moves in fast and hard, it could break the lines. The 'catchers'll be so busy getting back in order and trying to handle that, they'll be even more thrown by the other two attacks."

"That's a whole lotta *if*," Talbot says. "And even if all that does go right, here's what else will happen: one side will inevitably start pushing in further than the other. Then whatever's left of the center squad will fight in that direction to close the gap and rejoin with us."

"Which'll leave the opposite flank in the dust," Damian says. "Although then we'll have a single larger force to push through toward them."

Talbot scoffs. "And the entire Council army between you. I don't like it."

"I don't either," Damian says. "But it's the only one

that makes sense. There's no way out of this without massive losses. We have to coordinate those losses to our favor as much as we can."

"Spoken like a true Council bureaucrat," Talbot growls.

Damian fixes him with an icy stare.

Riley pounds the table. "Enough. D is right: it's the best plan we got. The question is, who gonna roll up front and center?"

"We are," a ragged, throaty voice croaks. We all turn. There in the trees, a small army of ancient, robed spirits stands. Their muted luminescence flickers in the cemetery gloom. Each one is tall, with long limbs and hunched-over backs.

"The Marcus Garvey Park spirits," Riley says, a wary smile breaking out across his face. "The fuck y'all doing here?"

The lead spirit warbles something in a language too old for me to even fathom.

"That was all the English they know," Riley reports. "This one's name is Rathmus. He an ancestor of Carlos's. Says they're joining the cause and they want to be the front punch roll."

Riley shakes his head sadly.

"It's a suicide mission," Talbot mutters. And I see what he means: the park spirits don't look like they have much fight in them—they move at a lethargic crawl, and those arms are long but look ready to snap.

Cyrus nods at them and says something in warble, which Rathmus responds to. "Yes," Cyrus says with a pained smile. "This is the way."

"I'm with them." It comes out of my mouth before it's a full thought in my head. Maybe it's because Carlos hasn't shown up since he went tearing after Caitlin Fern, and some little piece of him lives in Rathmus, however distant. Maybe it's because I know Flores will be back there somewhere, and the center strike feels like the clearest shot at him. It doesn't matter—deep inside me, I know this is right, even if it ends in slaughter. Which it probably will, considering I'll be waging war with Team Senior Center.

Riley side-eyes me. I nod at him: *Yes, I am sure.*

He shakes his head, then shrugs. "Kaya, Damian, Talbot, take your troops to the western flank. Vincent, Saeen, take the east. Cane, you good to fight?"

The huge detective has been lurking off to the side the whole time. He gives a thumbs-up and a big smile, but it looks like it took some work to make it happen.

"You roll with them. Cyrus—"

"Me and the remaining Burial Ground troops will join Sasha and the Old Ones," Cyrus says. And that's that. Riley might be the supreme commander, but no one challenges Cyrus Langley.

Riley lets a half smile creep over his face. "Aight, boss man."

"Where you gonna be, Commander?" Saeen asks.

His smile becomes full fledged and grim. "Wherever the fuck I'm needed most."

"Us Burial Grounders will make the first push," Cyrus tells us as we gather at the edge of the woods. "But y'all can roll up along either side of us like a sleeve once we break the front line. Feel me?" He gazes up at the gigantic, wrinkled faces of the Old Ones. They confer in quiet flapping noises, then nod. It makes sense—I don't think these guys will be able to keep pace with us in the initial rush, and the sleeve maneuver should help widen the battle zone around us once the fight slows our roll.

Should.

Forsyth Charles, somehow still dapper amidst all this killing, and Dag Thrummond stand to one side of Cyrus. Dag's still got that war hammer of his, and I make a mental note to steer the hell clear of it. A woman in a head scarf named Tam and a tall, older woman with skeletal face paint stand to Cyrus's other side. We regard each other with quiet nods, and then Cyrus turns toward the enemy line, draws his blade.

We make it halfway across the snowy expanse in front of the Council army before the alarm goes off, and by then it's too late. Forsyth, Dag, and Tam lead our thin column of warriors in a breathless bum-rush straight into their front lines. The 'catchers are just getting it together when Dag swings that hammer in a wide arc, obliterating an even dozen. Forsyth Charles and the skeleton-faced woman hurl into the fray behind them; the sharp clang of ghost blades fills the air as yells and commands erupt around us. And then Cyrus gives me a grandfatherly wink, and we pass out of the peaceful field and into the realm of war.

'Catchers on all sides. I'm deflecting blade swipes and charges, barely registering any of it. The Council's troops look worn out, terrified. They slash and parry and then fall back or are chopped down, letting out desperate bleats as they fall, then fade.

They weren't ready for us, but this won't last long. The rest of the Burial Grounders pour in behind us. We push outward, blades swinging, then pull back suddenly, an ever-expanding and contracting snake, all the while carving deeper into the Council ranks.

"Any time now," Cyrus mutters, shoving a Council blade away with one blade while he swings his other one upward through the 'catcher's face guard. They crowd in harder now—their confusion has become fury. A blast of pain ignites across my left arm, and I yelp, then throw myself backward into our ranks as another blade flashes inches from my face.

"You okay?" Cyrus asks without taking his eyes off the enemy ranks.

The wound sends a sharp, urgent throb through my shoulder, down my arm, but it didn't reach deep. "Fine," I growl, and lurch back into the fray blades-first, skewering a 'catcher in the neck and another through the gut. They fall, and it seems like five rise up in their wake. It occurs to me that sheer exhaustion might do us in if we're not cut down first.

"Where them old spirits go, then?" Cyrus says. He tries to steal a glance back into the fray, but there are too many swinging blades. "Not sure how much longer we can hold out."

"All squads of the revolution!" Riley's voice seems to claim the entire night sky as its own; for a moment, it's all I know. *"CHARGE!"*

The Council should be bracing for a full-frontal assault now that we've got them pointed forward. Unless their spies let 'em know what's coming. Or the rear assault showed up before our troops could move into place. Or some other unforeseen shit went down. I shake off the endless maybes, parry two attacks from 'catchers, and then duck as Dag's hammer comes whooshing past overhead.

"Good timing," Cyrus says. His eyes are smiling, even if his mouth is clenched.

Riley pops his head up from the chaos behind us. "Thanks!"

"Riley!" Cyrus and I yell at the same time.

"The hell you doing here?" I demand, shoving some blades away and moving in front of him.

"I said I'd be where I'm needed. And anyway, low key, if anything happens to you and I wasn't there to at least jump in front of the blade and get got too, Carlos would kill me."

I roll my eyes. "Except he knows I'd come back from the Deeper Death and kill him for hurting you for such a dumbass reason."

"Mighty kind of ya," Riley says. "And anyway, I wanted to be where the action at."

"You found it," Cyrus says. "Just don't get got. We need that booming voice a little while longer, aright?"

Riley's about to respond when a shining rush of motion blurs around us. "The fuck?" he yells, and then "Oh!" as the blur slows, resolves itself into the towering forms of the Old Ones. "Oh damn."

The ancient spirits have their backs to us. They shove forward into the enemy ranks rhythmically, slicing away and then pulling back—much like we'd been doing earlier but way, way better. The Council army seems to collapse around them.

"So much for that theory about them being slow and ineffective," Cyrus mutters.

"Damn," Riley says again.

Up ahead, the Old Ones have cleaved a clear path straight through to the cemetery gate, and there, standing amidst a squad of primes, is Juan Flores. My whole world curves around that singular figure. I clench my blades. "He's mine" is all I say as I brush past Riley and Cyrus, then the front lines of the Burial Grounders.

"Fine, but don't die, dammit!" Riley yells after me. "Dag, keep her company."

I hear Dag grunt, and then I'm out in this strange no-man's-land that the Old Ones' double-column assault has created—a perfect tunnel leading right to the heart of the Council's leadership. I could cry, but first I have to kill. The twins, Carlos, Trevor, those photographs of my family—they all make a cryptic kind of slideshow across my mind. Then comes Reza, Janey, Gordo. The few good Survivors I still cared about before everything went to shit. Maybe it's my way of saying goodbye, but somehow it just feels like they're cheering me on, wherever they all are. I catch Dag charging forward in my peripheral, a massive, unstoppable steam engine beside me, hammer raised.

Up ahead, the commander's men break their huddle and move into defensive positions. The lead two crumble beneath Dag's unblockable swing. I burn past their fading corpses, block a downward cut from another guard, and dart straight for Flores. He steps forward to meet me, broadsword raised, one hand out, beckoning me to stop.

"Aisha," he growls. "Don't do—" I'm on him before he can get the *this* out, both my blades clanging against his. He parries easily, but I can tell he's tired, torn between his duties as general and warrior. The armies stretch out to either side of us, an ocean of turmoil.

Dag clobbers another Prime while I press my attack, cutting, thrusting, dodging, thrusting again. Even winded and wielding that ridiculous broadsword, Flores moves fast. Still: he can't hold up much longer on pure defense. I feint to the left and manage to slice into his shoulder with one blade. The wound electrifies him: whatever dam had been holding back all his rage against me must've finally shattered. Flores roars and charges, swinging wildly. I hurl his blade to the side with mine, sidestepping as he hurls past and cutting deep across his thigh.

We've switched places now, and from here I can see the two battles waging to either side of the Old Ones' warrior corridor. At the far western end of the field, what's left of Talbot's and Kaya's troops are scattered throughout the Council army, fighting desperately in small clumps. The eastern front is faring much better: the Black Hoodies and Saeen's 4s pushed hard against the 'catcher ranks, forcing them into the Old Ones' blades. The Burial Grounders have swept out of the corridor and now wreak havoc on the Council's rear guard.

Still: we are outnumbered. And have lost who knows how many . . .

Flores charges again. His downswing carries all the wrath of an endlessly rejected lover, a man who still rules the broken world he created even as his plans collapse at every turn. I block, but the sheer force pushes my blade down, slashing it against my own shoulder. I shove forward, bodychecking him out of my way, and then stumble back to get some distance while I regain my footing.

He doesn't give me the chance, rushing in with a series of vicious swings and jabs.

"*Push west!*" Riley's voice blasts out. "*West! All troops to the western front!*"

It's still anyone's battle. We could eke out a draw. We could be crushed. We could win. But I will kill Flores, one way or another. At the sound of Riley's voice, Flores pulls back from his attack and glances across the battlefield. 'Catchers on the western end of the field begin rushing toward the corridor, reinforcing their lines. Flores must've sent out a silent telepathic blast.

I've never understood Carlos's obsession with throwing that blade of his. Like: You throw your blade, and then what? Maybe you hit, maybe you miss, but either way, you're down a blade. In fact, you mighta just given it to the person trying to kill you. Sure, I carry two, but not so I can hand one of 'em over.

Still: sometimes it's good to break patterns. I run toward a headstone, leap on top of it, and then hurl into the air as I let one of my blades fly at Flores. He only barely registers it in time and has to swat it away with an awkward, one-handed swing of his broadsword. Which leaves him wide open when I come hurtling out of the sky, blade-first at him. The point goes through his face guard, into that emptiness, and pierces out the other side of his helmet. My empty hand pulls out a dagger as we collapse into the snow, and I stab his chest again and again until there's barely any Flores left to pester my nightmares and day terrors.

Panting, I stand over the crumpled, fading mess that used to be my husband. A roar goes up from the rebel army. Word traveled fast. Dag stands a few feet away, wounded and breathless from his own tight victory. He's still got that hammer, but one arm hangs useless at his side. He's smiling.

"Commander Flores is dead!" Riley announces across the midnight sky. *"PUSH!"*

But the Council troops fight with renewed vigor. They must realize how much is at stake suddenly. Superior numbers made them sloppy, but now they're fighting for their collective lives. The initial flood of rebel squads falls back beneath a desperate tide of screaming 'Catcher Primes. The revolution's western front is all but obliterated. I don't see Damian or Talbot anywhere. Kaya and Big Cane fight off a rising onslaught with their few remaining troops.

I see Big Cane growl and launch directly into the Council throng, blades flashing. He's cut down in seconds as Kaya hollers and pulls further back toward the trees.

"PUSH!" Riley urges, and I can hear the desperation in his voice. The Council pushes too, crushing several Old Ones in their counterassault. A few river giants stalk the battlefield, untroubled by the now-wiped-out throng haints, but there aren't enough to turn the tide our way.

This will be a close thing.

I'm following Dag back into what's left of the Old Ones' corridor, about to launch into the fray when a rush of wind shrieks over my head. At first I think it's Riley, and he's been wounded and somehow broadcast his own death call across the skies. Then a heavy thud concusses the world, followed by a sharp blast. Council 'catchers hurl upward, screaming, in pieces, and a mushroom cloud rises from their ranks.

I duck as another shriek cuts through the air. Another explosion rocks the Council army. From the edge of the battlefield, a single thread, barely visible against the darkness, reaches upward. I follow it to where a huge, somehow familiar-shaped void is expanding across the night sky.

And then mangy, translucent hounds pour out of the void, yelping and yipping and growling. They flood into the Council ranks as a third projectile streaks past, exploding not far from me.

"Booyakah!" Krys yells as her mohawked head appears in the crisp emptiness taking over the night. That bazooka is on her shoulder, and there's a tall ghost beside her, one of the Burial Grounders. Fighting erupts around me—the 'catchers are in disarray, but they still have the numbers, and Riley's rallying for the final push. The hellhounds run rampant through the fray, snapping and snarling. Krys hurls downward, drawing a pistol and a blade, and her friend follows.

I count four ghostly threads leading from various parts of the cemetery up to the edges of the void above us. Small shapes shimmy along them into the sky.

Ngks.

And then the whole plan clicks into place.

Mama Esther wasn't just setting into motion a strategy for the revolution to win—victory will be a happy by-product of the larger plan.

She was putting all the pieces in place, aligning each element for a singular event.

Mama Esther has arranged for an upheaval of the natural order, which really isn't so natural at all, and the Council just happens to be standing in the way of her plan. So she's removing one element and in the process bringing in the ones she needs.

Her laughter echoes across the battlefield as I smile,

placing each piece together in my head. She'd been planning this all along. And now there's only one last piece left to complete the puzzle. The ngk threads pull loose from the ground and begin coiling upward toward the void. I break into a run, cut two soulcatchers out of my way, and then jump, grab the nearest thread, and let it haul me into the sky.

For a few outrageous seconds, the whole battlefield spins beneath me, then the whole cemetery, and then . . .

You came! Mama Esther's voice surrounds me, becomes the world.

"You invited me," I say. Or think. I don't know which. Everything is Esther. Am I still holding the thread? Doesn't matter.

I wasn't sure if my message would come through clear. Things accelerated faster than I thought they would.

"Some of that might've been on me," I admit. It's been weighing on me, to be honest, but I'd been pushing it aside. "I pissed off their head war honcho just before they came at you. I didn't think—"

No! Her voice booms through me, expands outward in waves. *None of this is on you, Sasha Brass. You are the balm.*

I shake my head, laughing or maybe crying—I can't tell the difference anymore.

Each of you played your parts. And of course, we must credit that old fool Sarco with giving me the idea of getting rid of the barrier. He was onto something brilliant, just a shit way of going about it.

I remember having the same thought, back when it was all going down. Pretty sure Carlos was on the fence 'bout it for a minute too. And of course, Trevor was all in . . .

but the inevitable disaster once the throngs of needy dead poured through the newly opened breach between the two worlds—that was always the downside. "How'd you clear all those masses of spirits out of the first level of Hell?"

Credit young Krys with that. She followed the plan I left, released the hellhounds, and that sent the mezzanine spirits scattering. They'll come back through, but it won't be the deluge that would've caused mass havoc. And you . . . well, you got the message, I see.

Somewhere below, ghost troops thrash back and forth in the final throes of the battle to end Council rule; it seems so far away. "Thought you were dead," I mutter. "Deeper Death dead."

Close, Mama Esther chuckles. *But not quite. Something else. Something in between, you could say.*

I muse on that for a moment, or maybe ten moments, picturing Mama Esther's impossible journey from grounded ghost to this being of the sky. Whatever it is, the reverie is broken by her voice: *You ready?*

I pause, catch the words *for what?* before they slip out. Instead I nod. The Mama Esther–shaped void stretches all around me, but it's not everywhere. There's an edge where the regular sky begins. I move toward it, float-swimming through cloudy ether.

Carlos stood in the same position a little over a year ago, except he was on a rooftop and it was Sarco urging him to step into the role of the Divine Gatekeeper.

This is the same recipe at work, but a whole 'nother chef entirely.

"Will it hurt?" I ask as I approach the line between the sky and the void.

You will feel amazing. You will feel the whole world pass through you and open up into what it was meant to be.

"I wasn't talking about for me."

Oh. Ha . . . pain isn't really an issue for me. Don't worry about me, Sasha. This is bigger than me.

Hard to imagine anything being bigger than Mama Esther, in whose expanse I'm just a speck at the moment, but I get it: this is about the future. The line between life and death hangs by a thread.

Draw your blade.

It's already in my hand.

A humming sound rises around me; I don't know if it's Mama Esther or the sky itself or the soldiers below.

I place my blade against the edge of the sky, take a breath, and cut.

Carlos

Caitlin's broken, smiling face keeps blitzing across my vision as I make my way through the snowy fields of the dead. The bus caught her full on, and her whole body flipped upward and through the sky like a rag doll, landed on an SUV halfway down the block, spiderwebbing its windshield. Its alarm screeched into the night as the bus driver jumped out, yelled, "No! No! Oh God, no!" and ran to where Caitlin lay crumpled.

He stood over her, blubbering into his radio for help, and then just burst into tears. A small crowd gathered, mostly folks from the bus; then an ambulance screeched around the corner, emergency lights blazing. I watched them put a plastic C-collar on her, strap her to a back-board, scoop her up, and place her on the stretcher. I followed along from behind the cemetery gate as they lifted her into the back of the ambulance.

I saw her smile.

It was just a flash. She pulled herself up, ever so slightly, straining against the straps and tape. She caught my eye. That broken face. She smiled. Then she screamed and shook her head back and forth, as if she was trying to clear a noise out of it that wouldn't stop. "Noooo!" she screamed as the medics tried to calm her and tell her to be still so they could get her loaded up.

"Stop!" she yelled. "Bitch, stop! I killed you! Be gone!"

I didn't see no ghosts on her, though.

The medics shook their heads, loaded her up, and then peeled off through the snow.

I make it back to the battlefield just in time to see the woman I love swoop up into the air at the tail end of an ngk thread. I yell her name, trying to figure out what the hell is going on with the sky—some strange void seeps open across it—but then there are Black Hoodies all around me and the yells and clangs of fighting take over.

"*Keep pushing!*" Riley's voice cries. I let a little wave of relief slide over me: he's still alive. We burst through a line of those ancient park spirits—no idea when they arrived or how they survived this long; those guys must be slow as hell in a fight—and then, a few rows ahead of me, I see the front line of Black Hoodies clash with the Council army's rear guard.

The 'catchers look harried. Their swipes and parries are desperate now, and sloppy. I'm guessing Flores is down, but what about Sasha? I look up, and all I see is that unfathomable emptiness. No Sasha. No sky. Just nothing. More and more nothing.

CHAPTER EIGHTEEN

Krys

Redd and I aim for a spot right in the middle of the Council army. We come down cutting, drop three as we touch snow, then turn to see an entire squad reel toward us. Chaos rules here—there's no organization, no direction. As quickly as the squad heads our way, two run off, and a third gets tackled by one of the hellhounds. We dash forward, meet the remaining nine head on, clanging ghost steel to ghost steel. I send one spinning out of my way with a slash as she charges, hack off another's arm, and then something slices my cheek and I reel back.

And then the sky shatters.

No. "Shatter" isn't the word. It's like a dirty film peels away and suddenly, for the first time ever, the true sky stares back at us, and it's resplendent, glorious, crisp, unfiltered.

The fighting stops.

Weapons fall to the snow. All of us, 'catchers and rebels alike, just turn our heads skyward and gape like children at winter's first snow.

There are spirits all across the sky. They're not Council spirits—there is no more Council. And they ain't renegades either. There are no more renegades. They're just spirits, floating back and forth through the air with newfound freedom. They came from that first layer of the Underworld, like Redd and I just did, except there is no first layer of the Underworld, because the wall has come down.

We aren't one or the other now; we just are.

Redd slides a hand around my shoulder and grins down at me; I take his face in my hands and pull him in for a kiss.

"We did that shit," Redd whispers.

"We sure helped." A trail of tiny fires erupts along my shoulders and arms as I wrap around him and kiss him even deeper. All across the battlefield, 'catchers and rebels shake their heads in wonder as the new world we created begins to take shape around us.

CHAPTER NINETEEN

❦

Sasha

After the first few days of wild debauchery as that initial layer of the Underworld became one with the living world, everything pretty much calmed down and found its own equilibrium.

Imagine that.

Spirits, for the most part, can't be bothered to politic with the living. But now, if they feel to, they can. And something much deeper has changed, besides the breath of freedom of life without the Council. It's hard to describe, but it's something like a filter being removed from your vision that you never realized was there. Or maybe it's just been replaced by another filter. Freedom is something you feel in your muscles and bones. It's a certain ease you carry as you walk down the street and don't check each corner to see if you're about to get got. Freedom is the smile that rises suddenly, catching even you off guard, when you realize this new peace is here to stay.

One thing I do know: Mama Esther may not exist in any spirit or corporeal form anymore, but there's a little bit of her in everything. *Everything.* It's like she exploded across the world and some tiny shard of her seeped into each corner and cranny. Her wisdom, her laugh, her wry humor: it's with us. It's part of us.

Makes sense. She did this. We're living her legacy now. That master plan—it survived on a wink and a smile, but it worked. Mama Esther's dominion was information. She was wise as hell too, and that's no small thing. But her real genius was always in being able to see straight through a person, past all that flesh or ethereal goo and directly into their heart.

And me? Ha. The whole of El Mar gets quiet when I walk in. Even the damn DJ scratches her records to a stop, so the once-festive celebration suddenly becomes a hall of silent wonder, all because of me.

I flash a smile. "Stop, y'all. It's just me. I'm still me." Okay, yeah, I got a certain glow that (thankfully) only folks with the spirit Vision can see. And technically, I'm a kind of demigod, a keeper of the newly torn open threshold between life and death, a being of perhaps unimaginable powers (I haven't tried them all out yet). But I'm still me! Still Sasha Brass. I'm still a mom and a lover and a fighter. I still get hungry and irritable. Still get my damn period, for God's sake. Started yesterday while I was herding some of those hellhounds around. And shit: I'm hungry now. "Anybody bring cake to this New Year's Eve victory bash, or y'all too busy getting wasted?"

They chuckle, and then Riley's voice blasts across the room with that spirit megaphone trick—I'd throat punch whoever taught him how to do it, but it would probably kill them. "*Sasha Brass, ladies and gentleghosts!*" He's clearly wasted. "*The Divine Gatekeeper.*"

I shake my head. Not helping. The whole room explodes with cheers, and then Carlos is there, pulling me into a hug, and everything will be okay, somehow. We kiss, and the room goes "Ooooh!" and I roll my eyes at them. Then the DJ kicks back in with the old-school jams. She's alive—a slender black woman in a cowboy hat—and she's killing it.

The twins poke their heads out from behind Carlos's legs. They've fallen in love with him so quickly, just dove straight into the arms of their father with no hesitation and the intuitive abandon of toddlers. I scoop them up and hold them close, feel their tiny heartbeats against my skin and their tiny arms wrapping around my back.

"You guys okay?"

They giggle and coo, and I pass Xiomara to Carlos—she's already a daddy's girl, reaching for him and burying her little face in his shoulder when she gets what she wants. Gordo waddles up, Reza and Janey beside him. They're looking very pleased with themselves, I notice.

"Thank you," I say. "Thank you all. I'm sorry it was a lot longer than we thought it'd be."

"No worries," Reza says. "We had fun." Her grin speaks of the kind of fun only Reza can enjoy.

I try not to worry. Whatever happened, it's over. Then my momness kicks in and I can't help it. "Something happened?"

Reza shrugs that Reza shrug. "You could say that. But everything's fine."

"It got sticky," Janey concedes, and Reza scowls at her, looking betrayed. "But we handled it. You don't wanna know."

"I think I do."

"Later," Gordo says. "Tonight is for celebration." He

has one arm wrapped around the waist of a woman so tiny and frail I didn't even notice her at first.

"CiCi," I say. "Wonderful to finally meet you."

Small though she is, Cicatriz Cortazar holds herself like a gentle warrior—back straight, a subtle smile creasing her lips. "The pleasure is mine," she says. "I've heard many wonderful things. And I see you are . . . fully manifested now."

My turn to shrug. I like how she said that: fully manifested. Feels true. Means this, all of this, has been inside me all along, waiting to come out.

"¿A bailar?" Gordo says, offering CiCi his big ol' hand.

She smiles slyly at him. "Claro, mi amor." And they glide onto the dance floor and immediately rule it, improbable and ancient and adorable.

Two-D projections of our fallen line the walls, and you would think it'd be grim, but it feels right somehow, like they're here with us even though they're not. Little Damian's in there somewhere, and Big Cane. Talbot. Breyla. Many, many more. There are hundreds of them, and they smile out at us, and their smiles demand a promise: *We died for this*, those smiles say. *You must live for it.*

And we will, my own smile says as I take Carlos's chilly hand in mine and hoist little Jackson tighter against my chest and we watch the room rock with dancing, laughter, good food and drink, the excitement of a brand-new day.

Carlos

"How it feel to be king?" I ask Riley when the dancing slows down enough for us to catch a minute to chat.

"Man," Riley sighs. "You know it ain't like that."

"They pick a title for y'all yet, though?"

He shakes his head; we both light smokes. "We'll see. All that'll come."

"Word."

A heavy hand lands on my shoulder. "Carlos."

I look up into the single eye of possibly the last motherfucker I expected to see here. "Quiñones?"

Quiñones runs the Burgundy Bar, a busted old saloon where all the Council folks hang—used to hang in—during afterhours to talk trash. I'd just figured he took me for a lunatic all this time, buying extra rounds that sit beside me while I ramble to people who clearly aren't there. But here he is. "You can . . . you can see the dead?"

Quiñones flashes a rare smile, possibly his first. "Man, you don't tend bar at the Dead's number one hangout and not eventually end up seein' 'em."

"So all this time . . ."

He shrugs. "Pretty much. Anyway, I just wanted to say you guys did a good thing. Fuck the Council. If you ever have cause to ramble on back my way, drinks are always on the house, my brothers." He trades a dap with Riley and pats me on the shoulder, then heads into the crowd.

I blink a few times. "Did you—?"

Riley shakes his head. "But wow. All that time leaning over to sip my drink while it's on the bar like an asshole for nothing."

A moment passes. DJ Lynnee has switched to some kind of unstoppable Afro-beat mix that all the young folks are going bonkers over. Krys and her new friend Redd take center stage, Krys throwing a pretend lasso over Redd and pulling him in while the whole room cheers. Baba

Eddie even let the Iyawo jump in there, against all protocol, but I can see he's keeping a sharp eye on her. Baba's
husband, Russell, and Dr. Tijou whisper to each other over
the music. The Iyawo ditty bops happily in the corner
beside Jimmy; Reza and Dr. Tennessee spin past in a simmering tango that somehow matches the music perfectly.

"We did it," I say as it hits me once more. "We did it,
Riley. We won."

He nods, smiling. The long road we've traveled to this
moment right here stretches behind us; a whole other one
stretches ahead. "Sure as hell did."

"What happened to that detachment they tried to flank
us with from the rear?"

Riley laughs. "Man! Apparently some kids showed up
and like . . . handled 'em."

"Kids?"

"Teenagers. I guess Gordo and Vince both knew 'em
and someone put a call in? Our scouts say they threw
some kinda colors at the Council goons and it sent 'em
scattering."

"¿Qué?"

"Like paint? Iono, man. They handled business; that's
all that matters. One day we'll track 'em down and give
'em all a fuckin' medal of honor, seriously. We'da been
even deeper in the shits if those guys had come at us from
the rear."

I nod, shake my head. "Damn."

"We'da still fucked 'em up, though."

"I know it."

Cyrus slides over beside us and puts a pipe in his
mouth.

"You alright, old man?" Riley asks.

He nods, smiling that sad smile, but I believe him; it's not just for show. "Damian went how he would've wanted to go. Don't make me miss him any less, but . . . we knew there'd be a price to pay for freedom."

"Commander Riley!" Sylvia Bell hollers from the dance floor. "Report to the center of the conga line ASAP or you're in big trouble."

"Shit," Riley says. "Cyrus . . . you're the reason we're here."

The old conjureman shakes his head. "Just one of many, many."

"For *me*, man, I'm talking 'bout for me. You lit the way, Cyrus. For me."

Cyrus nods and stands, and they embrace, a hug that holds the whole terrible breadth and immensity of the war in it. When they're done, both men are wiping their eyes and smiling, and dammit, so am I.

Then Riley heads into the conga line and Cyrus and I just take it all in for a few moments. "Gray dude," Rohan says, strolling up with a rum punch in one hand and a Red Stripe in the other. "She here."

She. She? Oh! Oh, shit. All that happens in my head while I blankstare the guy.

"You comin'?"

Am I? I seem to be. I stand, nod at Cyrus. But I'm grimacing as I follow Rohan through the revelry.

"How'd it go at the botánica?" I yell over the music.

"Smooth, man. We played Uno all night. Jimmy beat all our asses. Baba Eddie passed out at ten like an old lady. The Iyaweezy and I kept watch till dawn. Council ain't fuck with us. Pretty sure they had their hands full with you guys anyway."

We stop in front of a wooden door that leads to some more back rooms at El Mar. I'm sure all kinds of nefarious shit goes on through here. Rohan says, "Oh yeah," and takes a sheathed blade off his belt, starts to hand it to me.

"Nah, man." I hold him off. "Keep it. I still got one and I don't plan on using it any time soon."

Rohan smiles wide at me. "You alright, C-dog."

One table takes up most of the cozy little back room. By cozy, I mean dim and cluttered with various flyers, upside-down chairs, and child seats. A slender, unimpressed white woman sits at the table, smoking. Jet-black hair hangs down either side of her face, partially obscuring one of her eyes. A half-empty bottle of Jack keeps her company.

"Carlos," I say, reaching out my hand.

She doesn't take it.

"That's how it works, man," Rohan says. "You touch her, she sees it."

"My death?"

"Both of 'em," the woman says, "in your case."

"You told her 'bout me?" I ask Rohan.

"Nah, man, she just be knowin' shit."

"Miriam," she says, and smiles. It's one of those smiles people who never smile whip out when they mean it, and I decide she's not rude after all, just surly. And I guess I would be too if I saw everyone's death who I touched.

"So, you know, here's how it would go," she tells me, offering the empty chair facing her. I sit. "I touch you, see the deaths. I tell you what I see, or maybe you can swing some halfie magic and see it through me." She takes a drag, shrugs. "That part's up to you. But, look, either way, it is what it is." Then she stares at me, and I realize her stare is a question.

And then I realize it's a question I don't know the answer to.

For years, I'd have given anydamnthing to see exactly what happened that night at Grand Army Plaza. Then I saw a snippet of it and it ruined my life. And now we've unraveled so much, put so much back in place—both the story and each other. So much has happened, and the knowing took such a toll.

I close my eyes, and the face I see is the woman with honey on her lips.

"Thank you," I say to Miriam, opening my eyes and meeting hers. "I'ma pass."

She grins, takes a swig of Jack. "Smart move."

I nod at her, and then Rohan, and then I walk out the door.

It's just past eleven p.m. on December thirty-first—that dizzy in-between time when we're not quite here but not yet there—and I put the past behind me forever and head down the corridor, back to the great hall full of the living and the dead celebrating freedom together, back to Sasha, to my family, and all that lies ahead.

ACKNOWLEDGMENTS

Many thanks to my terrific editor, Rebecca Brewer, who has believed in and helped bring this trilogy to life every step along the way. Thanks to publicist Alexis Nixon and the whole team at Ace/Roc Books, particularly the cover art department, who absolutely nailed it. Huge thanks to Eddie Schneider and everyone at JABberwocky Literary for all their hard work and excellent advice. Thank you beta readers: Kortney Ziegler, Troy Wiggins, Phenderson Djèlí Clark, Sorahya Moore, Isake Khadiya Smith. Shout-out to all the good folks on Twitter for keeping me laughing along the way.

Thanks to Chuck Wendig for giving Miriam the day off so she could come hang on Bone Street for the day.

The two musicians who appear in this book are real live people and very damn brilliant. You can find Akie Bermiss—who serenades Sasha in the coffee shop—at akiemusic.com and DJ Lynnée Denise at djlynneedenise.com.

Huge thanks to the great Mildred Louis for the awesome river giant drawing on the front of this book, and to Cortney Skinner for the Bone Street Rumba map.

To my amazing wife, Nastassian: I love you. Thanks always to my wonderful family, Dora, Marc, Malka, Lou, and Calyx. To Iya Lisa and Iya Ramona and all of Ilé Omi Toki and my good friends in Ilé Ashe.

I give thanks to all those who came before us and lit the way. I give thanks to all my ancestors; to Yemonja, Mother of Waters; gbogbo Orisa, and Olodumare.